THE GETAWAY

Sometimes, it's the secrets that save a marriage.

For Claire Fitzgerald, her monthly getaway at a remote cabin is a time to relax, unwind, indulge. Two years with Elliott Reyes have been good to her...but all good things must come to an end, and she can only hope this final weekend together will finish their relationship on a high note.

Elliott has other plans.

Having Claire once a month is not enough. He wants more of her. More *from* her. And, he's got a plan to show her just how good it could all be, if only she will let him make her happy.

Getting snowed in should be romantic, but tensions between the lovers rise. As a snowstorm traps them in the cabin and a menacing, unseen assailant launches an attack on Claire, both she and Elliott discover truths about each other they never suspected.

As it turns out, infidelity is not the worst thing that can be discovered about the ones you love. For Claire and Elliott, every truth comes tumbling out...and blood is spilled. Who will survive their weekend getaway?

And who will die?

THE GETAWAY

MINA HARDY

HOWLING
UNICORN
PRESS

For REB
The only one for me

ONE

"Have fun."

It was the last thing Troy had said to her this morning before she left the house.

Have...fun.

Nothing odd about his tone, nothing strange in the sentiment. Just a man wishing his wife a good time on her weekend getaway without him. Why, then, had his words lingered with her all morning, turning over and over in her mind, splintering her already fractured attention? Why, instead of her usual mounting excitement and anticipation about the weekend ahead, was Claire Fitzgerald thinking about her *husband*?

Almost three decades of marriage had created an easy compatibility, but it didn't always work seamlessly. There were still new things to learn about each other. Surprises.

Sometimes the secrets were what saved a marriage, after all.

Even so... "have *fun*?" It wasn't like him.

"See you when you get home" was Troy's usual reply when she called out her final goodbye before walking out the door for her monthly trip. That implacable attitude was one of the traits that both infuriated and also comforted her — steady, reliable Troy. Unemotional, unexcitable, unswayable, unshakeable Troy. He was the thinker in their relationship. Claire had always been the feeler.

This morning, she was definitely "in her feels" as Aviva would have said. Their daughter had turned out to be the best mix of both her parents. Practical like her dad, but also deeply driven by her emotions in the same way as her mother. Viva would have understood exactly why Troy's unexpected comment was digging so relentlessly into Claire's brain — but of course, Claire would never talk to her daughter about it. She was in this all by herself.

Knowing in advance that she'd have a hard time concentrating this morning, Claire had made sure to leave only the simplest of projects on her To Do list. Despite this foresight, Troy's casually tossed-off farewell played over and over again in her mind, interrupting every report she tried to read. Had she imagined his gaze trying to snag hers, trying to make her linger? Had his generally absent-minded kiss this morning been a little more...passionate? Insistent? Claire banished the thoughts.

She had other things to think about.

The box that had arrived at her office yesterday, for example. There was nothing printed on the plain brown box to give away where it had come from, no branding or advertiser's logo. The shipping label itself had been printed in a plain, nondescript font. Not even a return address. She'd still known immediately who had sent it, even if she had no clue what might be inside it. The box tempted her now, but there was no way she was going to open it here.

Claire gave up at last. She'd read this report three times without any of it sinking in. She wasn't going to do any good work today. Her heart thumped faster as she shut down her computer. Cutting out before noon felt like ditching school — illicit and furtive and exciting. It was one of the reasons why she never made it a habit to leave early on getaway Fridays, no matter how slowly the hours passed until she was able to leave.

She never wanted to call attention to the days she left from work for her weekends away. Never wanted to explain herself to anyone — there was no way to tell the truth about what she was doing, not without a whole lot of judgment she had no interest in weathering.

She pulled the package toward her, hefting it with both hands. The weight of it gave no hint about what might be inside. She touched the label again, her name spelled out in black and white. Her fingers toyed for a moment with the packing tape. She could risk taking a little peek, right? One freshly manicured fingernail slid beneath the tape, lifting it, her eyes going to the scissors stuck into the mug of pens on her desk. It would only take a few seconds to slice open the tape sealing the seams —

"Big plans this weekend?"

Startled, Claire spun in her desk chair to face the office doorway. The box slipped from her hands and bounced onto her lap, then bumped against the edge of the desk before it could fall to the floor. She imagined a rattle inside, the clunk of metal or clink of glass. The box had not been labeled fragile, but she grimaced, hoping she hadn't broken anything inside it. Carefully, she set it on the desk and turned away from it as though it meant nothing.

Her office mate Jean, chipper and upbeat as always, gave her a bright grin. "Early birthday present?"

Claire's return smile squirmed on her lips until she managed to force it into a neutrally curious expression. "Hmm? Oh. No, just something I ordered for myself. For the house. Just some kitchenware. I impulse-clicked on an internet ad."

Too many details. That's what liars did, added layers to their story as proof it was the truth. Claire pressed her lips shut on more words.

"Oh, you don't have to be embarrassed. I do that all the time. Send things to the office that I don't want Rick to see." Jean's voice dropped low, conspiratorial. "He gives me such a hard time about my online shopping habit. I tell him if I spent one-tenth of what he goes through with all his car parts and new tools..."

"Right?"

Troy never cared what Claire ordered, and he never gave her a hard time about spending money. Troy never did most of the things the women at work complained about, but Claire had learned a long time ago that saying so was tantamount to bragging. Married women, even the happiest, bonded over how terrible their husbands could be.

"I asked if you had anything fun going on this weekend?"

Claire shook her head. The box mocked her from the corner of her eye. She twisted her chair toward Jean to block the sight of it. "Not really. You?"

Jean launched into a rambling description of her plans to spend Saturday antiquing with her sister. A planned dinner out with her husband. The kids were coming over, and she thought one of them might have a pregnancy announcement to make. That would put Jean at four grandchildren.

"Sounds fun," Claire murmured. She closed her planner and slipped it into her bag. Jean would talk her ear off if allowed, and now that Claire had made the out-of-character decision to leave early, she was eager to get on the road.

"You're heading out already? It's hardly even eleven — "

"I have an appointment," Claire said.

Jean got the hint. "See you Monday, I guess. Have a great weekend, Claire!"

"You, too."

The strange feeling that had hovered around her all morning didn't disappear once she was settled behind the wheel of her car. If anything, she felt more ill at ease and unsettled by the break in her routine. She checked her phone for messages, half-sure she'd find one telling her the trip had been cancelled, but only Aviva had texted with some funny meme she'd thought her mother would enjoy, along with a string of heart-eyed emojis, a few fire balls, and, of course, a little poo.

Mindful of not texting and driving and knowing her daughter wouldn't necessarily expect an answer, Claire didn't reply. As she eased into the steady stream of traffic heading out of town, she tapped the buttons on the steering wheel that would allow her to make a call. Her fingers tensed until they ached, and she made a conscious effort to relax them.

She never called Troy on the way to her getaway, nor on the way home.

Never.

Seconds before the call would've been shunted to voicemail, he answered. "What's up?"

Claire hesitated at her husband's breathless tone. "Was I interrupting something?"

"Of course not. You sound like you're driving."

"I finished up early and decided to get on the road to beat the traffic." This was not entirely a lie; Friday night traffic could and sometimes did add another twenty or so minutes to the regular hour-ish drive.

"You're on the road already?" Troy's voice crackled, fading in and out. "...expect to...there?"

She looked automatically at the navigation screen. Still another forty minutes to go, if she didn't stop, and she planned to hit the grocery store before she got to the cabin. It was too remote even for pizza delivery, not that she'd be able to call for any once she got there. The phone signal was terrible.

"At least another hour or so." More electronic noises. "Hello? You're breaking up."

"I said, 'I love you.'" Troy's voice fractured again.

"Love you, too. Troy," Claire added, thinking he was going to hang up on her. "What...what are *you* up to while I'm gone?"

The silence lasted so long she was sure they'd been disconnected, before finally, he said, "Nothing much. Just thought I'd get caught up on some stuff around the house. You'll be back Monday, right? After work?"

She always went straight from her getaway to work and returned home at her usual time. This time, she'd taken Monday off as one of her floating holidays, because of President's Day. She'd still get home at the expected time, but she hadn't told Troy she was taking an extended weekend. He thought she'd be at the office Monday. "Yes, but —"

The line went quiet again. The phone beeped, signaling that the call had ended. Claire muttered a curse and almost redialed — but then, did not. In another hour or so, she'd be pulling into the drive of a secluded, romantic cabin in a beautiful forest, and there would be wine and cheese and chocolate, there'd be slow, soft music for dancing, there would be candlelight. There would be a box full of surprises.

There would be sex.

A full-body shiver rippled up and down her spine with such force she let out a small, involuntary sound of pleasure. Again, her fingers gripped the wheel, with a different sort of tension this time. A tingling, engulfing heat began at the base of her throat and spiraled down between her thighs.

Claire shifted in the driver's seat, aware of the black lace panties she'd put on this morning. The matching bra. Bare legs and feet slipped into heels too high for the office. Ridiculous shoes, really, for anything but being on her back.

Any weirdness she'd imagined was in her own mind, and she was only making it stranger. She never called her husband on this drive, and she would not call him back now. She was having her weekend, and he was having his own, whatever it might be. That was how it had been for the past two years, and that was how it was going to be this weekend. Monday evening, she'd greet him with a kiss and a hug, and if he asked her if she'd had *fun*, well...

She supposed she'd tell him yes.

Two

The man standing at the end of access road that led to the cabin stood at least six-five and wore his thick, bushy black beard halfway down the chest of his black snowmobile suit. His breath puffed out in plumes of white smoke as he waved her to a stop. He bent toward the driver's side window. Carefully, with a smile on her face, Claire rolled it down an inch or so.

"Hi there," he said. "You must be Mrs. Reyes. I'm Jay. You're earlier than I was expecting. Guess it's a good thing I decided to come out sooner than I'd planned."

Jay. The owner. Claire was not the one who'd booked the cabin and had never interacted with him. She didn't correct him about the name or the false assumption.

"Nice to meet you," she said. "It's not a problem, is it? Me being early? I wanted to get a jump on the traffic because of the holiday weekend."

"Nope, no problem at all. You're set up for early check-in and late check-out, same as you are every month. I was just unlocking the gate for you. We've had some problems with kids coming up here to the cabin when they think nobody's here, especially now that it's off season. I had to start keeping the gate locked. Doesn't always stop them, but you gotta try." His smile broadened, showing off an uneven spread of teeth and gums. "Wouldn't want you and the mister to get up there and find out the place had been trashed by some rowdy kids looking for a place to party, am I right?"

Her polite smile warmed into sincerity. "You are definitely right. Thank you. What about the cabin door? Is code that the same?"

"Same keypad, so no worries there. But I did just change the lock code. I sent it through the app."

"Oh, I don't access the app."

"Maybe Mr. Reyes sent it to you?"

Claire swiped her phone screen and frowned. No new messages. "He didn't. I think he assumed we'd be arriving closer to the same time. I didn't tell him I'd be coming quite this early. I thought I'd enjoy a little bit of time here by myself, I guess. It's so peaceful."

"It sure is." Jay stretched and looked around with a firm nod. "Ah, well, then, seeing's how you're here first, I'll write it down for you. The cell service here is terrible, I know. They keep telling me they're going to put up a tower, but I'll believe that when I see it."

He showed off the heavy padlock that hung from the metal gate before shoving it into the pocket of his snowmobile suit. "I'll be back Monday after you check out to get everything all locked up again. Hang on. I'll grab that code for you."

Jay went to his truck and brought back a piece of crumpled notebook paper with a series of numbers scrawled in thick black ink. She rolled her window down a bit more to take it, but Jay didn't release it at once. Claire tugged it briefly until he let go. His easy grin creased into a frown that rippled his forehead as he looked around again, his gaze stopping at the sky.

"We're supposed to be in for some weather," he said. "The propane tank was just filled last week, so the furnace should be fine. Unless you lose power."

"What happens if we lose power?"

Claire was not a camper. The cabin was already as rustic as she ever wanted it to be. Her chest tightened at the thought of facing the weekend with even fewer amenities.

"Furnace can't kick on without the electric. Same with the water heater. But I laid in extra firewood for you, so no worries about staying warm. Got plenty of candles in the kitchen drawers. A couple of battery lanterns in the linen closet, too. I'd make sure they're all charged up, just in case. You can use a match to start the stove. It runs on propane. The well has pretty good pressure, so you should still be able to get water, but it'll be cold. You'll have to leave the faucets dripping, just a titch. Stop the pipes from freezing. If we get a *lot* of snow, though..." He shrugged and looked apologetic. "It can take some time before anyone will be able to get up the drive and plow you out."

Claire frowned. She'd heard the weather reports, of course. Snow throughout the weekend. It had sounded sexy and romantic when she was imagining it. Not so much right now. "Surely by Monday afternoon, though?"

"No better place to get snowed in than a romantic cabin getaway, am I right?" Jay said, which was not the answer to her question. He thumped the top of her car and stepped back.

"Someone would come by Monday afternoon, right?" Claire called after him as he headed for his pickup truck.

Jay spun on his heel to face her car. "Depends on the snow. If you're really that worried about it, you could leave your car down here, and I can drive you up to the cabin. The main road gets cleared by the county, so they'll have trucks running often enough to take care of it. If you did get snowed in and needed to get out, I could always run up on my snowmobile and grab you, bring you back down to your car."

"It's just that I have to be back at work on Tuesday." And she'd told Troy she'd be home Monday night. It wouldn't be impossible to explain how she'd gotten snowed in so deeply she was stuck and couldn't make it home, but it would be...*awkward.*

"Sure. No worries. I can run you up there in the truck right now."

Weather could be unpredictable, but what she *could* predict was the panic if they weren't able to leave when they were supposed to. "You wouldn't mind?"

Jay shook his head. "Heck no. We're used to the snow around here. Pull into that little gravel area right over there. Your car will fit just fine, with plenty of room for Mr. Reyes, too. It'll be a lot safer for you both, I'd say, based on what they're calling for. I'll head up on Monday at check-out time to grab you up, get you out of there on time. How's that sound?"

"It's very nice of you, Jay. I'd hate for it to be any trouble."

He waved a hand. "Not a speck of it. I have to come up to do the housekeeping anyway."

"Okay then, thank you. It would be great if you could give me a ride." She parked in the spot Jay had indicated, pulling up far enough that the tail end of her car didn't stick out too far. She got out and pulled her weekender bag from the back seat, along with her purse. She popped the trunk and coughed, self-conscious about how much she'd brought with her for a single weekend, albeit a long one. "I have a lot of stuff with me. It's mostly food."

"Sure, sure, you gotta eat. You know, I thought about offering a whattya call it, a concierge service. Grocery orders in advance, have it all ready for guests when they get here so they don't have to pack it all. I was already offering the sweethearts package with the rose petals and champagne, and the candy. Just never got around to getting it set up on the site. Hey, you weren't kidding," he said when he looked into the trunk. "Are you staying for a weekend or a couple of weeks?"

"Better to have something you don't need than need something you don't have," Claire quipped.

Jay chortled, beard shaking. He gestured at the liquor store box filled with bottles of wine. "You won't run out of stuff to drink, that's for sure. C'mon, let me get you settled. You want me to grab that for you? Looks heavy."

In minutes, he'd helped empty her trunk and the back seat, loading everything into the bed of his capped pickup truck and helping her into the high cab. Jay eased the big vehicle past the metal gate and onto the narrow, winding road that was essentially a private driveway. He gave her a glance.

"It's hard as hell to keep the cabin rented during the winter. Oh, you get the folks wanting to spend a cozy, romantic Christmas or New Year's, but the rest of the time seems like people'd rather go to Mexico or someplace warm. It's even harder to find guests you can trust to keep your place nice, leave it in condition almost better than it was when they got there. You and the mister have been such excellent guests. I'm happy to have your business so regular. Once a month, like clockwork."

"Just like that," she murmured, looking out her window at the press of evergreen trees creeping up so close to the edge of the road that there was very little space on either side of the truck.

She normally didn't get a good look at the forest. When she was driving herself, she kept her eyes on the slender strip of asphalt, mindful of the road's sharp turns and how easy it would be to veer off into the ditches on either side.

She and Elliott had gone hiking here a few times. Nothing too strenuous, more like nice walks to look at the scenery. Sometimes, a picnic. Lovemaking on a blanket under a bright summer sky. The cabin's property butted up against state game lands all around it, and depending on which direction they headed, avid hikers could potentially spend entire days, hiking for miles, before reaching any sign of civilization.

They'd never meandered more than an hour or so from the clearing. She'd known the woods were dense, obviously, but the cabin had a nice clearing around it, and the trees didn't hover so ominously close to the house as they did to the road.

"It must be hard keeping the road clear all year round, not only in the winter," she said as the pickup bumped heavily over a rough patch.

Jay nodded. "I have a crew that comes out to take care of fallen trees, keep them trimmed back. It's worth it, though. For the privacy?"

"Yes," she said. "The cabin is extremely private."

In the time it took to drive to the clearing and the cabin, Claire struggled to find small talk. Jay didn't seem to notice. He chattered away about the road, the trees, the cabin, about everything but really nothing. By the time they finally emerged from the denseness of the forest and into the cabin's squared-off gravel parking area, he'd been yapping non-stop for the entire drive. He didn't seem to care that Claire mostly answered in noncommittal murmurs and nods.

"Well," he said now as he parked the truck. "Here we are."

He retrieved her boxes and bags and insisted on carrying everything to the porch for her, but then he stepped back. "I'll leave you to it. I know this is a private trip for you, so I'll head out and see you Monday at three. If there's too much snow, I've got the snowmobile, and I have a trailer I can hitch up to it, so don't worry about all your luggage. We'll get you out of here on time, no problem."

Jay waited, an expectant look on his face.

"Thank you so much," Claire said, wondering suddenly if she was meant to tip him. Surely not. He was the owner.

"Have fun," Jay grinned and winked.

She thought of Troy again. His words had been the same, but from Jay, Claire imagined a faint lewdness in his tone. She shook it off as her own self-consciousness.

"I plan on it," she said, perhaps a bit too blatantly cheery, too aggressively pointed.

What did she care about what Jay thought of the monthly getaways? She and Elliott had never claimed to be married to each other; if that was Jay's assumption, that was fine with her. And if it wasn't, if he knew the truth about these getaways, well...again, what did she care about what he knew? Or thought he knew?

"Hope the weather cooperates for you." Jay tossed the words over his shoulder with a wave.

And then he got into his truck and drove away.

A sudden chill swept over her. Icy wind stirred the trees. The sky overhead had gone gray and dim, promising the predicted snow. There'd be no hiking on this trip, she thought as she pulled the slip of paper with the new door code from her pocket. The string of numbers seemed familiar, but was way too long to easily remember. She'd have to keep the paper handy.

481-516-2342

Her pulse throbbed at the base of her throat. She was always a little jittery on these weekends. Not anxious. Excited. Anticipating. Eager. Today was no different. Her fingers moved clumsily on the keypad, and the door lock chastised her with an angry beep and a flash of red. Claire blew out a breath and watched it turn into silver fog. She pulled off her leather driving glove to try again. Her fingers were already numbing with cold. She typed slower this time. Pressed each button carefully.

This time, the lock rewarded her with a cheerful chirrup of a beep and a green light. She opened the door and stepped inside, breathing in the familiar scents of fireplace smoke and the fainter, floral smell that always lingered in the place. Pushing one of the totes of food in ahead of her with her foot, she left the door open and took the mystery package into the bedroom.

She set it on the bed and stared at it for a moment or so. Her breath caught. Her heart beat so fast she pressed a hand to her chest to feel the thump. She couldn't keep the smile from her face, not even when she covered her mouth with one hand. A small, infatuated giggle slipped out of her.

He was so, so good with the surprises.

There'd been times, many of them, over the past two years that Claire had told herself she was going to give this up. Give *him* up. They both had obligations that took precedence over what they did together here once a month. So far, they'd never had to cancel, but she knew at some point one of them would, for one reason or another. At some point, Claire had always assumed one of them would be "unable to make it" and simply not reschedule.

Something that felt this good couldn't last. It would be better to end things on the up note, before it turned sour, before they began to hate each other for being everything they'd promised each other they would always be. The end was inevitable, it always was, but this time she had delayed it over and over again. And why?

She had a good marriage. A loving husband, an amazing daughter on the cusp of her adulthood, and a terrific group of friends, none of whom knew about her weekend getaways. She wanted for nothing, financially. Her health was good. Getting older had only meant getting better.

Why, then, why continue with this dalliance that was sure to end in disaster? It couldn't only be the sex, which was so good that during the weeks between their meetings, Claire sometimes almost convinced herself that she was misremembering the way their bodies worked together. Because certainly, no two people could fuck so hard, so frequently, so passionately, without it getting stale. Predictable. Occasionally even boring. Yet every time, no matter how tired or unsexy she'd been feeling before she stepped into Elliott's arms, the instant he touched her, she was on fire.

This relationship was sustainable wholly *because* of the steady but infrequent scheduling of it. She was convinced of that. And the illicit thrill of it, too, of course. Keeping it a secret, something she couldn't tell her sister or even her best friends. That made a difference, too. What she did with and felt for Elliott never had the chance to get talked to death. Analyzed. Picked apart, shredded like potatoes meant for Hanukkah latkes.

This lasted because she didn't share it with anyone but him.

Claire shook herself free of the wisps of gloominess trying their best to infiltrate her. She would mourn the end of her relationship with Elliott the way she'd mourn the loss of anything she loved, but she didn't have to start today. She had the entire long weekend to enjoy and savor before that happened. Monday, though…

Monday would be the end of it all.

THREE

As much as it was killing her not to open the box, Claire left it on the bed without so much as lifting the edge of the tape. Anyway, she liked the anticipation. Her coat pocket hummed, finally, with a text as she brought the rest of her baggage in from the porch, but it turned out to be a phantom. No new message. The last text she'd had was from Aviva. Below it was the last one Troy had sent, a bare and simple exchange totally indicative of their marriage.

Butter

Unsalted?

Yes

Claire hesitated on the porch as the cold wind dipped and twisted around her, finding all the open places in her jacket. Shivers rippled through her at the icy touch. One foot inside the front door, phone in her hand, she considered texting him. Her fingers even tapped an emoji before she turned off her phone. She hung her purse on the hook right inside the door and tucked her phone firmly inside it. For good measure, she zipped the bag shut. There. Temptation and distraction put away.

She was supposed to be unplugged and out of touch so she could recharge and refresh. Friends and family knew about Claire's sacred once-a-month "me time." Nobody would be expecting to hear from her, and nobody would bother to try and get ahold of her. Not even Troy.

Especially not even him.

Claire closed the front door firmly behind her and locked it, then gave herself a moment to study the cabin, unable to contain her giddy grin and the upward rise of giggles that slipped out of her. An entire long weekend of nothing but decadence and debauchery, she thought with another secret chuckle.

Her own glee warmed her even better than the fire would, once she got that going. For now, she spun in a slow circle and allowed herself to simply revel in the joy that being in this place gave her. Delighted, as well, in being here by all by herself, at least for the moment. She relished the quiet peacefulness of a house in which she was the only living thing, a space she did not have to clean or maintain, a place she could enjoy but for which she needed to take no responsibility. Here, alone, she could take some time to simply be...Claire.

Belonging to no one, beholden to nobody.

That would change when Elliott got here, but not in a bad way. He was, after all, the reason she was here in the first place. He was, too, the reason why she was sometimes a different Claire. But there was no harm in enjoying the space to herself right now, letting herself imagine what it would be like to live by herself and not have to answer to anyone else, for any reason.

It was a fantasy she allowed herself to indulge in only rarely, because it was a dangerous dream. One that seduced but in the end, would leave her bereft. She was smart enough to know the difference between wishes and reality, to understand wanting more and being grateful for what you had.

A Claire who lived alone would not be as happy as the Claire who lived with other people imagined.

"Enough," she said aloud.

She'd always been prone to emotional highs and lows. It was her childhood response to being chastised by her equally emotional and volatile father for reacting to his outbursts. She'd rebelled by always embracing her feelings instead of stifling them the way he'd ordered her to.

Menopause had sent her into a roller coaster of emotional ups and downs wilder than she ever recalled from adolescence. Most of the time, Claire accepted the moodiness and emotional swings as part of herself, who she was and had always been, but right now she wasn't going to allow this moroseness to threaten her euphoric mood. She had only a brief bit of time to herself, and she wasn't going to squander it.

On the Homecation site, this cabin was described as "rustic and remote," and while both of those details were accurate, Claire had been thrilled to discover that rustic did not mean shabby. Comfy leather furniture, ample reading lamps, and shelves of books and games decorated the combined living and dining area. That main space connected to the kitchen, separated by a half wall that doubled as a bar with high stools. The cabin had only the single bedroom, a little too small for the king-sized bed, but it connected directly to the bathroom, which also had a door into the living room. The fireplace in the main space provided romantic ambience, but also much-needed warmth all year round — even in the summer months, the nights here in the mountains were chilly.

Jay had indeed laid in extra firewood and kindling, all of it set up neatly in the fireplace and the metal rack next to it. More wood lived on the front porch, easily accessible, and from past visits, Claire knew there was also an entire huge pile of it back behind the barn-like shed. They'd have enough to last all winter and beyond. Using the lengthy fireplace matches Jay also considerately provided, she got the fire going and sat for a moment, warming her hands, as she made sure it had caught and the chimney was drawing the smoke.

What she wanted was a drink. Opening the fridge to put away the bottles of wine she'd brought, Claire was surprised to find a bottle of her favorite white wine. All it needed was a label saying DRINK ME.

"And fall down the rabbit hole, I presume?" Claire murmured as she pulled the bottle of Briar White from the shelf. The brand was regional and not easy to find. She'd drink other brands, of course, red or white, but this was her favorite. Another rush of warmth flooded her at the thought of Elliott making the arrangements with Jay to provide her with the surprise.

It had even already been opened for her, the cork replaced but loosely enough that she'd have no trouble getting it out. Because he knew, she thought with a sudden hitching-in of her breath. He knew about her hands, and how they ached, and how hard it was sometimes for her to get the grip needed to use the corkscrew. She'd joked with him the last time about switching to brands that had screw tops, or boxed wine, forgoing her beloved Briar brand.

He'd remembered.

That was why what had been meant as a simple fling, something impermanent, had gone on and on, well past the anticipated expiration date. Because Elliott remembered the smallest things about her, and he acted on them. He figured out what would make her happy, and he did his best to give her whatever that was.

For a moment, the sting of unexpected tears blurred her vision, causing her to pause in pouring the crisp white wine into the glass in case she misjudged and spilled. Claire drew in a few quick breaths and put the bottle firmly on the counter. She wouldn't want to waste it.

"C'mon, take a breath," she admonished aloud. She pressed her fingertips below her eyes, looking upward to stop the flow of tears and preserve her mascara.

How could she end this, even though she knew it was for the best?

Her emotions swung again, melancholy merging and melding into something else she couldn't quite describe. Something akin to anticipation, although of a less joyful sort. Claire took a few more deep breaths and let it flow through and out of her. She focused on her anticipation of the weekend, all of the good and how it outweighed anything bad, and in a minute or so her happy warmth returned.

Outside, the gray sky had grown even darker, making it seem closer to dinner time than it was. She was still here hours earlier than she'd planned to be, earlier even than Elliott would have expected her. He wasn't due for another couple of hours, but she shot off a quick text to update him on what was going on, including the fact her car was parked at the bottom of the driveway and the reason why. The message stayed on DELIVERED without switching to READ, which was no surprise, considering her phone showed only a single bar of service that disappeared even as she watched. Hopefully, he'd think to check the Homecation app for any updates.

Connecting her phone to the portable speaker she always brought with her, Claire listened to music and sipped wine while she put away the groceries. In the bedroom, she efficiently unpacked her weekender, using the same drawers and hangers in the closet that had become "hers" over the past couple of years. At last, with tension thrum-thrumming all through her, no more reasons to delay, she turned to the bed and the box on it.

The first time he'd sent her a package to her job, Claire had been... upset was not the exact right word. Taken aback felt more accurate. Yes, she'd told him what she did for a living, and of course it would have taken no more than the tiniest bit of sleuthing to find the address of her office building. She hadn't told him *not* to find her. She'd never told him she would not accept gifts.

"I wanted to surprise you," Elliott had told her then. "I couldn't send it to your house, could I? I was careful, Claire. Of course, I was careful. Please forgive me."

She had. Of course, she had. That first surprise, a book of poetry she'd mentioned in passing, a bottle of her favorite wine, a candle in the scent she'd mentioned she preferred...clichés, but thoughtful ones. Caught up in that first dizziness of the affair, she'd been willing to overlook a misstep, and in the end, why was it such a big deal? She let him put his penis inside her — what difference did it make if he knew where she worked? It wasn't as though he'd shown up on her doorstep in person. Ever since, he'd sent her occasional treats to the office. Last month, he'd hinted to her there'd be something extra special to look forward to this time.

The cool wine slipped down her throat and stayed as sweet on her tongue as a kiss, but the warmth rising up the column of her throat crept into her cheeks as she contemplated the box. Carefully, already feeling the wine buzz, Claire put her glass on top of the dresser and allowed herself to caress the cardboard. She stroked the packing tape that sealed the seams. Picking at it would wreck her manicure. Instead, she fetched the makeup bag she'd put in the bathroom and found her nail kit. She used the tiny cuticle scissors to slice the tape. Putting the scissors on the nightstand, she treated herself again to a slow, sensuous sip of the wine.

Oh, how thoroughly Elliott knew her.

He knew exactly how to press each and every single one of her buttons. Knew how to make her laugh. Knew how to get her off. Knew when she wanted to be silent and when she wanted to speak.

What would the contents of this box reveal about what else he knew about her?

There was only one way to find out.

FOUR

"What's the filthiest, sexiest thing you've ever fantasized about?"

Elliott's voice is languid. They've finished fucking, but they will be ready to do it again soon enough. The tang of marijuana lingers in the air and the back of her throat, masking the taste of him on her tongue. Claire draws one more hit from the vaporizer pen and passes it back to him.

"I like to imagine myself tied up. Blindfolded. I'm wearing earplugs so I can't hear anything, either. I'm wearing the skimpiest lingerie possible, and it actually makes me feel more exposed than if I was naked. I'm waiting for a stranger to come and take me. No talking. I never see his face. He comes in, goes down on me until I come. Maybe fucks me, too."

"Why only maybe?"

"Only maybe," Claire says and laughs, "because it's my fantasy, and maybe I simply want to be taken care of without feeling like I have to reciprocate in any way."

"You want to be selfish."

"Yes," she says. "I want to be selfish."

"What happens next?"

"Then he leaves, still without speaking to me. I never hear his voice. I never tell anyone about it, never talk about it or discuss it. It's a completely *separate moment from everything else in my life, and I don't have to take a single bit of responsibility for any of it. I just get to enjoy it. And keep it to myself."*

"MY DIRTY LITTLE SECRET." CLAIRE'S VOICE HITCHED.

A head-to-toe shiver wracked her, a chill but also heat. Like a fever. Or something else, something like a deep-seeded relief, and she did mean seeded, not seated, because every time she was with Elliott, it was as though something that had been planted inside her only now was starting to bloom.

Inside the box, a froth of red and black greeted her. The nest of silky crimson fabric cradled several tiny bits of black lacy mesh that turned out to be a pair of sheer panties, so high-cut her cheeks would be on full display, but not a thong. She hated thongs.

Next came a matching teddy cut with a generous swing to the hem. She held it up to herself and turned toward the full-length mirror on the wall at the foot of the bed. The teddy would hit right above the waistband of the panties. Sexy. Classy. She couldn't say she'd have chosen this particular set for herself, but that was what made it even better — it was *not* what she'd have picked out in a store or from a catalog, but it was perfect, nonetheless.

Claire laid out the lingerie on the bed, then removed the next items. First was the coil of red silk ribbon, substantially wide and with enough length to be put to good use. Next, a matching silky scarf with fringe on the ends that tickled her skin when she drew it across her hands. A small case contained a pair of soft foam earplugs. Another small box contained a sealed pouch of two cannabis gummies, which made Claire laugh. He'd really gone all out. The wine was already moving through her veins, warming and arousing. She'd save the gummies for later.

Finally, she pulled out a square envelope of creamy, heavy paper with her name written on it in an elegant, unfamiliar script. Inside, printed instructions, not that she needed any, since Elliott had provided her with all the ingredients to fulfill a fantasy she'd already gone over with him in great detail. Overcome, Claire sat on the edge of the bed with the paper in her hand. It trembled, a little, while she took a few more breaths. The first instruction?

Enjoy your bath

Oh, she would.

The first time they'd stayed here, Claire had been delighted to discover the old-fashioned clawfoot tub. The separate single shower stall was utilitarian, but that tub held enough water to cover her entire body and the cast-iron kept the heat for as long as she wanted to soak. She'd told Elliott more than once it was one of the things she looked forward to on these weekends. She had an amazing shower at home, but a bathroom renovation there had come at the expense of a soaking tub.

Claire started the water running and finished off her glass of wine, then went to the kitchen to pour another for sipping as she luxuriated in the tub. From the kitchen window, a movement from behind the shed caught her attention. She pulled aside one charming lace curtain and saw a cascade of dead leaves eddying around the yard. A few fat flakes of white floated aimlessly downward, but only those few. Another quick glance at the sky showed a hint of blue here and there. Maybe the weather reports had mis-predicted. They were wrong all the time.

Taking her wine to the bathroom, she stripped down quickly and settled into the hot water with a hedonistic sigh. Steam bathed her face as she relaxed. The wine had gone to her head more than she'd expected, even on an empty stomach. She was tranquil. Languorous.

Inside her, soft petals unfurled. Vines of desire twisted and twined all through her. She shifted. The water slopped. Claire opened her eyes, searching for a clock, but of course there wasn't one in the bathroom, and her phone was still in her purse, hanging by the front door. Dripping, she rose from the water. She didn't want to be in the tub when Elliott got here.

The lingerie, as she'd expected, fit as perfectly as if it had been custom-made for her. Claire quivered, recalling the way Elliott liked to span her waist with his hands, fingers curling over her hips. Her nipples peaked as she recalled the way he cupped her breasts. He knew her body.

She admired herself, but critically, in the mirror. She was heavier in her fifties than she'd been in her twenties, of course, but that had translated into a full ripeness of curves that she'd lacked as a younger woman. Yes, her belly was lined with the faint silver scars of pregnancy, but daaaaaamn, wasn't her body still banging?

Oh, maybe she was a little tipsy, but she didn't care.

"You sexy bitch." Claire laughed at herself, cocking a hip and shaking her head so her dark hair tumbled over one eye. She admired the silver streaks at her temples. She'd never understood why age had to be such a burden. She'd never felt better about herself, her body, her sexuality, than she did right now. "You vixen."

She cupped her own breasts, thumbing the nipples hard through the sheer teddy. Her breath caught as one hand slid between her legs, fingers skating over the lace and the heat of her body beneath it.

Time was wasting. Quickly, breathlessly, Claire tugged down the patchwork quilt, fleecy blanket and flannel top sheet, then settled herself on the bed. The soft foam plugs went into her ears, muffling all sound.

It took her a few tries to get the pillows perfectly propped behind her. Every moment had become sharp and clear, outlined in glass. Quickly, she created two slip knots in the ends of the red ribbon and wound the length of it through the curving iron headboard, leaving each end accessible. Wrapping the scarf over her eyes sent another wave of arousal rippling through her.

The world became a hazy red. She could see shapes, but nothing more. Wriggling back onto the pillows, she managed to find the loose ends of the ribbon. She slipped her wrists through both loops and tugged the ribbon tight through the headboard. It cinched both her wrists. Experimentally, Claire shifted both her arms to pull on the ends of the ribbon. The knots got tighter, so she stopped and lay back.

She waited.

Silence.

Darkness.

The room was a little too cool for this outfit, but the heat of her anticipation was keeping her warm. Claire focused on her breathing. In. Out. She gave herself up to the moment. Trusting him.

She didn't quite hear the creak of footsteps as much as she sensed the vibration of them, along with the billow of a breeze from the direction of the doorway. She tensed, her wrists tugging the ribbon again. Her eyes opened wide, but she'd done an excellent job with the scarf and could see only the vaguest shape standing at the foot of the bed. When the bed dipped at her feet beneath the weight of a body, she cried out. She could smell crisp, fresh air. Snow, or at least the promise of it.

Hands chilly from the outside moved from her ankles up her calves and thighs. Claire's back arched when fingers skimmed over her belly. The bed dented between her legs; she spread them in invitation.

At the first breath of heat against her body through the sheer fabric of her panties, she drew in a breath and held it. Her body tensed again as she tipped her hips upward, offering herself.

Nothing.

Claire let out a frustrated rumble but loved the teasing. A light slap on her most sensitive spot shocked her into a muttered curse that turned into a gasping cry when rough hands snapped the spaghetti straps of the teddy. Another tug tore it way from her breasts. Then the scrap of panties, leaving her bared. Exposed. Open.

Ah, then yes, oh yes, there was his mouth on her, exactly as she'd imagined. Tongue and lips and even a hint of teeth had her squirming. The past hours of anticipation had readied her for this, and it felt like only moments before she was on the edge. Hips rolling. Trying to cry out but managing only harsh moans.

She tossed her head from side to side, delirious with not being able to see but loving it, still trying to get the blindfold to slip down, because the turn-on was in being unable to witness what was happening to her. She fought the ribbon binding her, too, for the same reason, not really wanting to be free but needing to feel as though she couldn't escape, even if she knew it wouldn't really take much to undo the knots she'd made.

This was a fantasy after all, her fantasy, come to brilliant, amazing life. Claire fell back against the pillows and gave in again to the onslaught of pleasure. It was too much. She was too caught up in it, and she couldn't...quite...get there. She strained toward that release, crying out...but her unseen lover withdrew.

The bed shifted again. Claire tossed her head, writhing. The press of blunt heat between her legs had her crying out again. He filled her with a single guided thrust. The weight of him covered her seconds after that. The buttons of his shirt pressed her skin. Elliott fucked harder for a few thrusts, ending with one deep, hard grind against her.

And after that...

Again, nothing.

He moved off her. Claire hadn't finished, but Elliott pulled the torn scraps of fabric off her, then covered her with the blankets. She waited for him to take off the blindfold or to undo the ribbon, at least on one wrist, but as the seconds ticked past and became a minute, then another, Claire realized Elliott had truly fulfilled her fantasy to the fullest. He'd left her alone in the room.

Now, what? Claire gave her wrist another experimental tug, but the bonds were tight. By tossing her head back and forth, she did manage to get the scarf to come off her eyes. The room had dimmed a lot. Now the light coming in through the window shone a soft, silver gray. Wind batted against the glass, but with kitten paws, claws sheathed. The living room glowed orange and amber from the fire.

She pulled out the earplugs. Had she imagined the sound of the front door shutting? The thud of footsteps on the front porch? She *had* said she wanted there to be silence, no conversation. She giggled. He'd gone outside, poised to come back into the cabin and pretend that nothing had happened between them.

This hadn't been perfect, but it had been damn close.

Claire would do her part to keep the fantasy going, which meant getting herself free. The wine had worked its way through her, and she had to pee. Also, her arms and shoulders were now starting to ache from the position. She didn't feel like giggling any more. With a groan, she rolled as far as she could to see if the nail scissors she'd used earlier were still on the nightstand. Thanking past Claire for help with present Claire's predicament, she stretched to reach them.

For a moment, the small set of scissors almost slipped from her fingers and fell out of reach, but she gripped them tight. It took a few quick, awkwardly angled snips to free her left wrist, and another few to loose the ribbon's grip on her right. Quickly, Claire stashed the scarf in her bag and remade the bed. She couldn't find the remnants of her lingerie anywhere. Elliott must have taken the shreds with him when he went back outside.

On weak legs, but moving fast, Claire went to the bathroom and used the toilet with a sigh of relief. She washed her face, brushed her teeth, used a washcloth to clean her other places. She paused.

He'd used a condom.

They'd used them in the beginning, of course, but they'd stopped a few months later. A shiver tore up and down her spine. She'd asked for a stranger, and he'd given her everything she'd asked for.

She was slipping into the robe she always packed when she heard the sound of the front door opening again. In the living room, Elliott stepped through the door and set down his overnight bag before opening his arms for her. She was in them within moments, offering her mouth for his kiss.

He shot her a grin and went back onto the porch to bring in two handfuls of plastic grocery bags. "I love the outfit."

"I was getting ready to hop in the shower." She peeked around him. The yard and road were both empty. "Jay brought you up?"

"I actually drove all the way up here, but got your text right as I pulled up. It sounded like a good idea, so I drove back down and got ahold of Jay. I should have unloaded all my stuff up here the first time, I guess. It would have saved some time. I texted you to let you know."

Claire checked her phone and tucked it back into her purse. "It didn't come through. The service up here is so spotty."

"It might be kind of exciting. Getting snowed in for a few days, just the two of us. You and me, all alone here. Nobody else. Just the two of us." In the kitchen, Elliott pulled out a loaf of French bread and set it on the counter.

He turned and took her in his arms again. His lips curved into a smile that didn't quite make it to his eyes. He looked past her, to the window. When his expression eased, Claire got the feeling he'd had to forcibly smooth it. She put a finger on his chin to turn his face to hers.

"It's always just the two of us," she said. "Are you okay?"

"Now that I'm here with you? I'm terrific," he said.

She didn't press him. They'd always talked about everything, she and Elliott. Hopes, dreams, their childhoods, jobs, families, friends, favorite movies and books and television shows. They'd bonded over unstable, judgmental fathers and mothers who didn't speak up. They shared sexual fantasies so dark and dirty she'd never even spoken of them to her closest girlfriends. But they had an unspoken agreement that neither of them ever pressured the other into sharing something they didn't want to. Never pried. It was the nature of this thing between them — everything they revealed to one another could only ever be offered. Never requested and definitely never demanded.

She turned back to unpacking the groceries. They always brought food with them, but this time... "You must be expecting us to get snowed in for a week. You brought enough for an army."

She lifted out another couple of loaves of bread, three blocks of cheese, an entire jar of kalamata olives. Inside the bags were packages of chips, tubs of dip, a going-soft cardboard carton of Chubby Hubby ice cream.

She lifted it and raised an eyebrow. "You don't like ice cream."

"But you do," he said. "And isn't that your favorite?"

This was Troy's favorite flavor. There were no subjects that were entirely off-limits, but they did usually avoid discussing their spouses. She had shared, once, her frustration with Troy's insistence that the things he loved were also her favorites even when the opposite was true. She'd probably mentioned the ice cream then, and Elliott had filed it away like he did every other thing he remembered about her.

Claire shook her head. "I actually hate it."

Elliott liberated the carton from her hand and took it to the trash can. He stepped on the pedal to lift the lid. "Then it's out of here."

"No, no," Claire said. "You don't have to waste it. If you like it?"

"It's not my favorite. But I don't want anything here that you hate. If I keep things around that you hate," he said, "who knows? You might start to hate me."

"I could never *hate* you, Elliott."

"Of course you could," he told her. "I just hope you never do."

"You don't have to throw it away. You can eat it. Or we can leave here for someone else."

In reply, Elliott gave her a smirk and dropped the ice cream into the trash like he was dropping a mic. "Boom. Done. Gone. Never to darken your doorstop again. See how I take care of you?"

"You do," she said. "You really do."

"Why don't you let me unpack the rest of this, and you go take your shower." Elliott waved a hand at her initial protest. "Let me finish this alone. Maybe there are some surprises in here that I don't want you to know about, Claire."

She laughed, already backing away. "More surprises?"

"Always more surprises," Elliott promised. "Some I guarantee you'll never see coming."

FIVE

"So much for the snow." Claire shielded her eyes to peer out the living room's oversized front windows.

She looked over her shoulder at him. Elliott, frowning, swiped at his phone. He looked up and caught her staring. Sheepishly, he made an exaggerated show of putting the phone on top of the coffee table.

"No service," he said. "I was just checking."

She didn't ask him checking what, or with who. Mobile phones had become so ubiquitous, it sometimes took her a little while to unplug once she got here, too. She pointed to the bottle of wine she'd put on the dining table set up in front of the windows. "Can you open this for me?"

"Your hands?" he asked at once, brow furrowing. He got a corkscrew from the sideboard set up behind the couch where all the barware was kept.

Claire nodded. She didn't want to talk about the growing ache in her fingers, the weakness in her grip. They'd talked about her pain before, but ill health was not a sexy topic. That was for the other Claire. Not the one she was right now.

Elliott uncorked the bottle with flair and poured her a glass of rich crimson. She held it up to the firelight to admire the color before sipping with a happy sigh. As Elliott mixed himself a gin and tonic with lime, Claire settled onto the worn leather sofa in front of the fireplace and patted the spot beside her.

"Let's make out until dinner's ready," she said.

His mouth tasted of liquor and lime and the distinct flavor of Elliott that Claire had never quite been able to identify. It, together with the way his skin smelled and tasted, was something uniquely him and not tied, so far as she could tell, to any kind of soap, cologne or lotion, not even to what he'd been eating. Purely Elliott, and she adored it. They hadn't kissed earlier, and she'd missed it.

"Mmmm," she murmured into his kiss. "Do you remember the first time we kissed?"

"How could I forget? You pounced on me. Practically ravished me."

She laughed and pushed at him. "Ha ha. That is *not* how I remember it."

"How do you remember it, Claire?" Elliott drifted his fingers down the length of her hair, twining in it before letting it go.

"You asked me out for coffee —"

"I asked you out three times before you said yes."

"You," Claire said, "needed to be persistent enough to show me you'd be worth my time."

Elliott smiled. "That was your reason?"

"Yes," she told him, not making a joke of it.

"Okay, then. I asked you out for coffee, and you finally agreed, because I was persistent enough to be worth your time. We met at that little place with the local art on the walls. The one with the organic pastries that aren't very good. We sat in a booth at the back where nobody was likely to see us, and you touched my leg with your foot under the table."

"Did I?" She didn't remember that. She recalled the coffee shop, one that was not a usual hangout. The scent of flavored coffees and toasting bread. The flavor of inadequate pastry. The murmur of singer/songwriter music in the background. She did not remember touching him until after they'd gone out to the parking lot.

"You were flirting with me," he said.

She puffed out a protest and rolled her eyes. "Oh, please. *You* were the one flirting."

"You kissed me by our cars as we were saying goodbye. I was surprised. Not expecting it at all," Elliott said, no longer making this a story to tease her with, but the truth.

Claire's brow furrowed. "You were?"

"I thought for sure you were going to tell me that you'd made a mistake. That you weren't going to see me again. We'd been texting and talking for a few months by that point, and it had been hard enough to get you to agree to meet me for coffee. I was a hundred percent certain that I'd disappoint you in person. "

She'd been worried about the same thing, but seeing him had only emphasized how attracted she was to him. She had not been afraid he wouldn't want to see her again. She'd already known what Elliott wanted from her.

"I'd already met you in person," she reminded him.

"That was different."

"I wouldn't have met you for coffee if I wasn't intending to kiss you, Elliott. By the time I said yes to coffee, I already knew I'd say yes to... whatever else you were offering."

A shadow eased over his features. Maybe the firelight flickering. Maybe something else.

Elliott downed the last of his cocktail and got up to make another. She watched him, admiring his easy but efficient movements as he poured the liquor. Adding tonic from one plastic bottle, a splash of lime juice from another. No ice. That was his personal quirk, and she shuddered at the thought of drinking room-temperature gin.

He returned to his spot next to her and offered his glass for her to clink. "L'chaim."

"Sláinte," she offered in return.

They kissed, slowly. Tantalizingly. She was still aroused from earlier, but even so, felt need to rush. In the first days, they'd basically walked in the door and fell on each other, ravenous, tearing off clothes and fucking hard and fast, sometimes without even making it to the bedroom. That had been exciting, but there was something nice in the way things had become less frantic without getting stale.

His tongue stroked hers and he replied against her lips, "I'm really glad you did. No lie, I worry every time I show up here that you'll have changed your mind, and I'll wait all weekend, alone."

"You think I would just...not show?"

He shrugged and sipped his drink. She took a sip of hers, too, not sure what to say or if she could even make a real protest. She'd ghosted people in the past, but that was usually the exception, not her habit.

"I wouldn't just not show up if I promised to meet you, Elliott. That's not who I am. I wouldn't ever just disappear. I told you that in the beginning, remember?"

"You said you'd never end it without at least telling me goodbye," he said in a low voice. "I know. But a month is a long time to go without seeing each other. I start thinking stupid stuff in the meantime. I miss you."

She snuggled against him, admiring the reflection of the fire in her wine glass. "I'm right here."

He kissed the top of her head. "You don't miss me?"

"Of course I do."

"Will you tell me?"

He sounded serious. Claire shifted to look at his face. She frowned, forcing the words to form. "Yes. I miss you."

Elliott didn't look satisfied. He looked brooding. The mood had shifted, and that irritated her.

"We only see each other once a month. Don't waste it being moody," she said crisply, moving away from him on the couch. Her father's words had come out in her voice, and she didn't like it.

He looked vaguely chastened and was silent for a few seconds. "Don't you ever wish we could meet somewhere else?"

"You don't like the cabin? I thought you said this place was perfect. Halfway between us both. Private."

No chance of them running into anyone they knew.

Elliott's brow creased. "It has been. It is. Don't you ever want a change of scene?"

He was her change of scene, but she wasn't going to say so. "Maybe Homecation has another place we could try. Maybe on a lake or something."

"We should go to Ireland together."

He was joking. He had to be. "Why not all the countries that start with an I?"

"Anywhere would be fun, if we went together. Because that's what you do, Claire. You make things fun." When she leaned to kiss him again, he drew back. "I wasn't kidding about the trip. I want to take you away somewhere. Longer than a weekend."

She said nothing. Despite the roaring fire, she wished that after her shower she'd put on something heavier than her sexy nighty and the robe. Her chill had little to do with the temperature in the room.

"I said —" he began.

"How much longer until dinner's ready?"

Elliott scowled. "You always do that."

"Do *what*?" Claire drew the robe closer around her throat and sipped more wine.

"Deflect," he told her. "Whenever I make so much as a hint that I want something more than this."

Carefully, Claire set her glass on the coffee table. "Don't start again, Elliott. Please. I thought we'd agreed —"

"You agreed," he said shortly. "*You* did."

For almost the entirety of this relationship, she and Elliott had not fought. When all you had with each other was the highlights, there was no need for arguments. No room for them.

"I don't believe in making promises that I'm not sure I can keep. I've told you that before." She turned away from him and placed both her hands on her knees. Her shoulders ached from earlier, a dull throb she hadn't noticed until now.

Elliott put his glass beside hers and got up from the couch to pace in front of the fire. "Right. I *know*. I just don't see what the big deal is about telling you how I *feel*."

If she laughed at him now, it would hurt him, so Claire held back the sharp chuckle that had nothing to do with amusement. Elliott was even more of a feeler than she was. "It's not about that, and you know it. Get ahold of yourself."

His gaze flashed as he faced her. He looked...surprised? Put off? She'd warned him in the beginning that she had a temper, but she'd always done her cautious best never to show it before now. She'd never had to.

"Then what *is* it about, Claire?"

She sighed. "Why does it always go this way? Why can't anyone simply take things for what they are and what they're meant to be? Why can't anyone ever be satisfied with it being enough?"

At his flinch, Claire bit her tongue. Hard. She *had* hurt him, despite her best efforts.

"I forgot you were an expert at this," he said. "Forgive me for not having a much shorter resumé than you do."

Claire touched the tip of her first finger to her forehead, between her eyes. She forgave him for being unfair and took it as her due for being unkind. "I've never lied to you, Elliott."

"No," he said. "You only lie to *him*."

The bitterness in his voice was so sour, so pointed, he might as well have tossed his gin and tonic in her face. Claire's startled gasp was too loud, but she stopped herself from clapping a hand over her mouth. Blinking rapidly to keep herself from letting the sudden tears slip down her cheeks, she lifted her chin and set her jaw. She had a protest to make, a defense to give, but she found herself incapable of making it.

"I'm sorry. I'm sorry, baby, I'm sorry, I'm so sorry." Elliott went to her, but when he tried to pull her close to him, she put out a hand to keep him at arm's length.

He got onto his knees in front of her. When she refused to let him take her hands, he put his on her knees, instead. He put his face against them. His shoulders heaved with an enormous sigh.

"I'm sorry," he said one more time. "I hate knowing you've done this before. I hate knowing this isn't as important to you as it is to me. I fucking *hate* it, Claire. I try not to, but I still do."

She threaded her fingers through his hair to cup the back of his skull. With her other hand, she dashed away the two tears that had breached her eyelids. She took a deep breath.

"Look at me, Elliott."

He would not.

She pulled his hair until he lifted his head. She was hurting him, but this time on purpose. His pain glittered in his gaze, but the press of his lips showed there was pleasure in it, too.

"I won't tell you that anything I did before I met you didn't matter, because that would be a lie. I *will* tell you that what I have with you is precious, and I cherish and value it, and I cherish and value you." She loosened her grip on his hair and slid her hand around to cup his chin, keeping him looking at her. "But I will *not* make promises I don't think I can keep."

"They're only words," he began, but she gripped his chin tighter until he went silent.

"Words can cut deeper than any knife, Elliott. What we say to each other is important."

He turned his face to kiss her palm. "What about the words we won't say?"

Without waiting for her to answer, he pushed his face forward, nudging open her thighs and parting the robe so it fell open. His hot breath caressed her. Claire's low sigh shuddered out of her when Elliott slid his hands up and onto her hips to shift her to the edge of the couch.

When his mouth found her skin, she cried out. Arched. Her fingers dug deep into the dark thickness of his hair again, pulling. Guiding.

Her rising pleasure overtook rational thought, and she was happy to let it go. This was what they were here for. This was what they *were*. Mouths and hands and tongues and lips and teeth and slick wetness, hard and deep and —

"Oh," she cried out. "Oh. Yes. There."

She could have gone over the edge in another few seconds, but Claire fought off her climax by pulling his head back again. Elliott's eyes were dazed. His mouth, wet. He made a noise of protest, but she hushed him with her finger over his lips.

"On your back," she said urgently, already moving. He obeyed, of course, as he always did, and she straddled him, fighting with his belt buckle until he helped her. Together, they worked to get his jeans open and shoved down to his thighs, and she got back on top of him.

That first moment, the joining of his flesh to hers, always urged a cry from both of them, and this time was no different. She seated him inside her. Then moved. His hands went to her hips, fingers denting the generous swell of her flesh.

They moved together in perfect coordination. Well-oiled gears, meshing without a single clash. Pleasure rose up and up and up, and this time she didn't stop it but instead let the ecstasy flood her until, shaking, she finished. He followed her a moment later, spilling inside her with a low, strangled groan that sounded very much like her name.

Claire had been unaware that she'd been digging her fingernails on both hands into the meat of his chest, but she released her grip, leaving behind small half-moon marks she soothed immediately with her fingertips.

"I'm sorry," she whispered hoarsely. "I promised you I would never leave marks."

Elliott took her hand and pressed the palm to his mouth. A kiss. Another. He kept her hand curled into his and put it on his chest.

"Too late," he said.

SIX

TWO YEARS AGO

"How long do we have to stay at this thing?" Troy was discreet enough to mutter this under his breath, but Claire elbowed him in the side anyway.

"Until the booze runs out," she said.

Troy groaned. "It's never going to run out. The Allweins are fucking lushes."

He wasn't wrong. Jack and Brenda Allwein had what amounted to a full bar in their living room. No television in there, either. Drinking was clearly their entertainment.

"All that liquor," Troy continued, *sotto voce*, "and they don't even have a decent whiskey."

He lifted his glass of what she assumed had to be something cheap.

Claire rolled her eyes and leaned against him for a moment. "Poor baby. Drink it faster, maybe it'll taste better."

Troy frowned. "Don't tell me you're having a good time. They've played 'Santa Baby' about eight times already. The Madonna version.

Anyway, you know they only invited us because they felt like they had no other choice."

The obligatory Christmas party invitation from the boyfriend's parents had come in last minute, a quickie message left on Claire's voicemail instead of the fancy printed card she knew the Allweins sent out at the beginning of October. They didn't travel in the same social circles, but that didn't mean she'd never heard of their legendary December parties. Claire and Troy had been standing in the corner by themselves since they'd arrived.

"So leave. I'll stay. I can grab a Ryde home," Claire said.

"You mean it?"

He looked so hopeful, so adorable, that she kissed his mouth.

"I mean it," Claire said. "We're only here because it's possible that one day we'll be related to these people. Might as well begin as we mean to go on, right? The sooner they figure out you're an old poop, the better."

He made as though to swat her but then laughed. He kissed her. The noises of the party swelled around them, laughter and music, the clink of glasses and silverware on plates. He put his hands on her hips, turning her to face him. He leaned close.

"I'll owe you one."

Claire made a face. "You will definitely owe me more than one."

Over his shoulder, she glimpsed Aviva's dark curls. Their daughter was in animated conversation with a group of people who looked to be her own age, although Claire didn't recognize any of them. They must be Brent's friends. Aviva glanced toward her mother, gesturing.

"I'll stay a while longer. For Viva." Claire kissed her husband and gently turned him, pushing his shoulder. "Besides, you old grump, I'll have a much better time without you here."

He looked over his shoulder as he let her push him toward the front door. "You usually do. What time will you be home?"

"That depends," she said with a smile.

Troy paused to face her. He put his hand on her shoulder, his eyes searching hers. "Please let me know if you're going to be late, that's all. You know I'll worry, otherwise."

She stopped teasing him and picked up his hand to kiss the back of it. "I know."

He looked around the room, then back at her with narrowed eyes. "You think you'll be late?"

"That depends," she repeated, softer this time. "But considering the locale, it seems unlikely, doesn't it?"

Troy kissed her cheek instead of her mouth, this time, and squeezed her shoulder. She watched him walk away. She make their excuses to the Allweins and go after him. She could even manufacture an Irish Exit and simply slip out the door to catch him before he reached the car.

Aviva waved again, this time a little more urgently. Claire sighed. Her daughter would understand that her father had ducked out of the party. He was no good at functions like this, preferring to be at home with his computer games or online conversations. His very-not-cheap-and-so-very-expensive whiskey.

Claire was the one who shone at parties, vivacious and effervescent and charming. She had worked very hard to cultivate what Aviva had inherited so innately. For Viva, social functions were truly fun; for Claire, she made a good show, but they left her drained for days after.

Well. She was here to support her daughter, who'd been dating Brent Allwein long enough that his parents must have accepted the fact she was sticking around. Hence the party invite.

Claire didn't much care about Jack and Brenda, one way or another, and all she hoped from their son was that he was kind to her daughter, who seemed to be in love with him. She remembered the burden of having a parent you couldn't count on not to embarrass you. One you couldn't actually count on at all. She'd vowed she would never let her daughter down that way. If that meant making nice with the boyfriend's parents, then that's what she would do.

"Mom!" Aviva gestured.

Claire made her way through the crowd to put her arm around Aviva's waist. "Hello, girly."

"Hey, everyone, I want you to meet my mom. Mom, this is everyone." Aviva leaned into her mom's embrace, and for a moment, Claire was struck with a sense of wistful gratitude so deep, so strong, it was as physical as a slap.

There were multiple reasons why Claire and her own mother had never been close, but it wasn't until she'd reached adulthood that Claire understood how common it was. So many of her friends weren't close with their daughters. Women she'd gotten to know over playdates and dance recitals and scouting and mother-daughter fundraiser breakfasts, women whose children had grown up alongside Claire's own. They spoke of how their babies had become strangers, or worse, enemies. It would kill her if that ever happened to her and Aviva.

"Hi, everyone," Claire said.

Brent's friends were...much like Brent, himself. Good-looking kids raised with privilege. They went to good schools. Drove nice cars that had been graduation presents. Aviva fit in well with them, and if Claire privately thought her daughter was more poised, mature, funnier, well-rounded...she'd never say so here and now. Now, she smiled and nodded and greeted the group of young men and women who'd been taking up so much of her daughter's time.

And then, of course, there was Brent.

"Ms. Fitzgerald," he said, appearing behind Claire and putting a familiar hand on her hip so briefly, so casually, there could be no reason for her to startle. He kissed her cheek, too, but moved to Aviva's side at once.

If he gave Claire a look, she pretended it was of no significance. What someone did after too many rum-and-cokes should never be held against them. Not even if that person was decades younger and now dating your daughter.

"Brent," she said as warmly as she could. "Always so good to see you."

"Where's Dad?" Aviva asked.

"He ducked out. He had some things to take care of at home."

Aviva rolled her eyes, looking very much like her father.

"Hey, at least he made it for a couple of hours," Claire chastised, her voice light for the benefit of the others.

"Was he *ever* any fun?" Aviva asked.

Claire recalled a time when Troy had, in fact, been a lot more "fun" than he was now. Loyalty prompted her to answer a little differently. "Your dad's still fun. He's just more fun when he's at home."

"That's nice. Hearing someone say something nice about their husband," said a girl whose name Claire had completely forgotten. "Lots of times, people think it's funny to be mean about their husbands or wives."

"Ms. Fitzgerald is never mean. She's always polite. Always kind." Brent lifted a glass in her direction.

"That's just really nice," repeated the girl. Britt, Claire recalled suddenly. Her name was Britt. "My parents are constantly being snarky about each other. I mean, I think they love each other," she added hastily, maybe embarrassed. "But they're kind of mean about each other."

"My parents have exactly the kind of relationship I always wanted," Aviva said. Her eyes gleamed, and Claire glanced at the glass in her daughter's hand. She was tipsy. She was happy.

When her daughter leaned against Brent, Claire looked away.

"You kids have fun. I'm going to find something to nosh on. I'm starving," Claire told them all and ducked away before anyone could say more.

She weaved her way through the crowd. The Allweins' oversized Victorian had been extensively renovated, but the interlocking rooms of parlor, dining room, and sitting room remained untouched here on the ground floor, and the party guests had made full use of the entire space. Festive holiday foods had been laid out on tables all throughout, but even if she wanted to hunt through the platters and bowls to find something amongst the seafood or pork-laden delicacies that she'd be able to eat, Claire wasn't really hungry. If anything, her stomach had gone a little tight. She should have gone home with Troy. Aviva didn't really need her here anymore. Claire was going to make her thank-yous and goodbyes and head out.

Brent's dad was holding court in a far corner of the kitchen, regaling some guests with what sounded like a story about vacationing in the Caribbean. It involved a lot of hand gestures and loud laughter. He saw Claire and waved to draw her over. To her discomfort, he put an arm around her shoulders and drew her close until they were hip to hip. He rubbed a hand up and down her arm, his fingers curled with too much familiarity on bare skin before he let go.

"Everyone, have you met Claire? She's Aviva's mother. Brent's girl," he added for the benefit of anyone who might not know. For Claire's, he said, "We think she's just something special, isn't she? Such a bright girl."

Claire gave everyone a wide, glittering smile. "We're quite impressed with Brent, too."

"Claire, tell me you know the Kogans. They go to...where do you go?" Jack snapped his fingers toward a man and a woman Claire did not know. "Beth Shalom?"

"No, sorry, we haven't met." Claire dutifully shook both the Kogans' hands without learning their first names. They all shared understanding looks.

"You don't have a drink. Let me get you a drink. Bourbon? Gin?" Jack snapped his fingers. "Wine. I bet you're a Wine Mom, aren't you? Live, laugh, love?"

She was not. At all. Ever.

"Wine sounds great," she said.

Fortunately for her patience, Jack was easily distracted after he poured her a glass of wine and went back to his stories, so Claire could slip away. The wine wasn't as terrible as Troy had said the whiskey was, so she was grateful for that. She eased away from Jack while he was launching into another story about some vacation he'd taken.

Claire looked for Brenda so she could at least say goodbye to the hostess, but Brent's mom was nowhere to be found. Too many people, too much going on. Claire ducked onto a sunporch off the kitchen, hoping that when she got to the dark and quiet space she'd have some time to simply breathe on her own while she enjoyed her drink and gathered her strength to go back to the party. When she got there, she found it already occupied. The dim glow of a cigarette lit a silhouette. A man.

"Oh," she said. "Sorry. I didn't mean to barge in on you."

When she stepped to the side, light from inside the house shone onto his face. He smiled. Gestured toward the padded benches lining the glass walls.

"Don't worry about it," he said. "I've been waiting for you."

Claire paused. Her lips pressed together in a smile. "Oh, really? For how long?"

"My whole life, I think," the stranger said and held out a hand. "I'm Elliott."

CLAIRE HAD BEEN DREAMING ABOUT THE FIRST TIME SHE AND Elliot had met.

They'd spent an hour talking at the Allweins' horrible Christmas party. Then another. He'd asked for her number and she'd given it to him, certain it would lead to nothing. He was at least fifteen years younger. Fit, with a long, lean and athletic build that spoke of outdoorsy adventures and regular workouts. He was classically tall, dark, and handsome, and too charming for his own good. It wasn't that she didn't think she was worth his attention. She simply hadn't thought he would be able to keep hers.

She'd known it was foolish to start up something with a man who knew people she knew. She'd always kept her secrets by choosing partners with no connection to her everyday life. Discovering that Elliott lived a couple of hours away from her helped. So did his jokes, his compliments, the way he'd started sending her "good morning" and "good night" texts, and the way he kept everything precisely distant enough that she could convince herself it was only a friendship. Nothing more.

She *had* made him ask her three times to meet again in person, and it *had* been so she could be sure he was persistent enough, but she'd had other reasons, too. That same charm and persistence was almost too attractive to her. It had felt...dangerous, and not in the good way.

Claire had always avoided that sort of danger, the kind that led to broken hearts.

So, why was she here now, two years later?

Claire blinked, looking upward into darkness. Getting into bed was no more than a hazy memory. A faint reddish glow from the living room told her the fire had been banked. At her side, the warmth of Elliott's naked body was a comfort. She had no clear idea of how long she'd been sleeping, but her bladder told her it had been a few hours. Her mouth felt dry, as though she'd had too much to drink.

White light lit the room on Elliott's side of the bed. Without moving her body, Claire looked his way. His shadow hand held his phone as he lay on his side. Scrolling? Swiping? Texting, she thought as she heard the sound of his fingers tapping the screen.

Was that what had woken her? The faint bing-bing of a text tone, or the light? She heard nothing now but the wind outside and what sounded like fingernails rapping at the window. Sleet, she thought sleepily. Not a witch's fingers. She really needed to get up and pee. When she shifted, Elliott moved quickly, tucking his phone away. He settled back onto his pillow, still facing away from her.

She waited for a few seconds to convince him she hadn't noticed him using the phone before she got out of bed and went to the bathroom. She shut the door quietly behind her. Two years of monthly getaways might have given them the comfort of being able to sleep together, but it had not yet been enough time for her to use the toilet in front of him. Some acts were never going to be okay for lovers.

The cold seat under her bum woke her up a little more than she wanted. She stifled a jaw-cracking yawn and looked below the door. No white light. At least he wasn't on his phone again.

It wasn't something they'd ever made a rule between them, but it had become their habit to turn their phones off when they arrived and put them away. This was the first time she could think of that he'd been so persistent about using his, and it was definitely the first time she could ever think of him trying to keep it hidden from her.

Never mind how he was managing to get service, why was he texting so much in the middle of the night? And who? It wasn't her business, she reminded herself. She made a little more noise than necessary, warning him of her return, when she washed her hands and drank a large glass of cold water from the tap. He rolled toward her when she got into bed. They spooned. His breathing slowed, and her mind softened back into dreams.

Outside the window, a flash of light bobbed up and down before going out. Claire blinked, wondering if it had come from Elliott's phone. But no, there it was again, a quick strobe of light that came and went so fast she couldn't be sure she'd imagined it. Was it lightning? The cabin creaked and groaned from the wind, but she heard no thunder. It wasn't the season for it, anyway.

"You awake?" Elliott's voice was little more than a whisper. His fingers curled, cupping her breast.

Claire didn't answer.

"Claire," Elliott murmured, lower even than a whisper, his voice little more than a dream. "I love you."

SEVEN

The faintest chirp of a ringtone tiptoed into Claire's unconsciousness. Her eyes opened, and for a moment, she wasn't sure where she was. If she'd been dreaming, she didn't recall it. The slanted ceiling, rough and knotty wood planks, swam into focus. Disoriented, she blinked rapidly and pushed up on one elbow.

The cabin.

For the first time in all the weekends they'd been coming here, she didn't wake up with a smile. She swept a hand over the empty bed next to her. Cool sheets. Elliott must've been up for a while, then. Time enough to brew coffee. She could smell it. She considered calling him back to bed for a morning snuggle that would certainly turn into something sexier...but she did not. Instead, Claire lay on her back and stared at the ceiling.

She'd feigned sleep last night so she could pretend she hadn't heard Elliott's confession. She suspected that he'd guessed she was faking it, but he'd only patted her hip and rolled away from her, after. He hadn't said anything else, but she'd still had a hard time going back to sleep. No wonder she was struggling to wake up now.

If she counted back the months to the first time she knew Elliott loved her, she'd need to use more fingers than she had on both hands.

The fact he'd fallen in love with her had not surprised her. Everyone said men were the ones who wouldn't commit, who didn't know how to love, the ones who were always up for a purely sexual relationship with no emotional ties, but in Claire's experience, men were the ones who attached too much importance to sex.

A one-night stand? Fine. But start sleeping with someone on the regular, and sooner rather than later, he was going to start equating that great sex with something that meant more. He'd try to tell himself *she* was the one with the emotional ties, and he was only along for the ride. Elliott falling in love with her had not surprised her; the fact he'd waited so long to say it to her aloud, however, did.

Two years. It explained his insistence on this trip being extra special. It was an anniversary that Elliott knew she wouldn't feel comfortable celebrating in any conventional way. Two years of these cabin getaways. Two years together. What was to stop them from having another year? And then another? Before they knew it, ten years might have passed, quick as a sip of wine, and how could anyone be expected to carry on two relationships for that long?

Something crunched on the gravel outside, and something else thumped the ground close to the cabin. She already knew the thin walls meant any noises from outside were often exaggerated — Elliott liked to joke that if a squirrel sneezed in the backyard, they'd hear it in the living room. This sounded much bigger than a squirrel, though. They'd seen deer a few times, far across the meadow and close to the trees. It didn't seem likely a deer would be pounding on anything near the house. That sound had been made by a human. She listened for more noises, but everything had gone quiet.

After a moment, she rolled onto her side and reached automatically for her phone. Her fingers swiped on the nightstand's bare wood. She really must be a little out of it — her phone was still, so far as she knew, in her purse. Tucked away for the weekend the way it always was. Elliott's was not on his nightstand, either.

The low murmur of his voice drifted to her through the closed bedroom door. She sat up, her ears straining. She couldn't make out the words, only the urgent rise and fall of his voice. He sounded upset.

Whatever was going on, Claire wanted no part of it. She lingered in the bathroom, making more noise than was needed, alerting him the way she'd done in the middle of the night. Although they often spent the mornings here in their pajamas, or naked, this time she got fully dressed to give him plenty of time to finish his conversation. She waited until she could no longer hear even the faintest hint of his voice before she left the bathroom.

In the kitchen, she found a pot of coffee and a plate of bagels set on the counter, together with cream cheese, lox, capers, sliced red onion, and tomato. He'd arranged everything neatly on a plate and added a fork to serve it with. This was only breakfast, but it squeezed her heart. Elliott always put forth such an effort to make everything special. An occasion. A celebration.

Love, she thought. Oh, what was love, anyway, but the thing your heart did right before it broke?

Elliott had been looking out the kitchen window but turned when she came in. No phone in sight. He smiled at her the way he always did, as though she was the most beautiful thing he'd ever seen. It was addictive, being so consistently desired. And easy for him, she thought, jaded. Easy to desire what you never get enough of.

"Good morning, beautiful."

"Look at you," she said lightly, "so impressive here, with the traditional Jewish breakfast."

"I know it's your favorite, and I also know you don't indulge yourself with it often. I've got some of those little cans of cinnamon rolls you like, too. Figured we could make them tomorrow morning. Or today, if you want. Whatever you want."

She crossed to him. Offered her mouth for a kiss. "When did you get up?"

"A while ago. I like the mornings here. Very quiet." He put his arms around her, hugging her tight.

She rested her face against the soft flannel of his shirt. Beneath it, his heart thumped steadily against her cheek. She toyed with a button and kept her tone casual. "Who were you talking to?"

Elliott's hand stroked down her spine, then up again to cup the back of her neck below the tangle of her hair. He kissed her temple. "Why would you think I was talking to someone?"

"I thought I heard your voice." She didn't push away to look into his face. She concentrated on his heartbeat. It stayed steady, but she knew he had to be good at lying.

"I must've been talking to myself." He pulled away to kiss her forehead, then the tip of her nose. Her mouth. His lips dallied on hers before skating away. "Coffee?"

She let out a small and grateful groan. "Of course. Any snow yet?"

"Nope. Not a single flake. Sky looks gray, though." He bustled with the coffee, pouring her a full mug and one for himself.

Claire went to the kitchen window at the back side of the house and pulled aside the curtain. "Was someone here earlier? I thought I heard something out back."

"I saw Jay's truck this morning while you were still in bed. He walked back by the shed. I think he was checking the propane tank. He didn't stop by."

"He doesn't usually, does he?" She thought of past trips and if there'd been even glimpses of the cabin owner. "Yesterday was the first time I've ever met him."

"If the weather is going to be as bad as he said, I think it's a good thing he's making sure we're prepared."

She sipped coffee. "Do you think it'll be that bad?"

"You worried?" He tilted his head to study her. "You're not thinking about cutting out early, are you?"

"No."

But wasn't she? It would be a good excuse. She thought again of her earlier musings — how one month, one of them would cancel and simply wouldn't reschedule. How could she have believed it would be that simple? Elliott would never let her end it that way. She'd be lucky if he *let* her end it at all.

Breaking this off was going to be ugly, and it would be all her fault. She'd seen the warning signs that their casual, once-a-month relationship was turning into something else, and she'd ignored them so she could keep indulging herself. Her selfishness had brought them to this point, and she wasn't the only one who was going to pay the price for it.

"You sure?" He eyed her before plucking a bagel from the plate and separating it into two pieces he slipped into the toaster. Without waiting for an answer, he continued, "I thought we could go for a hike today. Before the snow starts. Get ourselves nice and sweaty before we come back here and get nice and sweatier. You know what this place really needs? A hot tub. I think I'll make the suggestion to Jay. What do you think?"

He was talking too much. Too fast. Trying to distract her by changing the subject.

"That sounds like a great idea," Claire said.

"We can go up to the waterfall. It'll be frozen. I've always wanted to see it that way."

She nodded. "Sure. That sounds great."

"Good." He nodded.

The toaster popped up, breaking the tension between them they both wanted to pretend was not there. Elliott didn't ask her if she wanted him to prepare the bagel for her; he simply did it with the expertise one could expect from someone who paid attention. From someone who loved you, she thought, and had to turn away from the sight of him.

When she looked up, he was staring at her with an expression that told her he knew exactly what she was thinking. He didn't call her out, though. They'd never spoken of love except in the abstract...until last night.

Elliott turned back to the counter. His shoulders hunched for a few seconds before he straightened. When he turned back, he had two plates laden with bagels, piled high with all the fixings. He frowned and took the plates to the table in the living room.

"Claire, baby, what's wrong?"

"Nothing," she lied. "I guess I didn't sleep well last night. My stomach's a little unsettled."

"You did hit the wine earlier than I did," he teased lightly. "You want some plain toast instead?"

Her stomach still felt a little twisted, but she wasn't convinced it was from the wine. "And pass up one of those amazing bagels? No way."

To her surprise, Elliott pressed the back of his hand to her forehead. "You don't feel warm."

"I'm not sick. Anyway, serves me right for being greedy."

"I would never call you greedy," Elliott said.

They ate without speaking for a few minutes. He got up to pour her more coffee. She finished half her bagel and pushed the plate away, wanting more but knowing she'd regret eating the whole thing. When she got up to take her plate to the kitchen, it slipped from her hand and toppled toward the floor.

"Whoa. Watch out." Elliott caught it deftly with one hand, using the other to slap on top of the stacked bagel and keep it from flipping off the plate.

A single caper escaped and rolled away beneath the couch. They both stared at it. Claire tried to think of something funny to say. Something self-deprecating. She couldn't come up with anything.

"Do they hurt? Your hands?" Elliott asked.

Instinctively, she flexed her fingers. "No more than usual. I'm just clumsy."

He knew that wasn't the truth. Her autoimmune condition meant that her joints, especially her hands and fingers, were going to keep hurting more and more, and her grip was going to get weaker over time. She wasn't going to be severely disabled from it, but she could be inconvenienced.

"Did you bring any of that cream? The CBD cream. I can rub it into your hands for you."

Her response was clipped. "No. Thanks. I'm okay."

She held out her hand for the plate, but Elliott didn't give it to her.

"I don't want to talk about it with you," she said when he didn't speak.

"You can talk to me about anything, Claire."

"Can and want are different things." She'd explained a bit about them, early on, to let him know why sometimes she didn't want him to hold her hands. Why she had a prescription for medical marijuana. She'd kept the topic hushed for the most part after that, even though she'd always known he was curious.

"I only want to help you."

"It's not—" she cut herself off. Tried again with a nicer tone. "This is our weekend. I don't want to talk about my hands. They're fine."

He sighed. "I hate seeing you in pain. That's all."

Here was another reason to end this, before she deteriorated to a point where she would no longer be able to meet up with him. Better to end it while they could both remember each other as vibrant. Before he started seeing her as someone who needed caretaking instead of lovemaking.

Through the window, she glimpsed sight of Jay's black pickup truck rounding the corner of the cabin. She moved closer to the glass, twitching aside the lacy curtain. The cabin's owner drove the truck around the back of the shed.

"Jay's back," she said. "He's got his truck out there by the shed again."

"I told you, he's probably checking the propane tank. Making sure it's all okay. This is his business, Claire. If we're foolish enough to book a place on the weekend of a blizzard, he's got to be smart enough to make sure we're not going to freeze to death."

"Sure. I'm sure you're right," she said, still watching.

After a moment, Jay's truck reappeared. This time it pulled a trailer behind it. It had a snowmobile on it. He drove off down the road and out of sight.

"He took his snowmobile out of the shed," she said.

"See? He's making sure he can get up here, exactly the way he said he would. Feel better?"

She faced him, knowing he was going to hate what she was about to say. "Maybe we should think about heading out today."

Elliott frowned. "No, no. Listen, love, we're going to be fine. I promise."

Obviously, he didn't have the same idea about not making promises he wasn't sure he could keep. She looked again through the glass. Not even a flake of snow.

"We could be stranded here. For real," she said.

"Fine. If that happens, I give you permission to eat me."

Claire made a face and looked at him. "That's so gross."

"What?" Elliott pretended to be offended as he turned to slap one butt cheek. "This is prime meat right here. I'm a full-on feast. I mean, you'd have to kill me first. But I could feed you for a month, no problem."

She'd started laughing at his ridiculousness, but sobered quickly. "That's not funny."

His grin faded. "Sorry. Cannibal humor is too far?"

"Not that part. I could never kill you, Elliott. How can you even say that?"

"Anyone can kill someone," he told her, "if they felt they had no other choice."

EIGHT

"LET'S HOPE I WOULD NEVER HAVE TO MAKE THAT CHOICE."

He pulled her closer for a kiss. "You never know what you'll do in a situation until you're in it."

Irritated, Claire nudged him away from her. "Stop."

"Sorry," he said again.

"Do you still want to go on that walk?"

He nodded. "Yes. Absolutely."

"I'm not sure I'm going to be warm enough." Claire looked down at her skinny jeans. Her knee-high riding boots were comfortable enough for a stroll over flat ground, but not good for hiking. Her wool pea coat would keep her warm, but her leather driving gloves were fashionable, not practical. "This is all I brought."

Elliott frowned. For a few seconds, she saw his hesitation and thought he would be the one to bail out. "The waterfall's not that far away. It'll be good to get out into the fresh air. It'll make you feel better. But if you really don't want to go..."

"No. It'll be fine." She could give him this.

"I don't want you to do something you don't really *want* to do."

"Elliott," she said, trying to hide her irritation, "I *want* to see the waterfall. Give me a few minutes to get ready."

He nodded, holding her gaze for a moment. "I'll clean up from breakfast. Take your time."

She used the bathroom and pulled a long-sleeved shirt off a hanger in the closet. Spotting the high heels she'd worn yesterday, Claire shook her head. She had definitely planned for warmer activities. But although the idea of hiking through the cold in her inadequate gear was not top on her list of ways she wanted to spend the weekend, the idea did have some appeal if only because it would get them out of the cabin. Get them doing something other than fucking...or fighting.

In the living room, Elliott showed off a small backpack, then slung it over his shoulders. "I packed a thermos. Some snacks. I know it'll be chilly, but I thought —"

"You think of everything."

She'd tried to keep her tone light. Neutral. There must've been something a little more biting in it, though, because his eyes narrowed. Only briefly.

"I want to take care of you, Claire. That's all. If you really don't want to go on the hike, we don't have to go. We can stay inside by the fire and drink wine. Play games," he said with a glance at the bookshelf loaded with board games. "I could beat your butt at Monopoly."

"We've never played Monopoly."

"See?" he said. "There's always something new to learn about each other."

A kiss took the place of what she did not want to say aloud.

Outside, Claire took in a long, deep breath of crisp winter air. The hairs inside her nose froze. Her cheeks tingled from the cold, and the smell of impending snow, electric and sharp, invaded her. She blew out a white breath of smoke and shoved her hands deep into the pockets of her peacoat. The snow had not yet started falling, but the crisp bite of ice hovered in the air.

Her boots crunched on the gravel as they crossed the parking area and sounded a different sort of complaint against the frostbitten grass of the field. Elliott had taken the lead, walking ahead instead of beside her, and she was glad for that. She wasn't in the mood to hold hands and saunter. The waterfall wasn't far off, he was right about that, but that didn't mean she wanted to lollygag on the way there.

By the time they got to the tree line, her toes were protesting the onslaught of numbness. Her thighs burned with the kind of heat that came from being too cold. Many times over the past eighteen months she'd come back from a getaway with aches and pains, occasionally even bruises that hadn't been there before she left. This was a different way of working her body. Stretching and shifting and breathing, in and out, focusing on each step she was taking one at a time. Elliott turned back to offer her his hand. Her gloves were thin enough to let her curl her fingers into his, but she squeezed them only for a moment before letting them open.

When he looked back at her again, Claire forced a smile. "It's too cold for a leisurely stroll, hand-in-hand. Keep those hot buns moving, sexy. The faster we move, the warmer we'll stay."

Elliott stopped, pivoting. His heels crunched on the frozen grass. "Forget it. Let's just go back."

"Back? No. C'mon." She glanced behind her, toward the cabin and its plume of welcoming smoke.

Every relationship had a turning point. Sometimes, several of them. Here was one, and it seemed as though they both knew it, but neither would admit it. She surely didn't want to, anyway. Not here or now. Monday would be here soon enough.

"I want to see the waterfall," she told him and started moving with determined steps again toward the tree line. "I bet it's gorgeous when it's frozen."

After half a minute, he caught up to her. This time when he reached for her hand, she let him take it.

Beneath the canopy of trees, the forest floor was thickly laid with pine needles that cushioned their footsteps into silence. Everything was quieter here. Dim and shadowed. The few times they'd hiked here during the summer, those shadows had brought a welcome coolness — this high on the mountain, the sun seemed to blaze so much brighter. Today, the soft gray quiet wrapped around her like a cloak, cutting the breeze and warming her.

The path wound through the trees, wide enough for three or four people to walk next to each other in most places, occasionally wider or narrower. No markers designated the way, but the trail was clear enough. Several other paths broke off the main one, none of them marked, either. The forest around the cabin was not part of any mapped hiking trails, which meant that none of them were officially maintained, but they were nevertheless in decent enough shape.

"Look at that." She pointed to something strung between a few of the trees. A few tiny vines, dead now, clung to it. She moved closer. "Barbed wire?"

"Probably some kind of fencing. A property line or something." Elliott kicked at the ground beneath it, turning up pine needles and dead leaves. Something metal clanged against his boot, and he overturned it with his toe. "*No Trespassing* sign. See?"

"It seems dangerous. Without the sign there anyone could accidentally walk into that wire. Get really cut up." She stopped herself from actually touching the wire, which bore nasty looking barbs, all rusted. There were gaps, but more wire stretched between a few of the other trees. If it was meant to be a fence, it wasn't a very good one. She kicked the dirt below it again, this time turning up a *No Hunting* sign. "We should mention it to Jay."

"He's probably the one who hung up them up in the first place. Didn't you say he was having trouble with kids breaking in?"

"He should still know about it, so he can fix it."

They walked on. Claire didn't fully remember how long it took to get to the waterfall, but they'd been hiking for fifteen minutes. It had to be getting close. She listened for it.

"I can't hear it," she said, then laughed at herself. "Of course, I can't. Not if it's frozen."

"It's just beyond those boulders." Elliott tugged her hand toward a tower of rock that formed a narrow passage leading to the waterfall overlook.

Claire paused in the rock channel. Someone had spray painted graffiti, destroying the rock's natural beauty. Multiple colors mingled, dripping, distorting the ineptly painted skull and crossbones.

"Oh," she said. "What a shame."

A second later, her breath scratched in her throat. The splattered skull had perhaps been meant to menace, but the thing below it was what startled her. A spinal column, also painted, curved against the rock. A grinning skull, a real one this time, had been tucked into a niche in the rock an inch or so above the vertebrae. What looked like rusted barbed wired had been wound through the macabre sculpture to keep in place, along with twigs, dead leaves and bits of garbage — plastic rings from a six-pack, empty beer cans. A dented *No Trespassing* sign as bold as a middle finger. Revoltingly, what looked like several condoms.

"Kids," Elliott said dismissively.

"Why would kids do this?"

"Because they can? Maybe a hunter lost his prize, the deer wandered over here and died. They probably found the bones and thought it would be funny to try and scare people."

"There were *No Hunting* signs up."

"There were *No Hunting* signs down," Elliott corrected.

Claire grimaced. "This is totally gross. And creepy."

Elliott tugged her hand, moving her down the path, away from the gruesome display and through the tapering rock passage. Finally, they reached the final stretch of path that led to the rocky overhang at the top of the waterfall. Both of them stopped abruptly. Silent at the sight.

They'd been here last in the fall, with the leaves changing colors and glorious temperatures. The water in the wide creek bed had been shallow but flowing, creating ribbons of froth and splash that streamed over a shale overhang and into a boulder-filled basin below. The pool emptied out into an equally shallow, meandering creek. Easy enough to cross with barely getting your toes wet, but a nice place to cool off in the summer.

Now...

"Damn it. Fuck!" He jerked his hand from hers. "Fuck!"

The waterfall was...not frozen. There was no waterfall to speak of. Instead of icy ribbons, a jagged set of minuscule icicles ringed the jutting rock the water usually fell over. Several of them dripped, but that was the extent of it.

"It's still pretty —" she began, but Elliott's hoarse, full-throated cry cut her off.

"This was supposed to be perfect!" he shouted, shaking his fists at the sky. He whirled on her, sending her back a startled step. He punched one fist into his palm. "It's fucking ruined."

Claire thought of reaching for him but faltered. She'd never seen him so angry. She'd never seen Elliott more than slightly perturbed. She took another step away from him.

"I had it all planned out. It was going to be romantic. I have some wine, cheese, crackers..." He slung the backpack off his shoulders and put it down on the rocks at his feet. Something crunched inside it.

Troy's relentless emotional stability had never seemed so appealing as in this moment. Claire shoved aside that dangerous musing. Thoughts of Troy had no place here.

"It's still pretty," she repeated.

Elliott looked at her. To her alarm, she saw his eyes glittering. Tears? High spots of color stood out on his cheeks.

"I needed it to be perfect!"

"Calm down," Claire snapped, regretting the vehemence immediately. She lightened her tone. "Nothing is perfect. Ever."

Elliott scowled and kicked a rock hard enough to shoot it over the cliff. It hit one of the icicles. It shattered. She watched it fall into the mostly dry pool but said nothing.

"We could be perfect, Claire."

She sighed and pressed her fingertips to her forehead. "Let's have a a drink and a snack. Then we can head back. Okay? Nothing is ruined."

"It is."

"I've never seen you like this," she said.

"Sometimes," Elliott said, "I don't think you see me at all."

"That's ridiculous."

"Yeah. I'm being ridiculous. I can't help it. You drive me to it."

Her jaw tensed. Old feelings, decades old, fought to flood into her. She would not have it. "I am not in charge of managing your feelings for you, Elliott. Don't put that on me."

Immediately, he looked apologetic. "I'm sorry. I really wanted to have this perfect moment between us. I had this idea of how it was going to go, and now it's all ruined."

"What?" she asked, frustrated by this circular conversation. "How *what* was going to go?"

"I brought you out here to tell you how much..." he paused, his mouth working as though to form the words.

No. No. NO. Claire shook her head, willing him not to say more. Too late, Elliott found his voice.

"I love you, Claire. I want to be with you. I brought you here to tell you that I want us to try and make something...permanent. Something real."

Why, why, why did they always have to ruin it? Claire swallowed a rush of coppery spit that filled her mouth with a taste like blood. She had only one answer for him.

"What we have *is* real."

"We meet once a month. Never in between. We barely even talk in between, Claire. We used to talk all the time. Now, we come up here. We fuck. That's it."

"There's a satisfaction in being content with what you have," she told him.

"But I'm not content with what we have!"

His hoarse shout sent her back, back back, until her heel scattered stones and her other foot slipped and rolled on the wet leaves and pebbles, and all at once a vast space yawned beneath her and her arms flailed as she tried to keep her balance.

Claire's sharp scream sliced at her throat. Elliott swung at her, he was going to push her over the edge...but no, no, she was wrong, he wasn't pushing her. He was pulling. He grabbed her sleeve and steadied her, and when she turned to look over her shoulder, she saw there was still room between her and the edge of the cliff. Nothing she could call plenty, not what she could call room to spare, but enough.

"Elliott," she whispered, wishing there was more to say.

"Claire," he replied. "I just...thought if I made this some kind of perfect moment, if I could get you to talk about it...that you might actually hear me."

A shudder hit her that had nothing to do with the temperature. His expression didn't show alarm. He hadn't been worried about her falling over the edge, even if he hadn't grabbed her away from it. If there was perfection in this moment, it was not the kind she thought Elliott had been trying to create.

"Oh, baby," she said, and the endearment had the flavor of honey that had begun to ferment. Sour and frothy. Oh, it would intoxicate you, but the hangover would make you want to die. She stepped closer to him. Her heart ached, even as her mind whirled with how to find the right words. "I see you. *And* I hear you. How could you ever think I don't?"

He pulled her close. His cold mouth sent another ripple of shivers through her. He clutched her, hard, so her face pressed the front of his coat.

"We don't have to talk about this now." His words muffled themselves into her hair. "Let's just go back."

"See? That does sound perfect." She pushed up onto her toes to kiss the corner of his mouth and his cheek, not quite able to bring herself to press her lips to his.

Elliott's phone whirred with a ringtone. He pulled it from his pocket and swiped the screen with a frown. He shoved it back into his pocket.

"Everything okay?"

"Fine. Spam call."

"Figures, you get a few bars of service and the first thing you get is a robocall telling you it's time to renew your car's warranty." She forced a laugh.

Elliott smiled and slung an arm around her shoulders, pulling her close. "I'm sorry. I know we're supposed to unplug when we're here. I'll put it away when we get back, okay? I promise. Won't look at it again."

He was lighter on the trip back, not so frantic and emotional. He was trying, she thought, to get them back to the semblance of something normal. By the time they passed the spot where she'd seen the barbed wire, he sounded like his usual self, pointing out the sound of a far-off crow. Bending to pick up a heart-shaped rock that he pressed into her palm.

At the edge of the trees with the clearing ahead of them and the cabin beyond, they both paused. The sky had gone even more gray. Cloud-covered.

"Look. Snowflakes." Elliott's voice was light and casual, full of the wonder everyone seemed to share at the first sight of softly drifting flakes. "I guess we might be in for some weather, after all."

Claire followed him toward the cabin, pushing away her sense of unease about what had happened at the waterfall. Not because Elliott had tried to harm her — she was sure she'd imagined that. No, what stuck with her was realizing that she'd believed, for even a single moment, that Elliott was *capable* of pushing her over the side of a cliff. As she followed him across the field, she thought of what he'd said to her earlier today.

Anyone could kill someone, if they felt they had no other choice.

NINE

In the short time it took to get back to the cabin, the snow had started slanting sideways, soft and fluffy as a cotton ball but mingled with occasional frigid pebbles of ice that bit at her cheeks. Claire gasped at the wind's sudden slap. Elliott glanced over his shoulder but didn't pause as he tapped at the keypad lock.

Red lights flashed, and the lock made an angry, grinding complaint. He tried again. Same thing. Elliott cursed under his breath.

Claire touched his shoulder. "You have to give it a couple of seconds to reset."

A third time, the same red flash. The same snarl of the lock refusing to disengage. She nudged at him to get out of the way.

"Let me," she said.

"I can do it."

He stabbed at the lock, and this time, when the same thing happened, Elliott punched the door.

"Stop," Claire snapped and gave him a harder shove. "Move."

The solid set of his shoulders said he wasn't going to, but after a few seconds, he relented and gave her access. Claire tugged off her leather glove, her fingers stiff from the cold. She still had the paper with the numbers on it in her coat pocket, and as she pulled it out to double check the lock code she only vaguely remembered, another wind-fist snatched it away from her. The paper sailed off into the sky, whirling like Dorothy's house right before it came down and landed on the witch.

"Great. Now we're locked out. What a fucking mess." Elliott jumped off the porch's short couple of steps and kicked at the patch of gravel rapidly being obscured by snow.

Shivering, she looked at him. He was angry again, and it irritated her, but also set her back a step. She'd always thought of herself as a woman with little patience, and she knew she was easily annoyed, but even to her, Elliott seemed to be overreacting.

"If you can get any service here, you can text Jay for the new code."

"What do you mean, new code?"

"The new code," she said as patiently as she could, which was not very, under the circumstances. "Jay changed it because he'd been having trouble with kids, remember?"

"He didn't give me a new code."

She bit her tongue against a surge of impatience and drew a breath, silently counting to three. He'd never pushed her buttons this way before, with that seemingly deliberate ignorance so many men seemed to cultivate when they were not incapable of a task but simply did not want to do it. She had never understood how incompetence could seem like the better option.

"How'd you get in, then?"

"The door was unlocked when I got here."

Beneath the square keypad lock, the door handle was the sort you gripped while pressing a lever at the same time. She tried it. The lever depressed easily, no resistance, and the door swung open when she pushed it.

They looked at each other. Claire laughed first at the absurdity of it. If only all their problems could be solved so easily.

Inside, Elliott pulled her close before she had a chance to close the door behind her. "I was an idiot. I'm sorry."

"We must have forgot to lock it, that's all."

"I didn't mean about the door," he said.

Now was her chance to soothe him again. It was Claire's moment to do what women were expected to do when men apologized — make it all better and somehow excuse them at the same time. She knew his apology had not been about the door, but that didn't matter. He was still expecting her to fix this. Them. Well, she wasn't going to do it. She had her own emotions to handle, thank you, and she wasn't going to take on anyone else's.

When she said nothing, Elliott shut the door. He engaged the lock and double-checked it to be sure. He took off his coat and hung it up, all without looking at her, and when he finally turned to face her, he wore a smile she could tell was forced, but one she appreciated because it meant that at least for now, they were both going to pretend things were the same between them.

"I'm going to take a quick, hot shower and get warmed up. I want to change into something more comfortable," she told him. "Then how about some drinks and a game before dinner?"

It was her peace offering. She imagined he'd have preferred a blowjob, but she wasn't inclined to offer one. The first time she forced herself to give him sex she didn't really want to provide would be the end of her wanting to give him anything else. She didn't wait for his answer, but went into the bedroom and shucked out of her clothes quickly. She half-expected him to appear in the doorway, maybe make a joke about joining her, but he didn't.

Her shower was truly fast, more a rinse than anything luxurious or dawdling. She didn't even get her hair wet. She dried herself quickly, noting the chill in the bathroom and bedroom as she slipped into a pair of sexy satin pajama bottoms and a thin tank top she knew he loved because it emphasized her breasts. Fleecy pajamas were not for affairs. Damn it, though, she was going to be cold. She rummaged in her weekender bag, but she hadn't packed a hoodie or sweater. Her robe, too, was sexy and not utilitarian.

"Can I borrow a hoodie?" she called out to the living room.

Unlike the outfits she packed for the getaways, Elliott's sexy apparel consisted of V-neck T-shirts, zippered hoodies, faded jeans, bare feet he didn't have to shove into ridiculous shoes. Oh, and the more unshaven and rumpled, the better, the opposite of her routine that required so much plucking and shaving.

Without waiting for an answer, she found his duffle bag on the bedroom chair. Elliott never unpacked and instead lived out of his bag, another difference between them. She rifled through it, sorting out briefs and tees and a few pairs of balled-up socks, looking for the soft gray hoodie he knew was her favorite. The scent of fabric softener wafted to tickle her nostrils, and her heart seized without warning at the thought that Elliott's clothes had been washed and dried and folded by another woman's hands.

Claire, on the other hand, would never have to deal with his laundry.

She shoved away that thought as quickly as she tossed away the socks and briefs. Digging for the hoodie, her fingers brushed cold metal wrapped in leather. She didn't lift the gun from the duffle bag, nor the rattling box of ammunition next to it. He'd always assured her it would never be stored loaded, and she believed him. He was far too conscientious to take a risk with a loaded weapon.

Her hand discovered the softness of his hoodie. When she pulled it out, something flew out of the bag along with it. The small cardboard box popped open when it hit the floor, and she grabbed it up. Inside, before she could stop herself from looking, Claire saw the pillowy satin of a ring box. The glint of something shiny. Holding her breath and looking quickly toward the door, she opened the lid wider.

Rings.

Two, both silver or perhaps platinum. Diamonds glittered in the thinner band, while the thicker was plain metal. Complementary. Clearly meant to be a matching set.

She closed the lid quickly, fumbling and embarrassed that she'd seen what had been clearly meant as a surprise. One she was *not* going to enjoy, but what could she do? Hide them? Play dumb when he asked her if she'd seen them? She'd never pull it off.

Elliott hadn't bought these rings to keep them a secret. He must have had them with him earlier, at the waterfall, and put them back while she was using the bathroom. His hint about this weekend being extra special made even more sense, now. She'd assumed it had been about the package he'd sent to her office, the fulfillment of her fantasy. Clearly, that had only been one piece of it.

Claire closed up the box and shoved it back into the duffle, together with the hoodie. She zipped the bag and put it back where she'd found it, then slipped into her robe and belted it at the waist. She gave herself a second or so to look calm before going back to the living room.

Elliott was on his phone when she came in, but he put it away quickly and gave her a thin smile. "Hey."

So much for promises.

"Everything okay?" she asked.

"Yeah. Of course. I didn't want to lose my Spanish lesson streak. I thought you were grabbing a hoodie."

"I didn't want to dig around in your stuff without permission."

He shrugged. "You know you're welcome to anything I have. I'll grab it for you, if you want. We can build up the fire, too. You look a little chilly."

She went to the thermostat on the wall and bumped it up a few degrees, listening for the furnace to kick on. Her huff of relief at the sound of it caught her off guard. She must be more worried about the power going out than she'd thought. Yes, they had the fireplace, but something about being out here, so far from everything, in the dark and the cold...no way to get back to civilization. Jay, she realized, had even taken the snowmobile they might have been able to use in an emergency.

Claire jumped when Elliott handed her the hoodie. He gave her an odd look, so she laughed. "You caught me daydreaming, I guess."

"About something nice, I hope. Preferably me."

She shrugged out of her silky robe and into the hoodie, plunging her hands into the pockets with a sigh of happiness. "You're definitely nice."

He joined her at the large bank of windows in the living room as she shielded her eyes and put her face to the glass to look out. She could see vague whirls of what must be snow coming down, but night was rapidly falling. A flash of light from the tree line had her straining to see more.

"There's someone out there," she said.

TEN

Elliott moved to her side. "Who'd be out there in the middle of a snowstorm?"

"I saw a light. I don't know." She shrugged. "Maybe it was a reflection from the fire on the glass."

Elliott put his hands on her hips and turned her toward him. "Whoever it is, they can watch the show."

When she tensed in his embrace, he pulled away. "Hey. You okay?"

"Yeah. Just..." She looked again toward the glass but could see only their reflection. With the fire behind them, they looked like something out of a fantasy story. "I'm starving."

"Oh no." Elliott staggered back, a hand on his heart. "She's starving. She's gonna get hangry!"

"Hush." Her swat at him didn't land, but she laughed, too.

"See? I know you, Claire."

It was true, and she neither could nor wanted to deny it. "Let's put on some music and cook and drink."

"Sounds like the perfect way to spend a Saturday afternoon in a snowstorm," he said.

The tension between them eased but didn't disappear. They were fragile, she thought. What happened in the woods today had taken them to the edge of something with the possibility of changing it all, but they'd managed to stop themselves from plummeting into the abyss.

She connected her phone to the speaker and pulled up one of her favorite playlists. It would shuffle through slow dance songs interspersed with bump-and-grinds, upbeat pop, and some classic rock. Music for every mood.

Dancing her way into the kitchen, Claire put on a little shimmy and shake for him. Elliott laughed and shook his head at her antics, but he joined her. They danced together for a few seconds before he stopped.

"I opened a bottle of that red you brought. Here." He offered her the glass.

"Oh, the Briar Crimson. It's new. I haven't tried it yet." She tasted it. Held the glass to him, already knowing he'd decline. He was the cocktail drinker.

She danced her way to the fridge to see what they could cook for dinner. "How about quesadillas? Quick and easy. Ooh, you brought guac. Yum."

They worked together, slicing, chopping, sorting ingredients. She assembled the quesadillas but left the cooking to him because the ache in her fingers made it hard to hold the pan and flip it. She set the table with the cabin's sturdy stoneware plates and plain glassware but added a pair of candlesticks from the mantel. Now she needed to find some candles.

Every kitchen had a junk drawer. The one here was in the narrow cabinet supporting the end of the bar between the kitchen and the living room. She thought she remembered seeing candles in it, but the first drawer gave up only a few batteries for the TV remote, some notepads and pens emblazoned with the names of banks and hotels, and a few rubber bands. She tried the second drawer and found several folded maps and thick pamphlets that looked like instruction manuals. She saw one for the propane stovetop and glimpsed one for the DVD player. An advertisement for some kind of satellite service. A manual for a camera system. Everything but candles.

She finally found them in the bottom drawer. A cardboard box of thick, plain white wax rods that reminded her of Shabbat candles but longer. Emergency candles, she supposed, pulling out two. They were slightly misshapen, maybe from melting a little in the summer. She took them to the table and fit them into the brass candlesticks.

"Jay said there were battery lanterns in the closet. We should charge them up, just in case we lose power," she said.

A new flash of light from outside turned her toward the windows. Still unable to see beyond her own reflection, Claire flipped the switch by the front door, turning off the overhead track lights. It helped a little, but there was still a lot of light from the fire and the kitchen lights. She shielded her eyes to stare out but saw only shifting, drifting snow. Where had the day gone? The storm had turned this early evening into full night.

The windows rattled as the cabin rocked against a fresh onslaught of wind. She shivered at the imagined tendrils of frosty air seeping in from around the window frame. Maybe not imagined. She put her hand there and felt a small pulse of air. The walls didn't seem to be insulated. There really was hardly anything between them and the night outside except a thin pane of glass and the width of the wood walls.

Nothing much between them and the night at all.

"Food's almost ready." Elliott handed her the glass of wine she'd almost forgotten about and held up his own squat rocks glass shimmering with clear liquid. "Here's to good food, good sex, and a good night's sleep."

"Good?" She teased and clinked her glass to his. "How about great? Amazing? Mind-blowing?"

"All of that, too," he said. "Here's to Claire, the most amazing, mind-blowing woman a man could ever —"

His words were cut off by the cacophony of engines thrumming and roaring past the front windows. Lights flashed, bouncing. Snow and maybe even some gravel spattered up to hit the glass.

Claire screamed and flailed. Her wine splattered fine droplets over the back of her hand but fortunately, didn't entirely spill. Elliott leaped to his feet and flung open the front door. Snow and freezing air swirled inside.

Claire joined him, clutching the throat of the borrowed hoodie. A least half a dozen, maybe more, snowmobiles were doing donuts in front of the house and in the clearing beyond. Despite the light spilling from the front of the house and the headlamps on the snowmobiles, it was too hard to make out more than the dark figures of the riders. All of them were dressed in black and wore helmets.

"It's kids," she said, remembering what Jay had said. "I think it's local kids."

Elliott shut the door and kicked at the small pile of snow that had accumulated before going to the kitchen to get the broom and dustpan. "They're a pack of little assholes, is what they are."

He swept up the snow and dumped it into the sink while Claire moved again to the front windows. The lights had gone more toward the trees, but based on the wild, strobing way they flashed, she guessed they were still riding like maniacs.

"Maybe they rode up to party but saw the lights on and realized someone was staying here," she said.

"There should be curtains on those windows." Elliott scowled and joined her at the window. "They better not come back again."

"They're just kids," she soothed. "C'mon. Let's eat. And drink. And then I'm going to beat your fine ass at cards."

"Can't you just beat my fine ass?" He waggled it in her direction.

She laughed. "Only if you've been a bad boy —"

Another roar of engines interrupted their banter. The pack of snowmobiles flew past the front of the house again, this time circling around the back and all around. Snow flew up and hit the front windows but with a distinctive round shape. They were throwing snowballs as they drove past.

"What are they trying to do, break the fucking windows?" Elliott went to the front door again and opened it to shout out, "Get the fuck out of here! I'll call the cops!"

No answer from the snowmobilers, who probably couldn't hear him anyway and weren't likely to care even if they did. She remembered being a wild kid, bent on getting into trouble. Claire pulled him away from the door and shut it, making sure to lock it. She stroked her hand down his arm, getting him to look at her.

"They're *kids*," she said.

Elliott shook her off and went to the door in the wall next to the bookcase. He tugged the handle, but it wouldn't open. Tried again, cursing.

"That's the owner's closet," she said. "It's locked. What are you looking for?"

"Isn't there a supply closet with extra sheets and stuff?" Without waiting for an answer, he scanned the room and stalked toward the narrow door tucked between the bathroom door and kitchen. This one opened for him, and he pulled out an armful of white sheets.

"What are you doing?" Claire asked.

"I don't want those little pricks looking in at us."

She thought again of how so little stood between them and anything...or anyone, outside. Beneath the hoodie she wrapped more tightly around her, she became aware of the tight points of her nipples poking through the thin fabric of her tank top. They became even more prominent when she shivered, both from the frigid air that had come inside when Elliott opened the front door and from the unease she shook off as best she could.

They were safe here. The cabin felt far away from the rest of the world, but it really wasn't. Kids on snowmobiles could be expected to make mischief. And besides, she thought with another shiver, this time one that tried to rattle her teeth. She didn't need to worry about anyone trying to hurt them. Elliott could protect them.

After all, he had a gun.

ELEVEN

THE LONG STRING OF CURSE WORDS ELLIOTT SHOUTED WAS so vehemently creative Claire couldn't help but be impressed. Also a bit taken aback at how fiercely he'd lost his temper for the second time that day, when he never had before. He struggled with the sheets, trying to get them to tuck into the window frame and failing. With a growl, he threw them down and kicked them into a pile.

"Let me see if I can find something we can use to hold them up there," Claire said. A fresh gust of wind rattled the house, making her jump and then laugh, self-conscious.

She went first to the large corkboard on the wall between the front door and the kitchen. Jay used it to pin up maps of local trails, information about the nearest town, cleanup and checkout procedures, instructions for the lock, stuff like that. That garnered her eight pushpins, and a quick search of the drawers where she found the candles offered up a box of thumbtacks.

Working together, they hung the sheets, pressing the pins into the soft wood of the upper window frame. No more snowmobile noises or shouting came from outside, only the occasional spat of sleet against the glass. Once, from far off, she thought she heard a rev of engines, but it faded quickly.

"I think they're gone for the night," she said.

Elliott, still frowning, pushed the chair he'd been standing on back to the table. "Good. That's bullshit. I didn't come up here to be terrorized by a pack of Mad Max asshole kids."

Claire pressed her lips together. He wasn't trying to be funny; she didn't want to laugh. "They're gone. Forget about them."

Elliott sighed and dragged a hand through his hair, rumpling it so it stood on end. She wanted to smooth it but held herself back. He looked at her, his expression becoming a bit sheepish.

"This is not at all turning out to be the weekend I was expecting," he said.

"We've had so many perfect weekends, Elliott, it's ok if once in a while we have one that gets a little messed up. Because," she added after a second, hating herself a little for saying it, "we're going to have so many more."

Elliott took her in his arms and pulled her close. He kissed her. Her answer had pleased him, she could see that on his face when he pulled away. She hated herself a little more.

"If you don't feel up for cards, I brought movies," he said instead. "I have the entire Hammer Horror collection. What do you say you pour yourself another glass of wine and get comfy on the couch. I'll build up the fire and get the lotion, and I'll rub your feet while we watch some classic Christopher Lee and Peter Cushing."

Claire curled her fingers in the front of his shirt, holding him in place. Grateful that he seemed back on even keel, the Elliott she'd come to know. "You think of everything. Yes. That sounds amazing."

She loved that he volunteered to rub her feet, and that he'd do it for hours, if she wanted him to, without complaining or expecting anything for himself in return. She loved how he mumbled in sing-song to himself under his breath while he made himself a cocktail. She loved how he cleaned up after himself as he went, and how he shot her a smile when he caught her staring.

She loved so much about him...

But she didn't love him.

She kissed him as though she did, though.

Bottles in the fridge clinked when she opened the door and bent to look inside. She hadn't finished the bottle of Briar White he'd left for her yesterday, and there was enough left for a large, generous glass. No need to conserve it. She'd be the only one drinking it.

Soon enough they were snuggled on the sofa with the fire crackling and the TV showing a fun old scary movie. With a handsome, attentive man rubbing her feet and a glass of her favorite wine, Claire couldn't recall the last time when she'd been so content.

"I wish it could always be this way." She said this aloud, surprising herself since it had felt like only a thought. The wine was going to her head.

Elliott's strong fingers drew down the arch of her foot, sending tingles all through her. "It could be."

"No," she said, aware she was slurring a bit. Feeling owl-eyed, the way you do when you're drunker than you thought you'd be. "This isn't real life. We have jobs. An' families."

Elliott's fingers worked, worked, worked. On the television, Peter Cushing and Christopher Lee faced off, Lee's eyes bleeding. Claire blinked to bring the screen into focus, then looked at her wine.

"I'm a little tipsy."

He laughed. "You sound more than tipsy. You want me to take that?"

She handed him the glass without bothering to finish the last couple of swallows. She hated wasting it, but she definitely didn't need any more. Elliott patted her legs so she'd move them. He got up and took the glass to the kitchen. By the time he got back, Claire was almost asleep.

"C'mon, my poor tired girl. Let's get you into bed." Elliott helped her stand.

Claire kissed him, yawning broadly in the middle of it. "Sorry."

Elliott scooped her up. She clung to him, squealing, burying her face in his shoulder but loving it. He always made her feel tiny and precious, which was not how she felt in most of her daily life. In the bathroom, he guided her to brush her teeth and put her face cream on, then he led her, stumbling and laughing, to the bedroom. He pulled back the covers and helped her beneath them.

"It's not like me," she tried to explain as she snuggled deep into the warmth of the flannel sheets.

Elliott chuckled. "You're tired. That's all. We did drink a lot. Do you need some water? You know what, let me go put a glass next to your nightstand, in case you wake up in the night."

Once he'd set the water on the nightstand and climbed into bed with her, Claire turned onto her side to face him. She touched his face. Sometimes light came in through the bedroom window here, but tonight even if there was a moon, the snow blocked it. The room was very dark.

"You could be anyone," she whispered. "You could be a stranger. I would have no idea who you are."

"Don't say that."

She let her fingers trace the lines of his invisible face. "It's the truth."

"I'm not a stranger." He covered her hand with his to stop it from moving. He put it to his lips. Kissed it. "You know everything about me. The same way I know everything about you."

"That's not true."

Claire rolled onto her back and settled deeper into the pillow. She yawned. Her eyes felt heavy. When Aviva was little, she'd often tried to run ahead of her mother holding her hand. In this moment, it felt as though sleep tugged at Claire's hand the same way. Impatient to take her someplace she wasn't yet ready to go.

"What do you mean?" Elliot asked.

"There's a lot you don't know about me," Claire said. "And a lot I don't know about you. That's the way it should be. Keeps it mysterious. Ess...citing."

Elliott turned on the light and sat up. "I don't want to be mysterious. I want you to know about me, and I want to know about you. You can ask me anything. I'll tell you whatever you want to know."

The challenge in his voice punched a hole right through the sleepy veil that had covered her moments ago. Claire sat up, too. Wine sloshed in her belly. "Who were you talking to? On the phone."

"Nobody."

"You," she said with a tipsy laugh, "are lying."

His jaw set. She studied him. Obviously, he wasn't telling her the truth, both about wanting her to ask him anything and also about the phone call.

"How do you manage to get away once a month?" was her next question.

If he asked her that question, she would tell him everything. And then he would know all the truth about everything, and it would change their relationship, but that would be all right, because they were changing anyway. *Had* changed. *Would* change. Already did. Her stomach was upset, now, and she sipped the water he'd brought her to fend off any nausea.

"I thought we weren't supposed to talk about things at home," he said.

Claire sipped again. "You can't have it both ways. Either you're going to tell me anything I want to know, or you're not."

"Why is *this* what you want to know all of a sudden?"

"I don't. I just...my stomach's upset. I really just want to go to sleep."

"Again?" When he tried to touch her forehead, she moved her face away.

"I'm not sick," Claire said. "I drank more than I intended to. Those glasses are so huge. I finished off that bottle you left for me."

Elliott paused. "Huh?"

"The Briar White," Claire said. His brow furrowed. "In the fridge? Already opened?"

"Umm..."

She grimaced. "You didn't arrange for Jay to leave it?"

"No."

"Gross. I drank someone's leftover wine." She pressed a hand to her stomach. "Wine doesn't go bad, does it?"

"I don't think it spoils. But it can definitely go off. Do you think you might throw up?"

"Ugh. Don't talk about it."

She sipped more water, slowly. "You don't think Jay left it on purpose, do you?"

"Why would he do that?"

"I don't know. On the drive up here, he was talking about all the groceries I bought and how he'd thought about doing a concierge service. Maybe he was testing it out? He also said we were his best customers." She paused. "We do leave a lot of empty bottles in the recycling can when we leave. It wouldn't have been hard for him to figure out what brand I drink."

Elliott shrugged. "Seems odd he wouldn't have mentioned it."

"It was already open when I got here," Claire said. "You don't think he'd have put something in it, do you? Both times I drank it, I felt way woozier than I should have."

Both of them were silent for a few seconds, contemplating this idea, before Elliott leaned forward to brush her hair over her shoulder. He squeezed her upper arm gently. She leaned in for a small kiss.

"I'm sure he didn't drug your wine."

He sounded confident about it. She wanted to believe him. But what was more ridiculous, the idea that Jay had left her an opened bottle of wine to be nice without mentioning it, or that he'd left her an opened bottle of *drugged* wine?

"You're letting your imagination run away with you, Claire."

"Don't do that to me," she said sharply. "My father used to discount me just like that. Accuse me of overreacting to things."

Elliott was silent for a few seconds. "Sorry."

The wind howled around the cabin and rattled the glass. Claire frowned. "How much snow do you think we got so far?"

"A couple of feet. Nothing to worry about. It's only Saturday night, love. Plenty of time for the road to be plowed. Anyway...would it be so bad if it didn't?"

"We can't get stuck here, Elliott. That's just...foolish."

"Why? We always pack enough food to last for at least a week. Even if the power goes out, we have the fireplace. We have wine and snacks. We have each other. Not to eat, either. Except in the fun way."

She usually liked his offbeat sense of humor, but it was falling flat for her now.

"You're being ridiculous." She didn't mean to snap, but her words came out sharp, thorny as a rosebush but without the softness of any petals to smooth it. "You know very well why we can't get stuck here for a week. Can't you simply enjoy what we have instead of always thinking about what we don't?"

He turned away from her. "It's only a fantasy. Can't you indulge me? I've always done my best to give you yours."

He had. Always. In fact, he'd gone above and beyond in fulfilling them.

She sighed and pressed her cheek to his back. He didn't soften beneath the embrace. "Anything could happen to us up here. Nobody knows exactly where we are. We have no cell phone signal. There's no way to get in touch with anyone if there was an emergency —"

"I'll take care of you. We're going to be fine. I was an Eagle Scout, remember?"

She bit back more words. She *was* overreacting. "I'm sorry. I got carried away."

He pulled her closer. "It's okay. You're right. We could be in trouble here, but we're not. Okay? You trust me. Right? I promise you, it's all going to be fine."

He promised, but she did not believe him.

She wasn't sure she trusted him, either.

TWELVE

"Looks like it's going to be a lazy Sunday by the fire." Claire twitched the kitchen window curtain shut and turned back to Elliott.

Wearing nothing but a flowery apron that left his extremely cute bottom cheeks exposed, he stood at the stove monitoring the omelettes he was making. Claire's contribution to breakfast had been making mimosas, and she sipped hers now as she peeked back out the window. So much snow had fallen overnight that the trails left behind by the snowmobile gang the night before had fully disappeared.

The field between the house and the forest usually offered a nice view of the gravel parking lot, meadow grasses, and flowers. A trail cut through it to the tall evergreens beyond. Today, all she could clearly see was a vast wall of white so thick and tall that it blended in with the snow covering the trees themselves. She knew they were there, she simply couldn't see them.

"It's like being lost at sea or something," she said aloud. "Nothing but white all around us."

Elliott expertly flipped the eggs in the pan and set it back on the burner. "I can't think of a better way to spend any day other than inside here, with you."

"How did you get so sweet?"

She'd been careful not to let her voice shake or sound strange, but still, he gave her a glance. His brow furrowed. He slid the food onto a platter and turned off the burner. Claire had already set the table in the living room.

"What do you mean?" Elliott took the salt and pepper shakers from the back of the stove top and seasoned the omelette.

"I mean that you're sweet. You always know the right things to say. You're not afraid to compliment me, and I believe you mean it when you say nice things. You're sweet, Elliott." She shrugged and went into the living room.

He followed, setting the platter on the table and giving her a nice view of that bare ass when he bent over. His smooth, dark golden skin had prickled into gooseflesh. He raised his champagne glass of mimosa toward her.

"Cheers to being sweet, I guess."

She frowned at the hard edge to his tone. "You make it sound more like I was insulting you than complimenting."

He shrugged. "I guess I don't see much point in getting a big head about something that seems as though it should go without saying. What you're describing as sweet seems to be the bare minimum of effort, to me."

Claire didn't disagree with him, but the edge in his voice put a frown on her lips. "Well, I appreciate you making the effort. All right? It might be the bare minimum of effort, but I can tell you, not every man makes it."

His lip curled. "You have such a very low bar, Claire, you shouldn't be so surprised when I'm able to step over it."

She stared at him for a few seconds without speaking. He was taking a dig at Troy, which would have made her angrier if he'd been right. The truth was, Elliott had no real clue and had made his own assumptions about her marriage. They'd established early on that they didn't discuss their spouses. Not to complain about them, not to compare each other to.

She and Elliott never pretended they didn't exist; they simply did not talk about them. When she complained about past relationships, she wasn't including Troy in them.

"You look cold," she told him. "Why don't you go and put something warmer on. I'll dish up the food and make more mimosas."

"Kiss me, first."

She did, willingly enough, and rubbed her hands along his biceps to warm him. When he pulled her close against him, the thin fabric of the apron did nothing to hide his hardness.

"I'm hungry," she murmured into his kiss. She put her hands flat on his chest and turned her face with a laugh when he tried to deepen the embrace. She pushed him away, but gently. "Elliott."

He tried again, his hands denting the silky robe over her hips. His mouth sought hers, his tongue probing, and she accepted the kiss for a few surprised seconds before she pulled away. More firmly, this time.

"The food will get cold," she said. "And besides, we have the whole day. We don't want to wear ourselves out first thing."

Elliott's expression darkened, but only for a second or so before he smoothed it. Nodding, he backed away a few steps in the direction of the bedroom. When he turned away from her, giving her another full-on look of that scrumptious butt, Claire had an instant's regret that she hadn't taken him up on the offer of sex — but she was hungry, and they *would* have time later.

By the time he came out of the bedroom, this time wearing sweatpants and a long-sleeved henley, she'd poured them fresh mimosas and filled their coffee mugs, too. They both dug into the breakfast Elliott had prepared. Mushroom and Swiss omelette, hash brown patties, toast with butter and jelly.

The sheets they'd hung the night before blocked much of the snow-bright sunshine, something she appreciated. In all the months they'd been coming to this cabin, she hadn't realized how disturbingly bright it could be in the morning until now. Maybe it was the mostly sleepless night that made it so much worse. Fortunately, last night's stomach upset had faded and was gone.

"You cooked. I'll clean up," she said. "Go pick out a movie for us to watch. Or a game. Your choice."

"I'll help you," he insisted, following her to the kitchen with his plate in hand.

"You don't have to—"

"I only get to see you once a month, Claire. I want to spend as much time together as we can. Is that wrong?"

She frowned at his clipped tone. "Of course not. I just thought —"

"I'm here to be with *you*."

The insistence in his voice unsettled her, and for a moment, Claire said nothing. She turned instead to the sink and began washing her plate and silverware. When Elliott came up behind her, pressing himself to her back, she tensed. He nuzzled the back of her neck, sending a full-body shudder through her.

His hands slid up to cup her breasts through the silky robe, finding her sensitive nipples and thumbing them tight. One hand moved down, over her belly, to part the robe and find the heat between her legs. His lips mouthed the back of her neck again, this time with the press of teeth.

It had always been this way between them — hot as tossing a lit match on gasoline-soaked tinder. The smell of him. Taste. The feeling of his hands on her body. His breath in her ear, against her skin, pushing its way into her mouth when they kissed. Lust was supposed to fade away, wasn't it? But so far, two years into this, Claire wanted Elliott as much as she had the first time.

His questing fingers now rubbed, rubbed in slow, steady circles designed to tease her close to, but not over the edge. His other hand pinched her nipple. Claire gave a low cry at the sudden pleasure-pain, unexpected and unusual.

"I want you, Claire. Now." Elliott's voice pitched low and urgent in her ear.

Desire surged. They'd fucked in the kitchen before. She thought that's what he wanted this time, but Elliott instead turned her in his arms. He kissed her fiercely while walking her backward toward the bedroom.

She cupped him through the loose sweatpants, stroking. He loosened the belt of her robe and tossed it onto the chair in the corner. Pulled her nightgown over her head and tossed that, too. He turned her quickly, her hands flat on the bed, her body bent over it. Again, he pressed against her from behind, the soft fabric of his sweatpants jutting with his erection. Rubbing her ass. He pushed a hand between her legs again, finding her sweet spot and working it with that expert, perfect touch until all she could do was fall forward to bury her face in the blankets and offer her body to him.

"Tell me you want me," Elliott said.

Claire turned her head to press her cheek to the mattress. "You know I want you."

"I want to hear you say it." His fingers dipped inside her, then out again.

Claire shuddered and shifted her feet to widen her stance. "I want you, Elliott."

He groaned and withdrew his hand to shove down his sweatpants. He was inside her a moment after that, one hand guiding his thickness inside her, the other gripping her hip to urge her back onto him. Her fingers dug into the bed as she opened her body to him.

Elliott thrust hard. Fast. He touched her again between her legs, his body curving over hers so his chest pressed her back. The faintly rough fabric of his shirt caressed her bare skin; something about the fact he was still mostly dressed while she was naked turned her on even more. She moved in sync with him, hips rocking. She lost herself in the pleasure.

When she came, it was like glass shattering. Claire cried out, shaking. Elliott grunted out her name and buried himself so deep she jerked from the sudden pain that immediately dissolved into another wash of ecstasy.

A few seconds ticked past as she struggled to catch her breath. Elliott withdrew, and Claire eased herself up onto the bed. He joined her, still wearing his shirt but nothing below it. She rolled onto her side to put her hand on his belly, low, then lower to cup him. She adored feeling him when he was soft and still sticky, in those moments before they both went to the bathroom to clean themselves up. Breathing in the smell of what they'd done gave her an entire second round of pleasure that was almost as viscerally physical as the actual sex had been.

"I don't appreciate being compared, even favorably, to anyone else," Elliott said into the quiet.

Claire pushed up on her elbow to look into his face. His dark hair had fallen over one eye. She pushed it away and let her fingertips trace each of his eyebrows.

"I'm sorry," she said.

Elliott rolled onto his side and pulled her close to him. He buried his face against the side of her neck. "I don't want to think about you with anyone else, Claire. When we're here together, I don't want you to be thinking about anyone else, either. This is our time. Our place."

The roughness in his voice scratched at her. She pulled away to look into his face, alarmed at the glint of tears in his eyes. She kissed him.

This was not what Claire had ever wanted.

"Hey," she said now, murmuring her words between kisses, "I have an idea. Let's do something crazy."

THIRTEEN

"IT LOOKS LIKE SOMETHING OUT OF A HORROR MOVIE." Elliott stepped back, setting one foot at a time into the snow that came up to his knees, and put his hands on his hips. "I dig it."

The snowman had taken them an hour or so to build. They had no carrot or coal to form its features, so, faceless, the figure did loom rather menacingly with the arms they'd made from snapped-off twigs liberated from the kindling pile. Claire had added a knit cap at a jaunty angle, and tucked a dusty fake flower from a vase inside the cabin into the place that would approximate a lapel.

"I'm not sure we can even call this a snow *man*," Elliott continued. "It's more like a snow *thing*."

"Snow person, c'mon. Be polite. It doesn't matter how it looks. It matters that we made it together." Claire tossed a handful of snow toward him.

Neither of them had brought clothes truly appropriate for outdoor activities, but the sun had come out so bright it wasn't actually as cold as she'd expected. They'd both worked up a sweat forging their way through the knee-deep snow. Elliott made his way to her, taking huge exaggerated steps to clear the drifts. He put an arm around her as they both admired their handiwork.

"This was a good idea, Claire. Thank you. It was good to get outside for a little bit. This is what I mean when I say that you make everything fun." He leaned to kiss her temple. "Mm. Salty."

She leaned into him, enjoying the bright sunshine fighting back the cold air. Her feet were numb, and her jeans were soaked. "Let's go inside. I want to take a steaming hot shower. Then, I say we fix ourselves some boozy hot cocoa cocktails. I'm getting hungry again, aren't you?"

Before he could answer, a buzzing engine thrum reached their ears. It got louder. Claire tensed, and Elliott's grip tightened on her shoulders. It relaxed a bit when a single snowmobile appeared on the access road.

"It's Jay," she said, relieved they weren't having to deal with the pack of rowdy teens again.

Elliott raised a hand in greeting as the cabin's owner pulled to a stop a few feet away from them. "Hi, there."

"Heya. I came to make sure everything's all right. With all this snow, you know. Got a good three feet, more even than they were calling for." Jay pushed his goggles off his face to reveal ruddy cheeks. "Haven't lost power yet, have you?"

"I don't think so. It was on when we came out here," Claire said.

"It's the wind that'll do it, not the snow. We got overhead lines out here." Jay pointed to the wire that ran from the tall pole to the corner of the cabin. "But if it didn't go out on you yet, you should be ok. There should be plenty of propane, but I just thought...I'd come and make sure. I'll stay out of your way, I just need to go around back. Take a look at things."

"No problem," Elliott said.

"Are the plows coming?" Claire asked.

Jay looked at the sky and shrugged. "Calling for more snow later this afternoon. The main roads are plowed out, but my usual guy had a hernia operation last week, so I'm on a wait list for the kid that works for him. It could be a bit before he gets here, and if it starts up again, he'll just wait it out. You okay? Not trying to leave early or anything? If you wanted to leave, I told you I could get you down to the main road. Considering the circumstances, I'd refund your money, too."

"You sound kind of like you're trying to get rid of us," Elliott said lightly.

Jay shook his head. "Oh, no, nothing like that. If you're okay staying, I'm fine for you to stay on until Monday, like you planned. You're okay, then?"

"Oh, sure. We're having a great time," Elliott assured him before Claire could speak.

"Nothing...worrying you?"

"Just those kids you told Claire about," Elliott said. "They came around last night. Threw some snowballs at the house and stuff. But they left."

"Damn kids. Nothing else?"

"Nope," Elliott said.

"Jay," Claire said when the big man started the snowmobile again. "Did you leave a bottle of wine in the fridge for us?"

"Uh...yes?" He looked caught out. Surprised. "Was that okay?"

She could hardly ask him if he'd slipped her a Mickey Finn. "It was a surprise."

"You like wine," Jay said like that was an explanation. He gave them both another nod and drove the snowmobile around the corner.

"Feel better?" Elliott asked her.

She didn't, but couldn't articulate why. As they were kicking the snow off their boots and legs on the cabin's small front porch, he added, "we've been coming up here for months and never seen the guy. Now he's all over the place."

Maybe that was the reason for her unease. "He does seem to be checking up on us a lot. I guess that's a good thing. Right? But he did seem like he wanted us to leave early."

"He's being a good host, that's all. They get ratings, you know. You were worried," Elliott said. "Now you don't have to be."

Inside, Elliott went directly to the fireplace and added some logs to build it up. He warmed his hands while Claire headed to the kitchen to put together a snack and get the water heating for some hot chocolate.

Outside the kitchen window at the back of the cabin, Jay took big steps to walk through the deep snow. The snowmobile had been parked out of sight. Something thudded against the outside wall. Then again, louder. She could no longer see the cabin's owner.

"I'm sorry this weekend is turning out to be such a bust," Elliott said from behind her.

Claire turned, distracted. "What?"

"I'm sorry." He moved to embrace her. With his face buried in her hair, he kissed the top of her head. "It's just that I had something really special planned for this weekend, a really wonderful surprise, and I guess I'm still really pissed off that it didn't work out."

If that meant he'd given up the idea of offering her a ring, she wasn't going to complain about that. But had he forgotten the lovely surprise he *had* given her? "What are you talking about? I loved what you did."

"No, no," Elliott denied, shaking his head. "It was going to change things between us. I had it all planned out, and it just...didn't happen. I'm being an asshole about it, though. I promise I won't be such a jerk the rest of our weekend. Okay?"

"Okay...but..." she paused, unease creeping its brambly tendrils through her. Tightening into knots in her chest and throat. "I really liked it, Elliott. It was exactly the way I described to you. All of it. I don't know how you can say you messed it all up. I'd have told you how perfect it was when you got here, but you know, part of it was that we'd never speak of it —"

"What are you talking about?"

Another thump sounded from the back of the cabin. More noises, bumps, and rattles, surrounded them. Then, silence.

"The box. The lingerie? The mask, the ribbon? And I followed the instructions. It was..." Her breath jerked and caught. She swallowed, but couldn't clear the obstruction in her throat.

"Claire," Elliott said slowly, carefully, precisely, "I have no idea what you're talking about."

The floor dipped and swayed beneath her, suddenly as slick as ice covered in oil. She was slipping. Sliding. Elliott grabbed her by the upper arms to keep her sagging knees from giving out on her. Claire gasped in a few breaths, fighting for air.

"Tell me it was you," she said.

Elliott looked confused. "*What* was me?"

"Oh god," she said. "Oh, god. Oh my god, if it wasn't you...then who was it?"

FOURTEEN

"DRINK THIS." ELLIOTT PRESSED A MUG OF MINT TEA INTO Claire's shaking hands. "It's hot. Be careful."

He'd taken her straight to the couch and tucked her up in a plaid blanket, then tossed more logs on the fire while he put the water on for tea. He'd joined her on the couch, rubbing her feet. Also her hands, which had become ice. He didn't try to pull her close, and Claire was glad of that. She didn't think she could stand being embraced right now.

Now, she held the hot mug in her frigid hands but didn't drink it. Her stomach lurched, and she swallowed the rise of bile. She hadn't been sick yet, but the feeling was there, lurking, as if if she made one wrong move, she'd definitely throw up.

From underneath the floorboards came a flurry of thumping and what sounded, briefly, like a raised voice trying to be a shout. Then, silence. Elliott looked at her.

"Does this place have a basement?"

"There are doors outside. Storm doors, or whatever they're called," she said after a moment's thought. "The kind you have to lift up, with stairs inside going down."

"The bastard's down there."

"He said he was going to check the furnace."

Before she could say another word or try to stop him, Elliott was shoving his feet into his boots. No coat, no hat or gloves. He slammed open the front door and ran out, leaving it ajar behind him.

Claire heard the crunch of his feet in the snow and went to the front door after him, but he was already rounding the corner of the house. She shook from the cold air but also the rippling waves of disgust that still washed over her every time she thought of how willingly she'd put herself in that vulnerable state. How wretchedly she'd been violated. How could she not have known it wasn't her lover?

"Elliott!"

When he didn't answer, she shut the door and went quickly to the kitchen window overlooking the back yard. She gasped at the sight of Elliott yanking Jay forward by the collar of his snowmobile suit and screamed when Elliott punched the bigger man in the face.

Jay staggered back a single step, all he could take in the deep drifts. Basically trapped, he was clearly doing his best to fight off Elliott's furious blows to his face and body, but the attack clearly had taken him by surprise. Crimson spattered the white snow, and Claire muffled another scream. She turned away, panting, almost choking.

Her phone. She had to call the police. Where was her fucking phone?

Her purse hung on the hooks by the front door. She couldn't find the phone until she dumped the bag, scattering lip balms and spare change and pens. Her phone fell out onto the hard wood floor and she scooped it up, certain the screen would be cracked, grateful to see it was fine.

One bar of service.

Was that a shout from outside? The front door banged open, missing her only because she managed to leap out of the way. Her phone fell onto the floor again, and this time it skidded away beneath the table next to the front windows.

Jay shoved Elliott through the doorway, where he tripped and fell onto his hands and knees. Blood from his nose dripped onto the floorboards. Claire didn't even have time to try and reach him before Jay hauled Elliott up by the back of his coat. The men scuffled, swinging at each other. Landing punches. Jay clipped the underside of Elliott's chin so hard it sent him reeling, but Jay yanked him to his feet. With one big fist dug deep into the front of Elliott's coat, the other man hit him again. Again. Again.

"Stop it!" Claire shrieked. She got on her hands and knees to grab for her phone. The screen had cracked this time. She tried to swipe up for a call, but the tiny letters No Service made her efforts useless.

Behind her, Elliott sagged in Jay's grip. The bigger man dragged him forward, pulling out a chair from beside the table and shoving Elliott into it. Elliott made no effort to get free when Jay pinned his hands behind him and secured them with a zip tie he pulled out of his snowmobile suit pocket. Elliott grunted as Jay tightened the plastic tie, but his head fell forward, blood and drool dripping. He made no louder protest, not even when Jay did the same with his ankles, securing each one to the chair legs.

Jay turned to her, his hair and beard wild, his eyes blazing. He took a few threatening steps toward her, both his fists raised. "You gonna give me a hard time, too?"

Claire could only shake her head. When she took a step toward Elliott, Jay's menacing gesture stopped her. "Please, just let me make sure he's ok."

"He's fine. A little busted up in the face, but that won't kill him. He's pretty enough, he'll get over it." Jay spat a gobbet of bloody mucus on the floor.

Claire cringed, but drew in a breath and did her best to keep her voice calm. "Jay. Listen to me. I'm sure we can work this out —"

Elliott groaned. Jay spat again, then gestured at her. "Go get him some water. Get him cleaned up."

She did as ordered, careful to secure her phone in her jeans pocket. No service now didn't mean no service, ever. For all she knew, the wind could change direction and she'd be able to call for help.

For now she concentrated on wetting a dishcloth with warm water. She wrung it out, then got another towel from the drawer and some ice from the freezer. She worked slowly, giving herself time to think. She must've been too slow, because Jay came into the kitchen behind her.

"Move it," he said. "He's bleeding on my good floor."

Claire pushed past him, but Jay grabbed her arm. He plucked her phone from her pocket, looked it over, and tucked inside his unzipped snowsuit. Then he let her go. For a moment, Claire forced herself to meet his eyes.

"Jay..."

"I told you to clean him up."

With a quick nod, Claire went to Elliott. She tipped up his head and dabbed at the blood crusting his upper lip. He winced and tried to pull away, but she held his chin still. She leaned in, keeping her voice pitched low.

"Stop fighting. We need to figure out what's going on. Don't struggle."

Elliott blinked, his gaze clearing. He looked over her shoulder, his eyes narrowing. "You won't get away with this."

"Shut up," Jay snapped. He paced in front of the place, pausing to fully unzip his snowsuit and take his arms out of it so it hung to his waist. "Shut up and let me think. Okay? Why did you come after me, man?"

Elliott pulled his face away from Claire's ministrations. "You raped my wife!"

"She's not your wife," Jay said.

Claire swallowed a bitter surge of bile but kept her attention on cleaning Elliott's face. She pressed the cloth of ice to his split lip. If they wanted to get out of this, she had to keep her head. Not lose her temper. Not dissolve into hysterics.

"And I didn't fuckin' rape *anybody,*" Jay continued. He spun on his heel to pace in the opposite direction, muttering to himself. "None of this was supposed to happen, damn it. Damn it, damn it! Not how this was supposed to go."

Elliott jerked away from Claire's attentions again. His gaze sharpened on Jay. "Exactly how *was* it supposed to go? How long have you been planning this?"

Jay stopped and faced them. His expression transformed from subtly panicked to smoothly neutral. The change was terrifying. Claire's heart pounded so fiercely she had to blink away a surge of throbbing red in the edges of her vision.

She could not pass out.

"First of all, I don't have any idea what you're talking about," Jay said.

His eyes shifted side to side for a moment.

"You're a liar!" Elliott shouted, struggling against his bonds and rocking the chair so hard it tipped back on two legs.

Claire grabbed his shirt and pulled him down solidly onto all four legs. "Stop. Be smart."

He looked at her. His lip curled, splitting open a bit wider. More blood welled, but he turned his face away when she tried to dab it.

"Calm down, buddy," Jay said. "No need for you to go getting all riled up."

Elliott scowled and looked at him. "You tied me to a chair. You busted up my face. You assaulted —"

Jay moved fast for such a big man. He was across the room in seconds. Claire fell back as he grabbed Elliott by the front of the shirt and shook him so hard the chair legs squeaked across the floor.

"I told you, I didn't fucking touch her!"

"Stop it! Both of you, stop it!" Claire screamed.

To her relief and surprise, both men went silent. Jay let go of Elliott's shirt. Elliott swiped his tongue along the fresh blood on his lip.

"You got here early on Friday," Jay said to her.

"And you were waiting for me at the bottom of the road. How did you know I'd be here?"

Jay shook his head and shrugged. "You always book the weekend for early check-in and late check-out. I wanted to be sure it was open for you, that's all. I didn't know you were showing up then. It was coincidence."

Elliott let out a disbelieving snort. "No such thing."

"But you left the gate unlocked when you brought me up here in your truck," Claire said with a gesture at Elliott to stay quiet. "So... anyone could have come up here after you dropped me off and left. Someone could have come here before Elliott arrived."

"Someone came in here, and someone assaulted her, and she thought it was *me*." Elliott spat each word. He strained again at the bonds, making the chair creak, until he fell back, panting and red-faced.

He wasn't helping.

"Why would she think it was you if it wasn't?"

"I was blindfolded," Claire told him. "It was supposed to be a... surprise."

"Sounds like you got one, all right," Jay said with a grim smile that turned her stomach all over again.

Frustrated and disgusted at his lack of concern, Claire tried again. "Jay, please listen. Something really disturbing has happened to me, and we could use your help in figuring out who did it."

"I told you, it wasn't me —"

"I know it wasn't you."

Elliott let out an astounded, snorting gasp. "Claire, c'mon —"

"It wasn't him, Elliott." Her voice sounded too calm even to her own ears. Robotic, almost. "Jay has a full beard."

She shuddered, closing her eyes. Swallowing hard against another rush of bile. None of this was real, was it? It had to be some kind of nightmare. Every time she thought back to Friday afternoon, the memory of the pleasure threatened to choke her. Full ripples of revulsion swept her entire body, over and over, like the feathery touch of insect legs. She rubbed at her arms, hard, to rid herself of the sensation, but it wouldn't go away. It would never go away, she thought. She would never be able to have someone touch her that way again without remembering.

"The person who assaulted me didn't have a beard," Claire continued, since neither one of them seemed to be understanding her.

Elliott rocked in the chair again, this time with an irritated grunt. "I thought you said you didn't see who it was."

"I didn't have to see him. I could feel it."

Silence from both men while this sunk in.

"I *told* you." Jay sounded petulant and superior, and Claire wanted to kill him.

A text tone bleated from Jay's pocket, and he dug out his phone to swipe at the screen. His lips moved when he read the message. She couldn't make out what he was saying. His thick fingers tapped a reply.

"How do you get service here?" She could not stop herself from asking.

"Internet."

He didn't even look up at her, intent on whatever he was reading on the phone. He swiped away one screen and brought up a different one, although she couldn't see what was on it. More tapping. He squinted, pulling the phone closer to his face and scrolling. Paused. Used his fingers in a familiar widening "V" to zoom in on something. His mouth opened, then shut. He looked at her with narrowed eyes and another of those humorless grins that twisted his mouth.

What had he been looking at?

"This place doesn't have internet," Elliott muttered. "We liked it that way."

Jay put his phone into his jeans pocket and his hands on his hips. "*You* don't have internet. I hid the network so nobody could use it. Turns out, renting this place as an 'unplugged paradise' got me way more business than offering Interflix and WiFi. People like you just love to have an excuse for being out of touch with people who might need to get ahold of you. Don't you?"

The sudden, snapping chatter of Claire's teeth turned both men in her direction. Elliott struggled for a moment but couldn't do more than shake the chair. Jay stood, staring, hands still on his hips. His head swung back and forth as he made a series of muttering snorts.

He moved on Claire so fast she had no time to react. One big fist tangled in her hair, yanking her head back as he marched her toward the table. Without letting her go, he pulled out another chair and shoved her onto it. He forced her hands behind her back and secured them with another zip tie from his pocket before pulling the back of the chair, and her, about six feet away from Elliott. He slammed all four legs onto the floor so hard that Claire bit her tongue.

"Jay —" Elliott began.

"You shut up. Both of you. Or else, by god, I will shut you up. You need to let me think."

Elliott looked as though he meant to say something more, but a look from Claire stopped him. He sneered but stayed quiet. She rubbed the sore, bitten tip of her tongue against the roof of her mouth. Her arms and shoulders already ached from the position and being manhandled. She watched Jay pace, keeping her eyes on the pocket into which he'd shoved her phone. If she could find a way to get it from him —

"Where the hell do you get off, anyway, claiming you got *assaulted*?" He stopped and faced her, using air quotes. "It's what you wanted, ain't it? Someone to come in while you were blindfolded, get it on with you. That's what you said you wanted."

The bitterness on her tongue wasn't all blood. "How did you know that?"

For a moment Jay looked caught, before his face did that awful smoothing again, this time into an expression so solidly blank it was like staring at the face of a mannequin.

"You wanted it, and you got what you wanted. Now you want to cry about it? Now you want to get me in trouble about it? I can't let you do that."

"Answer me. How did you know about my...what I wanted?" Claire's voice shook, but she did her best to keep her gaze pinned on his.

Jay cut it away, looking sly. He ran his tongue over his lips before they skinned back over his teeth, startlingly white against the dark bush of his mustache and beard. He jerked his chin toward Elliott. "I heard you tell him all about it."

The junk drawer. The pamphlets. The instruction manuals. Her eyes darted around the cabin. Wherever he'd hid them, Jay had done a good job of it, because she could find no signs of a single one.

"Cameras," she said. "He's been watching us with hidden cameras."

FIFTEEN

"CAMERAS?" ELLIOTT ASKED. "WHAT...WHERE? HERE?"

"He has them set up in here. Probably in the bedroom and bathroom, too. I saw the manual for them in the drawer. I can't spot any right now, but they have to be here." Claire lifted her chin, steadying her voice. "I bet he's been watching us for a long time. Haven't you, Jay?"

"You sick fuck." Elliott sounded appalled. Disbelieving.

Jay grunted and stabbed a finger toward first Claire, then Elliott. "Who's the sick fucks? The pair of you, coming up here for your fling! Cheaters, both of you. Disgusting! I always knew about it, of course, even without the cameras. When you have to deal with people, you get to see the signs. Nobody who's married goes on a romantic weekend every single damned month, at least not if they're married to each other."

"I feel bad for your wife, if that's what you think," Claire said.

Jay backhanded her. "You shut your whore mouth."

"Don't you fucking dare call her that!" Elliott threw his body forward, but the zip ties held.

Claire probed the inside of her mouth with her tongue. More blood. Her teeth had cut the inside of her cheek. She had never been hit in the face that way, and the shock of it hurt as much as the wound the blow had left behind.

"Do you watch everyone? Or only us?" she asked.

"Sure, because you're so special?" Jay chuffed out harsh laughter that shook his shoulders.

"You do watch everyone, then?"

Jay said nothing and made as though he meant to hit her again. Claire flinched. The big man's laugh was higher pitched this time. Sounded a little desperate. His eyes darted from side to side without settling on anything.

"So you heard us sharing our fantasies, and you decided that this time, you were going to help yourself? Is that what happened?" Elliott asked hoarsely.

Jay's lip curled. "I would never. You think I want to get some kind of disease? A woman who will step out on her husband, well, what else will she do?"

Claire leaned as far as she could to deliberately spit blood at Jay's feet. Fuck his floor. "You have security cameras set up to watch people who trust you not to be an utter pig. You spy on their most intimate moments. You don't get to take the moral high ground, and you can't slut shame me."

His guilty expression told her she hit a mark of some kind. But there was something else there, too. A genuine fear. What was he afraid of... and was it something she needed to be afraid of, too?

"You *should* be ashamed," was all he said.

Well, she wasn't, and she wasn't going to let this man make her.

"Who was here with me on Friday?" Claire asked. When Jay didn't answer, she pressed on. "You have cameras. If you're in the habit of watching your guests, you had to see him. Was it one of the kids you talked about, the ones who were breaking in to party?"

"He said you'd agree to pay..." Jay shut his mouth hard with a click of his teeth. He paced again, boots thudding hard on the floorboards and rattling the dishes on the table.

"What's that supposed to mean? All this is about money? Blackmail?" Elliott asked.

Claire, though, had a different question. "Who's 'he?'"

"Just shut up and let me think."

For what seemed like forever, nobody spoke. Jay pulled out his phone and tapped in some more messages, looking frustrated. He put the phone back into his shirtfront pocket and let out a low string of curses. He looked at them both but said nothing.

"Who is 'he?'" Claire asked again. "What are we supposed to pay for?"

"Keeping quiet," Jay said.

Elliott's lip curled. "So you are trying to blackmail us."

"Only her," Jay said with a sneer. "*You* don't have any fucking money. Do you?"

More silence. Claire risked a look at Elliott, who'd dropped his head again, hiding his face. They'd never talked much about money, but she'd long suspected she was in a better financial position than he was. She was older, for one thing. Had an established career and a second income that contributed to the household. Elliott arranged to rent the cabin, but she always paid half the cost and contributed to whatever food and drink they brought. She'd offered to pay for the whole thing, but he'd always refused to let her. Pride, probably.

"That's what you like about her, ain't it? She's a classy rich bitch? Spends her husband's money on her boyfriend. Making him her little pet. She's your sugar mama, huh?"

That was so far from the truth it was laughable, but Claire didn't laugh. She and Troy were stable, but not what she would have ever called wealthy. "Whores get paid, Jay, so which am I? A whore or a sugar mama?"

Jay goggled at her. "You have a smart mouth, that's what I know."

"I also have my own money," Claire said, no longer trying to smooth and soothe him. Being called a whore had put a stop to that bullshit.

"He said that, too." Jay gave her a sly, sideways grin.

Claire snapped. "Who is this fucking 'he' you keep talking about!"

Jay's phone jingled, the ringtone insanely cheery and out of place for what was going on right now. Jay tore it free of his pocket and held it to his ear. One finger of his other hand went into the opposite ear. He barked a greeting into the phone, then stood, listening without speaking. He spun on one heel and stalked out the front door, slamming it behind him.

"Baby," Elliott whispered, "are you all right? He hit you. He hurt you. I'm going to kill him."

"Shh," she said. "Can you hear him saying anything?"

She could not. With the front windows covered by the sheets, she couldn't see him, either. She released the tension holding her upright and sagged in the chair. Her head spun.

"He won't get away with this, Claire. He can't."

She looked at him. "If he thinks he *can't* get away with it, he might do worse to us than tie us up."

"Why..." Elliott trailed off and shook his head. His eyes looked glazed. The bleeding from his split lip had painted his chin in streaks and drips, but it looked as though it had stopped now.

"Why what?"

He gulped in some air. "Why would you put yourself in a vulnerable position like that?"

"Are you blaming me?" she asked, incredulous and disappointed.

"No. Of course not. No," he repeated and shook his head again, but his voice was unsteady and he cut his gaze from hers.

Claire closed her eyes. "The box showed up at my office. Of course I assumed you'd sent it, especially after I got here and opened it. You'd already told me you were planning a surprise for me. Who else would have done it? Who else could have known what I told you about my fantasy? You're the only person I've ever told that to. The *only* one."

His breath wheezed in and out of him. He shook his head and gave her an agonized look that was tinged with a bit of what looked like satisfaction. "If I'd gotten here earlier, I could have stopped him!"

"But you didn't get here earlier," she said. "And you didn't stop him. So here we are now, and we have to figure out how to get out of this situation before one of us gets really hurt."

Elliott's rattling cough sounded thick and painful. Growing bruises mottled his tan throat. "You're absolutely sure you have no idea who it was?"

"How could I? Do you know who it could have been? Do you have any idea who might have known we were going to be here this weekend?"

"Of course not."

Claire had never asked him not to lie to her. The very nature of their relationship had meant untruths or half-truths or white lies would always be a part of it. Consequently, she had little experience in figuring out his "tells." But he was lying to her right now. She *felt* it.

"Are you involved with this? Because if you are, you'd better tell me right now, Elliott."

Elliott flinched from her cold words, hard as a one-two punch. "How can you even ask me something like that?"

She thought of how it had felt when she believed she was teetering on the edge of the cliff. When she believed he was capable of pushing her over. Of hurting her. They stared at each other without speaking. Did he guess what she was thinking?

The front door slammed open, and Jay strode in with a swirl of snowflakes and icy air following. He closed the door far more carefully than he'd opened it, making sure to engage the lock on the inside. He still had his phone gripped in one beefy fist, but he was no longer talking on it.

He got up close to Claire and shook his finger in her face. "Here's what's going to happen. You're going to transfer some money to me. And then you're going to pack your shit and get the hell out of my house, and I never want to see the pair of you filthmongers again."

"Filth...?" Claire could not stop the startled laugh that bubbled out of her at the old-fashioned term.

Spittle flew from his mouth as, red-faced, he screamed directly at her. "This isn't funny!"

She calmed herself by rubbing her sore, bitten tongue against the inside of her equally wounded cheek. She shook her head. "No. It's not funny. You're right."

"Do we have a deal?"

"How much money do you want?"

Jay frowned. If the sound of his thoughts could be heard aloud, it would be the creaking grind of rusty gears, she thought. He gave her another of those sly looks that told her he thought he was being oh, so clever. Oh, so smart.

"Half a million. Or I'll tell your husband, and *his* wife." He jerked his chin toward Elliott. "I'll blow your lives to bits."

Elliott barked out a noise. "Half a *million*?"

"How do you know I have access to that kind of money?" Claire asked. "Let me guess. The secret mystery man. Well, your sources are wrong."

The big man stuck his finger in her face again. "I don't think so."

"It doesn't matter. Even if I did have the money, I wouldn't give it to you," she said.

"Didn't you hear me? I'm going to tell your husband what you've been doing. I'll call him!" Jay cried, wildly waving his phone.

"How do you even have his number?" Elliott demanded.

Jay didn't hesitate, not even a second. "I have all your information. Name, address. All of it. You think a hilljack like me can't Google you?"

He waved his phone again, this time in Elliott's face. "I can call right now!"

Claire's smile hurt her split lip, but she couldn't stop it from spreading wide and wider. If anything, she welcomed the pain. It meant he hadn't beaten her. "Go ahead."

Jay hesitated, clearly suspicious. "What?"

"I said," Claire repeated carefully, "call him."

"You don't really want me to do that." Jay sounded uncertain.

"My husband knows exactly what I'm doing this weekend. He's always known it."

The big man's jaw dropped. "What?"

"What?" Elliott said, almost at the same time.

Claire's chin tipped up. "Go ahead and call him, Jay. I'm sure he could be here with the police in an hour."

"I don't believe you," Jay said. "You're bluffing."

She was, but only partially. "Try me."

"He knows where you are?" Elliott asked.

She kept her gaze steady on Jay and lied. Troy did not, in fact, know exactly where she was or who she was with. But he did know she was with someone for the weekend, and in what general area. Jay's threats were useless. "Yes. Of course he does."

Elliott's chair legs scraped on the floor as he rocked it. "How does he know where you are?"

"I told him."

Jay pulled her phone from his pocket and held it up in front of her, swiping the cracked screen. He shoved the phone in front of her to activate the Face ID function, then swiped the screen to tap on the settings. He kept his eyes on what he was doing while he spoke.

"I'm calling him. And if he does say he knows all about his wife being a whore, so what? He'll still pay to get you home safe, won't he?"

"From blackmail to kidnapping? Jay," Claire said, desperately trying to get him to stop all of this. She watched him connect the phone to a hidden WiFi network. "You don't have to do this. You don't have to ruin your life."

"You don't know shit about my life. So shut up." Jay's mouth twisted. "*Whore.*"

The word held no strength to sting her. She didn't give a single wee fuck what Jay thought of her sexual habits, her relationship with Elliott, or her marriage. What did slice at her was the vehemence in his voice when he said it. The smiling man who'd greeted her on Friday was gone, replaced by a man driven to desperation.

Jay was still afraid of something; she saw it in every drop of sweat on his forehead and every flickering cast of his eyes from one side to the next. And what did men do when they feared women?

Hurt them.

"You don't have to do this, Jay," Claire said.

"You really think you can spy on us. Record us. Blackmail us, tie us up, assault us —"

"Elliot. Shut up!"

Jay waved the phone again, pounding at the screen with his fingers to bring up her favorite contacts list. Even if he didn't know Troy's name, he could make a good guess. "I'm calling him. I'm going to tell him what a whore he married, and if he does say he knows, well, I'll just hang up. He doesn't know who I am. And no matter what you said, I don't think he knows where you are."

Jay put the phone to his ear. Claire said nothing more, too tired and aching, saving her strength.

From beneath her feet came the sound of phone ringing.

At first she assumed she was hearing the ringing from Jay's phone, but it wasn't that. It was a ringtone, a familiar one. It filtered up through the floorboards. Jay slapped her phone to disconnect the call. The ringing stopped.

Befuddled, Claire looked at her feet, the place where the ringtone had originated beneath her. "That's my husband's ringtone."

Sixteen

"My husband's phone is ringing from the basement." The statement came out of her as calmly as an observation about the sky being blue.

She and Jay stared at each other, neither of them looking away. Claire was vaguely aware of Elliott's hoarse voice rising up and up into the sound of something tortured. She could make out each word, but she could not string them together into any sense of coherence. He shut up abruptly when Jay hit him in the face.

"Why is my husband in your basement?"

Did she speak aloud? Claire could not be sure. The words slipped out, over her teeth and tongue, but hung in the air like dust motes dancing on a ray of sunshine, and as easily blown away with a breath. At any rate, Jay didn't answer her, and Elliott seemed to have been punched into a silent submission.

Pulling a ring of keys from his pocket, Jay went to the locked owner's closet and opened the door to reveal not shelves or hangers, but a narrow set of stairs, almost a ladder, descending into the basement. Claire gasped. Elliott dropped a curse, heavy as a boulder.

"You said," he began, but she cut him off.

"How was I supposed to know what it was? It was always locked!"

Jay maneuvered his bulk through the doorway and disappeared down the stairs. She heard the rumble of his voice berating someone but could not make out the words. She worked harder at flexing and relaxing her wrists, desperately trying to loosen the ties.

If she could free herself, she could get to the bedroom and Elliott's duffle. She could get the gun before Jay got back up here. She had no idea how to load it, much less fire it, but simply having it would be a deterrent. She could fake it —

"Claire!"

She ignored him, rocking the chair now in her desperation at loosening her bonds. Jay had called Troy. Troy's phone had rung from the basement. Why was Troy's phone in the basement?

How had he found out where she was?

Why had he shown up here?

"Claire, damn it!" Elliott shouted. "Stop. Look at me. I have to tell you something —"

More shouting filtered up through the floorboards. Claire tipped herself forward, as if that would help her see through the cracks in the floor and into the void below. The ties binding her to the back of the chair cut into her wrists, already hurting. She'd have to pee soon. Would Jay come back in time, or would she have to embarrass herself? She let out a low, frustrated cry, but forced her lips to close tight over any other sounds of distress.

"Claire," Elliott repeated. Softer this time. "Please look at me."

She did, and her heart ached, and if it wasn't love, it was something close to it, because if you couldn't find some love for the person who was with you when something really, truly bad was happening...when could you? Her breath rattled in her throat. Her eyes burned.

"I love you," Elliott said. "No matter what else happens, promise me you'll remember that."

Breathe, she counseled herself. Focus. One thing at a time. She didn't say she loved him, too.

Elliott let out a long, frustrated growl and rocked in his chair, slamming the front legs up and down as he fought the zip ties on his wrists and ankles. He went silent again, head hanging, hair shielding his face. "What are we going to do?"

About this. About them. About everything.

"He has my husband down there," she whispered. "Why is he in the basement?"

"You said you told him where we were," Elliott began, but she interrupted him.

"I didn't tell him the address. He didn't...he couldn't have known."

"You said he knew about us. Is that true or another lie?"

She tried to clear her throat, but her voice came out rough and scratching. "That's the truth."

"When...when did you tell him?"

Claire let out a low, soft groan that became a horrible, grating chuckle that tore at her already raw throat. "He's always known, Elliott."

"I don't understand," he said. "You told me that we had to be secret. We could only ever meet once a month. You said he couldn't ever know."

"It's complicated," she cut in.

Was she awake? Had she hit her head, gone unconscious? That seemed to be the only explanation for this surreal landscape, the absurdity of it all. Nothing made sense.

For as long as she could remember, Claire had experienced moments of blurriness she thought of as unclarity. Not a true psychological dissociation, although it was a feeling of being displaced. As though she were not really awake, but only dreaming. She'd taught herself to lucid dream to counter the times she felt this way, learning the tricks to wake herself when she wasn't sure if she was actually here. Now, she tapped her fingertips against her palm three times in quick succession, the most reliable way to force her out of a dream, if she was in one.

She was not dreaming.

She closed her eyes for a few seconds and focused on Elliott's harsh panting. She drew in all the smells of this cabin — woodsmoke. A lingering hint of the onions and peppers from the quesadillas they'd had for dinner the night before. Her own body odor, tangy and sharp with the scent of both fear and fury.

"He knows that when I go away for these weekends that it's to meet someone."

Elliott made a strangled noise. "What else does he know? Does he know my name?"

"No. I don't tell him the details. That's our agreement."

"You've been fucking me once a month for two years, and he knows all about it, but he doesn't know my name?" Elliott sounded outraged.

"I've never told you *his* name," Claire said. "Why would I ever have told him yours?"

"You lied to me."

"I never said I wouldn't," Claire told him.

Elliott looked away.

"Jay can't keep us here forever," Claire said. She had not forgotten that ringtone. She was not ignoring the fact Jay had someone in the basement, and she thought it was Troy. She was simply trying her best to figure out what the hell to do next. "Even if he does have my husband down there for some reason, there are other people waiting for us. If we don't come back when we say we're supposed to, they'll have to start looking. Right?"

"How will they find us, Claire? Have you ever told anyone where we go on these weekends? Anyone?"

She pressed her lips together again, hating the irritated tone of his voice, but refusing to allow herself to rise to it. "Of course not. But if you go missing, certainly the police will be able to...I don't know. Look at your phone records, your browser history, hell, your credit card statements? They can check out your internet history or something. Right? Won't they be able to find the Homecation charges?"

"Nobody's going to notice me missing for a long time."

"What do you mean? Of course they will. *She* will."

"Heather won't be looking for me."

It was the first time he'd ever said her name aloud. It changed something else between them. Everything was different now, and no matter what happened here, it would never be the same.

Silence twisted between them, broken only by the crackling fire. The sound of his breathing. The sound of hers. Her heartbeat threatened to deafen her, and to Claire's alarm, her vision spotted with hazy red flickers. She was on the verge of passing out.

Tap, tap, tap, her fingers touched her palm, reassuring her she was, in fact, awake. She could take little comfort from knowing it. A nightmare would have been better than this.

Claire licked her lips. "Why won't she be looking for you?"

"We're not currently speaking."

The world swam. She choked on her own spit as her heart hammered in her chest. She asked the question she was sure she already knew the answer to. "Why are you not speaking to your wife, Elliott?"

"She's not my wife anymore."

Her entire body jerked and shuddered. She closed her eyes. "Since when?"

"What difference does it make?"

She didn't bother tapping her palm again; she was more than awake. She didn't ask him why, because she thought she already knew. She didn't open her eyes. She could not bring herself to look at him, or at this cabin where they'd spent so many wonderful weekends together. She could not look down at her own body, the blood from her head and split lip on her own hands, her dirty clothes, the floorboards beneath her feet that kept her from seeing what was happening below them.

"What," he prodded. "You're not going to talk to me now? You can't find anything to say to that?"

"I don't think I have anything to say to you."

His forced laughter gritted and grated. "Fair enough."

She wriggled again, but the ties were tight. They weren't cutting off her circulation or anything like that, but the position was putting a strain on her joints that would soon become unbearable if she couldn't move. She let out a low, frustrated cry, fighting tears. She refused to allow herself to give in to despair. If she could not figure out a way to get out of this, she was damn well going to find a way to get through it.

"Are your hands hurting?"

She looked at him. "Do you care?"

"Of course I fucking care," Elliott snapped. "I might be angry with you, but that doesn't mean I don't care."

She fought her bonds again. Did she imagine them loosening? Maybe. She tried again before she answered him.

"Angry with *me*? Why are you — you know what? Never mind. *I* don't care."

"Right. Of course you don't care. You don't care about anything but yourself."

Voices rose from below them. A sob tore out of her. Claire hung her head for a moment before looking at him.

"Why didn't you tell me that you'd left her?"

"Why do you think I didn't tell you?"

She pressed her lips together and shook her head. Elliott shot the question at her again, then again, until finally, she spat out her answer. "Because you knew if I found out, I'd want to know why, and if I found out why, I would end it with you."

"But you were going to end things anyway," he said.

For a moment, she didn't answer. Then, she nodded. "Yes. I was."

"Because I was getting too attached."

"Yes," she said. "And I had a feeling you were going to ask me for what I would never be able to give you."

"Why can't you give it to me, Claire?"

"Because," she said with a sigh, "I don't want to leave my husband. I will never leave him."

"Even if you love me?"

"I don't love you," she said.

It was his turn for silence.

"We need to figure out how to get at least one of us free," she said when he didn't speak. "Before Jay comes back. We need your gun."

Jay's raised voice came up again through the floor, louder this time. A minute or so later, creaking footsteps on the stairs had Claire tensing in anticipation. In the next, she gave a hoarse cry at the sight of a familiar silhouette. Jay shoved him forward so he stumbled up from the stairs and into the room.

Troy was bound with his arms behind him. Crusted dark blood had dripped down the side of his face and clotted in his dark hair. The skin around the wound looked angry, bruised, but the rest of his face was too pale. A couple of days' beard growth had sprouted. He wore the clothes she'd last seen him wearing, two days before.

Troy took another shambling step into the room, his lurching gait so unsteady she was sure he was going to topple headfirst into the fireplace. Jay yanked him by the back of his jacket and set him on his feet before shoving him forward. Troy cried out when he put his weight on his left foot and limped a few steps.

"Git," Jay said. "Go on."

Claire tried to shout out her husband's name, but all she could manage was a whisper.

Elliott's voice, on the other hand, was loud and fierce, the single word shooting from his mouth like a bullet from a gun. "Troy!"

How did he know Troy?

Her husband's head swiveled, taking in the scene. The bandanna stuffed into his mouth kept him from speaking, but the muffled noises of his voice said he was trying to. Troy took another wobbling step and limped at a slow run toward her...but instead of reaching Claire, Troy went to Elliott and fell onto his knees in front of him.

"Oh, baby, oh, fuck," Elliott said in a voice thick with horror. "I thought you'd decided not to come."

SEVENTEEN

This was not happening. It could not be happening. What the hell *was* happening?

For Claire, everything seemed to be stuck in amber — clearly visible and held solidly in place, but as it turned out, not for an eternity. Only for the span of one breath, one beat of her heart, then another and one more. The sound of her own gasps filled up her ears but could not block out the sound of her lover murmuring comfort to her husband, who still knelt in front of him.

"What in the holy hell?" Jay looked as stunned as Claire felt. He turned to her. "*This* is your husband?"

She opened her mouth to reply but only a hiss of air came out, followed by a strangled garble.

"Troy, love, are you all right?"

Elliott's murmur turned her face toward the two men. Troy had put his head in Elliott's lap. His shoulders shook, and hoarse, rasping gasps spilled out of him.

In twenty-seven years of marriage, Claire had never seen Troy cry.

"What the fuck is wrong with you?" Elliott screamed at Jay. "What did you do to him? He's cold as ice, he's probably in shock. His head is bleeding. Did you hit him? Don't just stand there, untie me so I can help him."

Jay didn't move anything but his big fists, which opened and shut helplessly on empty air. "This was not supposed to happen. This was not supposed to happen. This was —"

"None of this was supposed to happen, but it is happening." Claire had found her voice. To her shock, she sounded calm and soothing. In control. Steady, the way Troy would have sounded if he were capable of speech. The way he *should* sound, she thought, shoving aside that idea before it could rise up and hit her over the head.

In every awful moment of her life for the past three decades, Troy had been the one to pick her up when she had fallen. Troy had been there to keep her from falling in the first place. They'd faced every crisis together as a perfect team. Troy handled the practicalities, and Claire took care of the emotional labor. If she let herself sink into this, she was going to be lost.

Claire could not afford to let herself be lost.

She said Jay's name and waited for him to turn toward her; when he did not, still focused on Troy and Elliott, she said it again. Firmer this time, like a teacher or a doctor, or a mother. "Jay. Can you please untie me? Troy clearly needs some medical attention. I have a first aid kit in my bag. If you let me get up —"

"I'm not going to do that." Jay's bushy bearded face swung back and forth, reminding her of a bison she'd seen in Yellowstone National Park the year they'd taken the RV road trip. Back and forth, back and forth, squinty eyes daring anyone or anything to come at it. It had charged a car that had stopped too close while the driver tried to take a photo. "I can't do that. I don't know what I'm going to do yet, but if I let you loose, you'll —"

"You took our phones," Claire cut in, but gently. Still soothing. Still calm, although a shriek was trying to force itself up her throat. She swallowed it and made eye contact with the big man, who she hoped would be more reasonable than the bison had been. "We have no way of calling anyone. The snow is far too deep for us to try and run, especially with Troy's injuries. But we can talk about this. I'm sure it's all just a misunderstanding. Let me help Troy, okay?"

"Sit there. Be quiet. He's fine."

"He's not fine." Elliott fought the zip ties still binding him. "He needs stitches. How hard did you hit him?"

Jay dragged both hands through his hair. "He surprised me."

To Claire's relief, Elliott turned his attention fully to Troy after that. His weeping words were low and soft and meant only for Troy, but still audible, if she tried hard enough to listen. She didn't want to hear what he was saying. She definitely didn't want to hear her husband's replies, not now. One thing at a time. First, she had to get through to Jay.

She drew in a breath to steady her voice and tried again. "Whatever happened, Jay, I'm sure we can figure out how to fix it. Okay? You know none of us here are going to want to get the authorities involved. That would be messy and embarrassing for all of us."

Jay looked at her and finally, really saw her. "*You* said you didn't care if I called your husband and told him what you'd been getting up to. Why would you care about what the authorities think?"

She was getting through. Claire spoke as calmly as she could, doing her best to keep Jay focused on her. "I didn't care if you called Troy because he already knew I was here. That's the truth. You can ask him about it, if you want. But that's the truth between the two of us. It's not something we'd want anyone else to know about. I'm sure you can understand that, can't you?"

"How am I supposed to know what you kinky freaks care about?" Jay sounded more petulant than panicked now, and although Claire took umbrage at the name calling, she could let that slide.

"We have families and jobs and friends, Jay. Our private business is private. We wouldn't want to embarrass ourselves, would we?"

Jay's lip curled, parting the fluff of his beard and mustache. "Maybe you shouldn't do things you're too embarrassed for anyone to know about, then."

"You're so right," she said, the words bitter and spiteful and a lie. She was not embarrassed by the life she and Troy had made for themselves, but other people might be, if they found out. People she loved and cared about.

"Just let one of us free so we can help him," Elliott demanded.

"Shut up, or I'll shut you up. Why's he over there with you, anyway, and not her?" Jay turned to Claire. "Huh? Why's your man crying like a little bitch with your boyfriend?"

At least with this, she could be completely honest. "I don't know."

"This was not supposed to happen," Jay muttered again. He strode to the corner of the living room next to the bookcase and shouted, seemingly to nothing, "you'd better get your ass up here! I ain't handling all this by myself!"

Was there someone else in the basement? Claire looked, but saw nobody on the stairs. Heard nothing from below. The camera must be hidden somewhere close to it. Jay was shouting at whoever was in on all of this with him, the mystery man who'd told him there'd be money from her, to the utterly ridiculous tune of half a million dollars.

Jay stalked to Troy and yanked him to his feet. Troy slumped in the bigger man's grip without struggling. Jay practically carried him to the couch and threw him onto it. Troy groaned and fell back onto the cushions at an angle, hampered by his hands zip-tied behind his back. Jay jerked him upright, manhandling him into place and shaking him by the shirt front. It didn't matter. As soon as Jay let go of him, Troy fell over again until all she could see was his legs behind the couch's arm.

"All of this a real cockup. And I'm telling all three of you kinky fucks, I'm not taking the fall for any of it. You hear me?" Again, he shouted to the cabin as a whole. "You hear me?"

Elliott fought his bonds, rocking the chair as if he hadn't tried that half a dozen times already without success. "You're going to regret every single thing you've done to us."

"Elliott, for fuck's sakes, shut up," Claire ordered.

His face twisted in disgust when he looked at her. She'd never seen anything like it, not from him. Until this weekend, Claire had never even seen Elliott mildly annoyed with her.

"Stop telling me what to do," he said.

An immediate retort rose to her lips, but she stopped herself before she could succumb to her emotional response. Jay, on the other hand, was not keeping control of his emotions at all. He stormed into the kitchen and yanked open a drawer. He pulled out a roll of silver duct tape and returned with it to Elliott. He tore off a piece and slapped it over Elliott's mouth, then turned to Claire.

"Please, don't," she said. "I won't scream. Even if I did, there's nobody to hear me."

"That's what you think," Jay said grimly, and covered her mouth with tape.

Claire screamed into the duct-tape gag. She fought the plastic tying her wrists. Jay hadn't thought to pin her ankles the way he'd done to Elliott, so she kicked out, catching the big man in the knee. He grabbed her by the hair and pulled so hard she thought he was going to come away with a handful of it. He shouted at her, but she couldn't make out the words over the sounds of her own hoarse and panicked shouting.

She fought the gag, trying to work her jaw, teeth and tongue, but it was stuck so firmly she couldn't budge it. Jay was still shouting at her. Her vision blurred, his face along with it. The tears she'd been holding back until now streamed freely down her cheeks, and her nose clogged with snot. She couldn't breath. She was going to suffocate. Her head lolled, but Jay's grip in her hair wrenched it back up.

"You ever kick me that way again, I'll kill you. Got it?"

Claire turned her face away from the stench of his breath, but she stopped fighting. Jay backed off and dug in his pockets, but his fingers came out empty. He cursed and whirled away. One big boot struck out, kicking at nothing. He went into the kitchen again, this time slamming open a bunch of cupboards before he found what he was looking for.

When he came back, he bore a hank of slim white cord in one fist. He used the rope to tie her ankles to the chair legs, cutting off the extra length with a hunting knife he pulled from a sheath on his belt. He straightened with a groan, a hand on his back. He was practically panting. Her own breathing wasn't much slower. She couldn't see exactly what he did with the rest of the cord, but she suspected he was using it to tie up Troy.

Elliott shrieked, but, muzzled by duct tape, all he could really manage was a series of guttural shouts. Troy was silent. Her eyes drifted shut, but when the front door slammed, they startled open. Their coats were missing from the hooks by the door. So were their boots. The roar of a snowmobile engine came next, getting more distant. Jay had left them, but for how long?

She looked at Elliott. His head hung again. She couldn't see his eyes.

Sweat dripped from his nose. He'd tired himself out. She couldn't see Troy, but he was still quiet.

A tsunami of fury rose inside her, forcing away the terror and despair. It wasn't at Jay. Not even at the situation. She was furious with Troy. For not helping her.

For being hurt.

For being *here*.

Her own panic at the idea of suffocating to death had faded, but barely, and not because she was convincing herself she would not. Her anger at her husband had spilled over into her fear and diluted it enough that she could focus on it instead of terror.

There were three of them here, and they would have to work together. When she gave out her own muffled cry, though, neither man responded. Frustrated, Claire yanked again and again at the plastic ties. She pushed past the ache in her hands and wrists which now radiated into her shoulders. She rocked the chair until it squealed a protest. The plastic ties weren't giving way, but the chair seemed to be.

Fine, then, she thought, this was how it was going to go, and before she could stop herself with worry about how it would feel, Claire rocked the chair off its right front and back legs hard enough to tip her over.

She fell, hard, and hit the wood floor with her shoulder and hip. Something cracked inside her. She screamed into the duct tape but fought away the tears. If her nose got stuffed up, she *would* suffocate. She concentrated on calming herself. She could hear Elliott hollering again. Still nothing from Troy.

She gave herself only until the count of five to rest. Jay could be back at any minute. At the end of the count, she tried moving. The chair back had broken. She wriggled. Still bound to the chair itself, she was nevertheless able to work the back free of the seat. She rolled, taking the back of the chair with her.

Her ankles were still tied to the chair legs, but it took only a few kicks to free her left leg. That was enough to let her get to her knees. The slatted chair back hung from her wrists, pulling at her damaged shoulder, but she managed to twist and kick her right leg also free.

Panting, she tried shaking her arms to see if it would free the ties from where they wove between the slats. When that didn't work, she went to the front door and swung her arms behind her, hitting it with the chair back. Wood splintered and cracked, but she couldn't tell if it was from the door or the chair pieces dangling from her wrists. Claire geared up, drew in a breath, and let it out in a primal shriek that vibrated the duct tape on her mouth as she hit the door again.

The chair back split into two pieces. One slipped free of the cord and hit her ankle and foot. The other remained tied to her wrists, which were no longer bound together.

A hitching cry of relief surged out of her, but Claire would not give herself time to celebrate. She worked her wrist free of the remaining bits of the chair and tossed it down. Elliott was rocking his own chair, too, but she couldn't tell if it was to get her attention or to follow her lead. It didn't matter.

Working the tape free of her mouth, Claire limped as fast as she could to the bedroom. She dumped out Elliott's duffle bag onto the bed and searched frantically through his clothes and toiletries. She found the ring box and tossed it aside. But no matter how she sorted the pile of Elliott's belongings, she couldn't find what she needed.

The gun was gone.

EIGHTEEN

ELLIOTT HAD NOT YET MANAGED TO TIP HIMSELF OVER. He was afraid of hurting himself, Claire thought with a curl of her lip. *Coward.* The insult launched into her mind like an inflatable raft held beneath the water and then released, and she grabbed onto it the same way. Surprised, but clutching at it the way she would anything else that would save her life.

A man who was too afraid to risk breaking his nose on the floor in order to get himself free was not a man she could count on.

When Elliott saw her in the doorway, he sent a volley of grunting cries her way that sounded far too similar to demands for her taste. She ignored him and went instead to Troy. Jay had taken his boots, too. His eyes were closed, and he lay slumped in the same position Jay'd thrown him in. For a horrible moment, she imagined him as a corpse.

"Troy. Can you hear me?" She tapped his cheeks lightly with the back of her hand.

He didn't respond right away. She slapped him a little harder. His eyelids fluttered. Opened. He struggled, face contorted into an expression of terror clear even around the tape gag covering his mouth. She pulled at it, wincing at his low cry of pain as the sticky glue pulled at his skin. There was no way to do this gently. She ripped it off, cringing at his hoarse shout.

"Where is he?" Troy cried.

"I don't know where he went. He's probably going to be back soon. We need to get you taken care of." She touched the seeping wound on his temple, but Troy jerked from her touch with a snort of pain. He struggled to sit up, and she helped him.

"Where is he?"

"I told you —"

"Not the guy who put me in the basement. Elliott!" Troy fought her grip, trying to twist around to look behind her. With his hands tied behind him, he couldn't.

Claire flinched. Her fingers gripped the front of her husband's shirt to keep him from falling over. She looked at Elliott, but didn't ask Troy how he knew her lover's name.

"He's here," she said.

"Is he okay?" Troy squirmed for a moment in her grip.

"He's fine." Her voice came out clipped and severe. She shook him to get him to look at her. "First, we need to get you untied and that wound taken care of. Are you feeling faint?"

"Head hurts. I'm starving. I pissed myself," Troy said after a hesitation. He blinked, and his vision seemed to clear. His gaze honed in on hers. "What are you doing here, Claire?"

"What am I —?" Claire cut herself off with a shake of her head. "First things first. Let me find something to cut you free."

"Claire, wait!"

She left him despite his protest. In the kitchen, she wet a clean dishtowel from the drawer and wrung it out. She considered one of the knives from the block but plucked the kitchen shears from their slot, instead. She took a few steps toward the living room before turning back and also grabbing the carving knife. Without the gun, she still needed something, either to threaten Jay or defend herself.

Using the shears, she quickly snipped the plastic ties off her wrists. Then Troy's. With an agonized sigh, he pulled his arms in front of him, rubbing the raw marks on his skin and rolling his shoulders to get the tension out. He sat up higher but pitched forward, almost as though he was going to fall over. Claire pushed him back, and if it was a little rougher than necessary…well. She wasn't quite herself at the moment.

"Let's take a look at your head. Okay?"

Troy went still. His gaze searched hers, and he didn't struggle to get away from her as she pressed the wet cloth to the swollen bruise and gaping slice on his temple. His nose looked bent, dark crust rimming the nostrils. Blood had also dried and flaked on his upper lip.

They'd been together for almost thirty years. If you'd asked her this morning, she would have said she knew this man up and down, inside and out. Looking into his eyes right now, Claire had the sinking feeling she didn't know Troy at all. Their secrets had been the salvation of their marriage, so why, now, was she starting to feel as though discovering what Troy had kept hidden from her was going to destroy it?

She whispered his name in a voice full of yearning, although for what, she couldn't be sure. An explanation? Reassurance?

Troy closed his eyes. He winced away from her touch when she dabbed again at the wound, which had now begun seeping fresh blood. Claire bent her head, fighting a sob at the sight of his wounds but also at the way he'd shielded himself from her.

"What were you doing here?" Her voice came out twisted and strangled, but he heard her. She knew he did. And yet, he didn't answer her, at least not with words. Troy opened his eyes, but not to look at her. His gaze shifted for a few seconds toward Elliott before he closed his eyes again.

She also looked at the other man, who'd stopped rocking the chair and shouting. He was staring at them, brow furrowed, eyes narrowed. She squeezed Troy's shoulder and got up. She went to Elliott.

She tore the duct tape off his lips. Before he had time to say a word, she slapped him across the face. Fuck not leaving a mark.

"You did this," she said.

Elliott used his tongue to poke out the inside of his cheek beneath the handprint. His smile curved without humor, its usual charm becoming something darker. Almost cruel. "I told you I had a surprise for you. It wasn't one of your fantasies, though. It was mine."

Her knees gave out; she gripped the back of the chair to keep herself from falling. She sagged, helpless to stand against this. Whatever *this* was. She shook her head and used the shears to free one of Elliott's hands, then left the shears in his lap before she went back to Troy.

She cupped his chin and gently turned his face to get a better look at his injuries. "Is it only your head? Did he hurt you other places?"

Troy grimaced. "He hit me on the head and tossed me down the stairs. I busted my hip pretty good. My elbow. My wrists and ankles hurt from being tied up down there. I think I sprained the left ankle. Maybe broke it. Everything hurts, to be honest."

"How long have you been here?"

"Since Friday morning," he said, with a pause, adding before she could ask, "I left the house right after you did."

"Were you on the way when I called you?" She thought she already knew the answer to that, but when he nodded his affirmation, her chest squeezed. She hung her head, thinking of that call. She'd known he sounded off.

His gaze drifted again over her shoulder. Looking at Elliott, who was working on freeing himself.

"Find something we can use to clean this up," she ordered Elliott. "Peroxide or alcohol. Or at least a soapy wet cloth. Any bandages you can find."

Elliott loomed over her. "Is he okay?"

Without looking at him, she said, "if you want to help him, Elliott, you'll get what I asked for."

To Troy, she said, "You probably need a stitch or two, but it looks like it's clotting. Do you feel dizzy or nauseated? Are you going to pass out?"

"No. I need a drink. Food. A shower." He pulled a face and looked into her eyes.

She wanted to kiss him, but did not, too aware that Elliott had not yet moved away from them. "Elliott. Please, go."

"I don't understand what's going on," Troy said.

"We'll figure it out."

Elliott returned from the bathroom with a small bottle of rubbing alcohol and a package of cotton balls. He had a handful of small adhesive bandages. "This was all I could find."

She could not bring herself to look at him, but she took what he'd brought and set it out on the coffee table. She tried to remember if she'd brought a sewing kit. Even if she had, she didn't think she had the guts to stitch the still oozing gash in Troy's temple.

Elliott knelt next to her in front of Troy to take one of his hands. He didn't quite push her out of the way, but it was close. "Are you okay? What the hell is going on?"

"I think you're the one who's supposed to tell us that," Claire said.

Elliott fell back onto his heels, his back knocking against the coffee table and pushing it away. The bottle of rubbing alcohol rocked without falling over. He let go of Troy's hand and got to his feet. "I'll get him some water."

Claire didn't argue. She bent to the task of soaking alcohol onto the cotton ball. Troy gritted his teeth when she dabbed it to his temple, and one hand shot out to grab her arm to stop her.

"Sorry," he said through clenched jaws and released her. "Hurts."

"I'm trying to be careful. This looks a little infected. What did he hit you with?" She tried again, blowing on the wound the way she'd done for Aviva when she was little and skinned her knees rollerskating in the driveway. Troy have never had a high tolerance for pain. She looked toward the kitchen, but Elliott had gone into the bathroom and shut the door behind him.

"I don't know. He was in the cabin when I got here. I guess I startled him. We had a little tussle. He was shouting that I wasn't supposed to be here. Next thing I knew, I was getting shoved down the basement stairs. It's all hazy after that." Troy put up a hand to stop her from pressing again at his head wound.

"He tied you up down there?"

"Yeah." Troy let out a long, shuddering breath. "Not on a chair or anything. Just on the floor. He brought me down an old sleeping bag, but that was it. He brought me some water yesterday, I think."

She paused with the saturated cotton ball held to his head, then finished swiping away some of the dirt and blood. What looked like a splinter jutted from the slice in Troy's head. Her hand shook, and she put it on his knee.

"Did you park up here? Next to the cabin?"

"Where else would I park?"

Quickly, she outlined meeting Jay at the bottom of the road, how he'd been messing with the gate. How he'd warned her of the impending weather and told her to park at the bottom. "But your car wasn't here when I got here."

Troy patted his jeans pockets, letting out a groan as his body twisted. "My keys are gone. He must have taken them. Moved the car."

"It doesn't matter. The snow's too deep to get a car down the road anyway." She chafed his cold hands for a few seconds.

He gently pulled them from her grip. Elliott was still in the bathroom. Troy lowered his voice. "Claire...I don't understand what's going on. What are you doing here? How do you know Elliott?"

"He's my getaway." Her voice snagged and shredded on the words.

Troy blinked again and fell back against the cushions with a groan. He covered his face with his hands. Alarmed, Claire moved to sit next to him. She put the cotton balls and alcohol on the coffee table.

"Troy?"

"Claire," he said. "This is so fucked up."

"How do *you* know him?" she whispered frantically, pitching her voice low to stop Elliott from hearing them.

Troy dropped his hands to look at her face. "He's my getaway, too."

NINETEEN

The first time Claire Fitzgerald met Troy Levy, he was dancing with another man. Lips locked, hips grinding, both of them shirtless and sweating and covered in the fine dust of glitter that floated down from the ceiling every now and then. The music was throbbing, the drinks were flowing, the drugs were circulating.

"There he is. C'mon, I'll introduce you." Janelle, Claire's best friend, pointed.

It had been close to a year since they'd been able to go out dancing this way. Janelle had gone to school in Florida while Claire had stayed marginally closer to home in New York State, but this summer, both of them were working in Ohio. Cedar Point Amusement Park hired from far and wide, and the two of them had both decided to spend their summer away from home. They'd even signed up to be roommates.

For Janelle, it was simply a matter of economics — she didn't have a car and would have been stuck babysitting for a family in her neighborhood for the summer instead of earning minimum wage. For Claire, the choice was a little more complicated. After spending her first year away at college, spending even a few months at home had seemed more like a prison sentence than a summer vacation.

Claire had snagged a job in one of the hotels, cleaning rooms and earning tips that were never big enough. Troy and Janelle worked together on ride crew for the Magnum, one of the park's most popular roller coasters. They'd hit it off the first day, but different schedules had kept Claire from meeting Troy until tonight, when a group had gathered to carpool the hour-ish drive to Cleveland and the club there that catered to the gay crowd and allowed underage kids in to dance.

"Troy!" Janelle waved, but he didn't hear her.

Mesmerized by the muscled men wearing nothing but gold lamé shorty-shorts who were dancing in cages, Claire didn't actually care about meeting Troy in that moment, but her friend grabbed Claire's arm and leaned in close to say into her ear, over the throbbing beat of the music, "let's go dance."

So they did.

By the end of the night, Troy had abandoned the guy he'd been with and was dancing only with Claire. They managed to get rides home in the same friend's car, hip to hip, knee to knee, squeezed into the backseat with more people than there were seatbelts. She'd pressed herself against the car door, praying she'd locked it and wouldn't go tumbling out onto the highway they'd been speeding down.

Back at the park with everyone stumbling away into their own dorm rooms, Claire had looked for Janelle, but she was giggling and smooching with a guy in the group whose name Claire could not remember. Troy had linked his fingers through Claire's, and when she tried to head for her dorm, in the opposite direction from his, he planted his feet and stayed in place until she stopped moving, too.

"I thought you were into guys," she whispered as he tugged her gently, step by step, toward him. She held back, but it seemed that against Troy, much like the Borg, resistance was futile.

"I am."

She laughed, then. "So what are you doing with me?"

"I'm trying to kiss you, Claire," Troy said.

"But I'm not a guy."

His mouth had met hers lightly, gently, the hint of the tip of his tongue teasing at her lips as he spoke. "I know."

That first kiss had lit her up inside. They became inseparable for the rest of the summer. At the end of it, Claire had assumed they'd break up. Troy would not hear of it. After a semester of long-distance dating, he'd transferred to her college, an act that had infuriated and frustrated his parents and was the last truly impulsive thing Claire could ever recall him doing.

They'd been married right after college graduation in a traditional ceremony, in a synagogue with a chuppah and a rabbi and a cantor and all of it. Their honeymoon had been a two-week tour of the East Coast, ending in Maine, where they'd found it difficult to get a good meal that wasn't infiltrated with lobster in some way or another, but they'd still managed to have a great time. For twenty-seven years they'd been having a great time.

For twenty-three years, they'd been sleeping with other people.

The getaways had been Claire's idea. When you love someone, you want them to be happy. She loved Troy. He loved her. There'd been a few rocky years around the time Aviva had been born when neither one of them had been happy and both of them had been too afraid to admit it. They'd never talked about splitting up, although she'd thought about it and honestly sometimes, still did. The getaways were supposed to fill the places in each of them that would otherwise have remained empty.

Getaways were supposed to be a reprieve.

"How long has he been your getaway?" was all she had the chance to say before the bathroom door swung open and Elliott came out.

He brought both a glass of cold water and a hot soapy towel. He handed the first to Troy. The second to Claire. Then he took a couple of steps back. It was obvious he'd taken the time in the bathroom to wash the blood from his face. His hair was wet and slicked back. His shirt was wet too. She could see his pulse throbbing at the base of his throat. Bruises were already blooming around both eyes, the skin turning navy and purple.

"Is that what you call me?" Elliott asked.

So, he had heard at least some of what they were saying, after all.

"I don't care," Elliott said when neither of them answered him. "Actually, I prefer to know it. It tells me a lot."

Claire frowned. "It doesn't tell you anything."

Troy pushed off the couch and went to Elliott. Their embrace looked awkward at first, even from where she was sitting, but when it melted into something more intimate, Claire turned her face away. She concentrated on her hands, curling into fists on her knees. There was blood grimed into her knuckles, but she didn't know who it belonged to.

"You stink," Elliott said, and she looked up. Elliott supported Troy with an arm around his waist. He looked at Claire. "We should get him into the shower. Then some food."

"We should try to figure out what we're going to do before Jay comes back," Claire began.

Elliott shook his head and held up a hand to cut her off. "He has our phones, we have no vehicle, much less one that could manage the snow, and Troy needs to be taken care of before we do anything else. He took our coats. Our boots. We have to be smart."

She shut up. He was right, but she hated him for his dismissiveness and the implication that she was going to be anything but smart.

Elliott shifted Troy's weight against him. "I'm going to help Troy get cleaned up. Why don't you make us something to eat."

Troy pushed away from Elliott and hopped on his good foot. "I need clean clothes. I don't know where my bag is, but probably in my car. Can one of you get me something to wear?"

"You brought a bag with you?" Claire asked abruptly.

Troy and Elliott shared a look she could not interpret. She thought about what Troy had told her Friday morning, about how he was going to catch up on some work while she was gone. But instead, he'd packed a bag and come here. Not to check up on her or confront her, because there was no need for that. He'd come here planning to stay. To be with *Elliott.*

"You lied to me," she told him.

The accusation hit him hard, based on the hunch of his shoulders.

She turned to Elliott. "You both lied to me."

Neither man denied it. Claire's low chuckle hurt her throat. She gathered up the discarded cotton balls and the papers from the adhesive bandages. Her entire body throbbed with pain, but that was nothing compared to the growing agony in her heart.

Elliott spoke first but to Troy. "C'mon, I'll help you get cleaned up."

"No," Troy said, but softened his tone to add, "Can...can you go see if he put my car in the barn out back? Get my bag? My clothes?"

Elliott hesitated, looking back and forth at both of them. His expression twisted before settling into a forced neutrality, but he made no further complaint. He gave Troy a curt nod.

"It's going to be cold as hell out there," he said. "And I have no boots or coat."

"Then I guess you'll need to be quick," Claire said.

In all the ways she'd imagined things between them ending, Claire had never thought it would be like this. With high emotions, yes. With disdain and accusations and maybe even a threat or two. But not this thinly hidden fury. The look that flashed in Elliott's eyes was fierce, verging on violent enough that she took a physical step back. He looked as though he wanted to hit her.

That was fair, she thought. She wanted to do the same to him.

Without another word, Elliott shrugged Troy's arm from around his shoulders. He stalked past them and went out the door. He slammed it behind him and didn't lock it.

Troy groaned, rubbing at his eyes. He balanced on his right leg, but he was already teetering. Claire got up and offered her support — she took the opposite side Elliott had, and she didn't think it had been on purpose until Troy's arm settled on her shoulders. He turned his face to kiss her temple.

"I'm sorry," he said.

She deserved more than that, but he'd started shaking. Elliott was right. They needed to get Troy settled and in good shape before they could really plan to do anything else.

Together, she hopped him along into the bathroom, then unbuttoned and unzipped his jeans to push them down over his thighs. He wasn't wearing his usual boxer briefs but had gone bare under the denim. She didn't mention that she'd noticed, but as she helped him sit on the toilet, their eyes met. He knew she had.

His sigh of relief was so loud and long it almost echoed. Claire tugged his dirty jeans off over his calves and feet. He grunted again at the pull of the fabric on his swollen ankle. When she took off his socks, the left ankle looked obviously...not right.

"Do you think it's broken?" he asked her.

She didn't want to probe it. The bruised flesh looked soft, like rotten fruit. "I don't know. We should treat it as though it's broken, maybe. It's at least a horrible sprain."

"It feels worse than that. Like something's grinding inside it."

"How long?" She got to her feet and kicked his dirty clothes into a pile near the sink.

"Since he threw me down —"

"No," Claire interrupted. Gave him a second to understand her, a moment to stop pretending he didn't. "How. Long."

Troy put his elbows on his knees. Face in his hands. "Just over a year."

She turned away from him, incapable of processing this. She and Elliott had been coming to this cabin for an entire year longer than that. Other than that parking lot kiss, they hadn't been physical with each other before that first trip, although they'd been texting and talking on the phone for three or four months before the day in the coffee shop.

She faced him. "How did you meet him?"

"We go to the same gym," Troy said, sounding a little confused.

"You didn't know him before that?"

"No. Why would you think I knew him?" Troy asked.

From the bathroom window, she could see the path of Elliott's footprints in the snow. The angle of the cabin compared to the shed meant she couldn't see the big double doors without craning her neck, but when she did, she saw Elliott in front of them. The snow had started again, big fluffy flakes of it that slanted sideways in what the creaking cabin walls and roof told her was a fierce wind.

"I met him at the Allwein's house. The night of their house party. You were there, too. I thought maybe —"

"I left early," he told her. "You stayed by yourself. When you came home, you had that look, the one I knew meant you'd met someone, but you didn't tell me anything about him."

"I never tell you anything about them." Her voice rose, hoarse with sudden tears she dashed away from her cheeks with her aching hands. "That's our deal. That's what we agreed to!"

Troy made as though to get himself off the toilet but sat back with a small groan. He gave her a helpless look. "I didn't meet him there."

"You had no idea he was mine?"

"No," Troy said. "I promise you, I would never have started anything with him if I'd known he was with you. I would never cross-contaminate us with anything like that. You have to know that."

Three days ago, she would have known it, but now...now, Claire had no idea. She peered again out the window. Elliott, hunched against the wind, was marching back through the snow. It had drifted so deep in places that it went all the way to his hips, and more was falling even faster than a few minutes ago.

"Claire." Troy said her name sharply. "What's going on out there?"

She looked at him. "The storm is getting worse. We're stuck here until someone comes to plow us out."

TWENTY

"I'm fine. You can leave me alone." Troy cut off a small groan as he hopped to the shower and twisted the knobs to start the water.

"I should stay."

"I'm not going to pass out," he said sharply, then hung his head. "Look, the shower's narrow enough for me to lean against the wall and take the weight off this ankle. I'll be fine. I promise you. Go see if Elliott found my bag."

There'd been a time when Claire would never have doubted a promise from Troy. Things had changed. Still, she backed off.

In the living room, Elliott stamped his feet in front of the door. He slapped at his body as he blew out big, shivering breaths. Snow had frozen in his dark hair, even in his eyelashes.

"It's frigid out there. Could barely see anything. I couldn't get into the barn." He made his way to the fire with stiff-legged strides, a man made of ice blocks, unbendable. He sank to his knees on the rug in front of the flames and held out his hands. "Big l-lock on the door. Padlock, needs a key."

"Damn it."

He rocked a little, back and forth, before sinking onto his heels. His teeth chattered around his question. "Where's Troy?"

"In the shower. He'll have enough hot water for a few more minutes."

"You left him? He could fall —" Elliott made as though to get up but went back to his knees with a mutter when Claire stepped between him and his view of the bathroom.

She'd closed the door, anyway, to keep the steam inside. To give Troy some privacy. To give her some privacy with Elliott.

"He's fine. He's banged up, but he'll be okay," she said.

Elliott's lips thinned, but he nodded. "I'm worried about the cut on his head."

"His ankle's in worse shape. It's probably broken, and I don't know what to do for it. Make a splint?"

"Yeah, that's right. You were never a Girl Scout," he said in a low voice.

She frowned. "This isn't the time for smartass remarks, Elliott."

"No," he said, looking at her. "I guess it's not."

She had kissed the man in front of her. Held his hand. Done every sex act imaginable. Shared meals, played games, watched movies. They had slept in the same bed, spooning, and she'd grown accustomed to the weight of his body when he dreamed. The smell of him. She had clung to him as something precious, and she could still see all of that. She could still remember how it felt to want him.

"He knew about me all the time?" Elliott asked her.

She shrugged. "He knew about you in the abstract. Nothing about *you*, specifically."

A soft grunt slipped out of him. He leaned again toward the fire, head down. The snow and ice in his hair was melting, trickling over his face and into his collar. A few drops spattered onto the floor.

"You never told me," he said.

"It wasn't anything you ever needed to know," Claire replied. "Kind of the way I guess you didn't think I needed to know that you'd left your wife?"

He looked up at her, his expression grim. "You thought you could keep me in line by telling me you could only get away once a month, you couldn't talk on the phone or see me the rest of the time? Did you think if I knew he was okay with it that I would have asked for more from you?"

"You would have."

Elliott sneered. "Because that's what all the others did, the ones before me?"

"Yes," Claire said, exasperated, "and it's what you would have done, too. It's what you *did*."

"I hate that you lump me in with them. I fucking hate that I'm..." His fists clenched and he pounded them lightly onto his knees. He hung his head again. "I was just one of many."

Of all the multiple lovers she'd had over the years, none of them had been what Elliott had become to her. If she told him that, would it cause more harm than good? It would still probably not be enough for him. It wouldn't make him feel better, and it wouldn't change her mind.

It wouldn't change what they were going through now.

"He said you met at the gym," she said instead.

Elliott looked into the fire instead of at her. "He did meet me at the gym."

"That's an awfully long way to drive so you can work out," Claire said.

"The gym's only about ten minutes from my place. So, not really."

She moved closer to the fire herself and warmed her hands. She looked down at him. "Either my husband started going to a gym a lot farther from home than he used to, or you're lying."

"I'm not lying. I live about ten minutes away from the gym where Troy met me." His voice was steady. Unwavering.

Too calm. Suspiciously, she watched his profile, but his expression, too, had gone far too emotionless to be the Elliott she knew. Had thought she knew, anyway.

"You told me you live in West Chester, Elliott."

He shrugged. "I used to."

"Tell me it was all coincidence," she said. "Tell me it was crazy, random happenstance. Please."

His silence was not the answer she wanted, but it was the one she'd suspected.

The sound of running water shut off. Claire took a step toward the bathroom. Elliott snaked out an arm to clutch her by the ankle, effectively stopping her by almost tripping her up. He got to his feet faster than she'd expected him to move. He pushed his way in front of her.

"I can help him," Elliott said in a voice that brooked no argument. "You should make us something to eat."

"I —"

"He's bigger and heavier than you are, and he'll be wet getting out of the shower. If he slips and falls, he's going to take you down with him, and we can't afford for you to get hurt, too. Can we? We have to keep our heads about this."

Claire and Elliott had only occasionally ducked beneath the waves of vanilla sex, never diving into the depths of BDSM play — but if she'd had to put a label on each of them, she'd have said she was the D and he was the S. Always willing to serve her. Always wanting to. Not necessarily submissive in the way it looked in porn or the media, but if one of them had ever the control in their relationship, it had been Claire.

It looked as if that had changed.

"No. I guess we can't." She ducked her head and backed away, giving him a single glance over her shoulder as she went to the kitchen and he entered the bathroom.

Her mind raced as she tried to lay out all the possibilities of what was going on. Clearly, both men had lied to her. But had they also lied to each other? Or had Elliott only lied to Troy?

She heated a couple leftover quesadillas in the microwave and added some sliced fruit. What was taking them so long? She went to the bathroom door and put her ear to it, but could hear nothing. A few seconds later, the bedroom door opened, startling her. Elliott helped a limping Troy through it. Troy wore some of Elliott's clean clothes.

The two men were of similar height and weight, but had very different styles. Troy leaned toward business casual, khakis and button downs, polos in the summer. His jeans had wide legs and his t-shirts were usually from concerts he'd attended — classic rock and sometimes, a little modern country.

Elliott, on the other hand, favored skinny jeans and novelty tees. His clothes fit tighter. He preferred boldly patterned sweaters but also plain, oversized hoodies, like the one Troy now wore over a shirt featuring a faded Sasquatch drawing with the words *I believe* in script lettering beneath it. Seeing her husband in her lover's clothes tightened Claire's throat.

Once, a few months ago, Troy had worn a similar shirt, one with a funny picture and phrase. She'd commented on it at the time, noticing it had not been his usual style. Troy had played it off, saying he'd picked it up on sale, but she'd never seen him wear it again. It had remained in his drawer, though, beneath all the others. She'd seen it while putting laundry away, but hadn't thought much of it, until now.

Troy and Elliott had shared clothes before.

They were not supposed to keep lovers' gifts at home, where they could be dwelled on or obsessed over, where they would take up space in the place that was for Troy and Claire, not anyone else. That had been part of the agreement she and Troy and decided together, early on when they were still figuring out how it should all work. Anything Elliott had given her, Claire used or kept at her office, and if she couldn't do that, she gave it away or took it to the cabin and used it there. She'd always been careful to keep to the terms of their agreement, but Troy had not.

"Sit here at the table. I'm going to wrap your ankle." Elliott helped Troy limp to the small table in front of the windows.

Troy settled into the chair with a groan. "It needs ice."

"Let me check it out." Elliott knelt at Troy's feet while Claire watched from the kitchen.

Troy put a gentle hand on Elliott's hair and the other man lifted his head. The look they shared was tender. Gentle. Full of emotion she didn't want to see.

She focused instead on finding a plastic bag and filling it with ice from the trays in the freezer. She sealed the bag and wrapped it in a dish cloth. When she handed it to Elliott, he gave her a grateful smile.

"It doesn't feel broken. Just badly sprained," he said. "But I'm not a doctor. I think you should still wrap it and put ice on it. Claire, do we have anything we can use to wrap it?

She thought of the length of crimson ribbon that she'd used to bind her wrists. It was long enough. Tied tightly enough, it would provide nice support for Troy's ankle. If it worked for ballerinas, it should work for a sprain.

"I might. Hang on."

In the bedroom, she dug through her bag and pulled out the ribbon. She clutched it to her chest for a moment, her eyes closed, flashing back to early Friday afternoon, when she'd thought she was being treated to the fulfillment of a fantasy. She ran the length of it through her fingers before coiling it into her fist. She'd made it through what happened to her then. She was going to get through whatever else came her way, too.

"See if this will work." Back in the living room, she gave it to Elliott.

He looked at it. Then her. His expression darkened.

"Just use it," she said.

Troy grunted when Elliott shifted. "What's wrong with it?"

He didn't know.

Of course he didn't know, but the last, tiniest, residual scrap of hope she'd had that somehow it had been Troy with her on Friday, that somehow he'd sent the box, arranged the surprise, that Jay had attacked him after Troy had been with her in the bedroom...Claire hadn't even realized how fiercely she'd been holding onto that thought until this moment.

Elliott pushed up the hem of the jeans he'd lent Troy. At the sight of the swollen, black and green and purple flesh, Claire let out a soft cry. Troy grunted again at the press of Elliott's fingers as he wrapped the red ribbon over and around Troy's foot, taking it up around the ankle and down again. He put a hand on Elliott's shoulder.

"What is it?"

Elliott sat back a bit. "Tell him."

"Someone sent me that ribbon in a box of other things I was supposed to use when I got here on Friday. So, I did. I thought Elliott had sent it to me."

"But he hadn't?"

"No."

Troy winced as Elliott tightened the ribbon his ankle and pulled the jeans down over it. "Who did?"

"We don't know."

"Someone assaulted her," Elliott said. "Someone convinced her to blindfold herself and get into bed and wait for him. And she did it."

"And it wasn't you," Claire whispered.

Troy jerked away from Elliott, but stayed seated. "No. Claire, are you okay?"

"Of course she's not okay," Elliott snapped. "Someone..."

If he couldn't bring himself to finish, how was Claire expected to? She did, though. She coughed into her fist and lifted her chin, meeting Troy's gaze head on. Later, she might break down over this. Later, she might scrub herself raw and never be able to wash off the feeling of crawling ants all over her. Right now, she had to deal with what was going on.

"It was someone who's been watching us here. It had to be. Because everything in that box, every piece of it, was something I'd shared only with Elliott."

Both men looked at her, then.

She kept her voice steady. "But if Jay's got cameras hidden here, then he...or anyone, could have been watching us. Listening. Clearly, someone heard us talking about it. Someone else knew we were coming here together this weekend, and someone set me up."

"But...how would anyone know I was going to be later getting here than you? How could someone be sure I wasn't going to walk in on them...taking advantage of you?"

Again, she coughed into her fist, wishing suddenly and desperately for a drink of something cold. "I don't know. Maybe they just wanted to cause trouble or freak us out. Maybe they were watching, saw that I got here early and decided to take advantage of the chance. I don't know."

"Jay said he didn't do it. You said Jay didn't do it," Elliott added. "So, who, then?"

Claire shuddered. "I don't *know*. But whoever it was, they're probably still watching us right now."

They were all quiet, then. Snow spatted against the windows as the winds rocked the little cabin. For a moment, the lights flickered.

"If the power goes out, nobody will be able to see us," she said.

Troy rubbed his forehead. He looked tired. Worn out, exhausted, in pain. He shook his head. "Why did you have me meet you here this weekend? Was it a mistake? Did you get your schedule confused?"

"No," Elliott said. "I brought you both here on purpose."

Twenty-One

 that I never meant to hurt anyone, especially not either one of you," Elliott said.

"That sounds like what someone would say when they know what they're doing could hurt someone else," Troy replied. "It sounds like an excuse you make in advance."

"I need a drink before we start talking about anything. And Troy needs food." She brought him the plate of leftovers. "Start with this. Go slow."

Troy's hands shook as he lifted the folded tortilla. "This looks perfect. I haven't eaten since Friday morning.

He stuffed the food into his mouth. Chewing, he said, "Are the two of you going to stand and stare at me while I eat?"

Claire had no appetite. She did pour herself a glass of wine and sipped it slowly, hoping it would steady her nerves. Elliott went into the kitchen to fix himself a plate that he brought back and put on the table. He took the seat opposite Troy, which relegated Claire to the wobbly chair, the one usually tucked out of the way. The extra chair, the side chair, not the main seat. Elliott might not have meant it as a statement, but it felt the same as one.

Troy had finished his food, and Elliott, without asking, scraped half of his quesadilla and guacamole onto Troy's plate. Her husband dug into that portion too, a little slower this time. He gave a happy sigh.

"This is good, babe," Troy said.

In all the years they'd been together, she could not recall Troy ever calling her babe...but Elliott did. Same as the borrowed clothes, it seemed her husband had picked up some turns of phrase. She had no idea which one of them he was talking to, so she said nothing. Elliott got up to pour a glass of water for Troy, who drank it thirstily. It was her place to serve her husband, but Elliott was doing it. He was taking care of Troy the way he'd always taken care of her.

"Have you come here together before?" Her voice broke through the sounds of chewing and swallowing.

Troy's fork clanked on the plate. He took a long drink of water and wiped his mouth with the back of his hand. "This was supposed to be our first weekend away together. We usually see each other on Wednesdays."

Seeing each other could have meant anything. Grabbing coffee or going to the movies, hooking up in the backseat of a car. Sending love gifts.

Falling in love.

The wine in her glass splashed a bit as she lifted it to her lips with a shaking hand. She grimaced at the sour taste, very aware of Elliott's gaze on her. She returned it boldly, waiting for him to speak.

"After the gym, I guess," Claire whispered. Troy's Wednesday schedule had been in place for the past few months. She'd suspected he might not be spending the entire time, if any, at the gym, but of course she'd never asked. The same way Troy never dug too deeply into the details of her weekends away. "Every week?"

"Yes," Troy said.

Elliott pushed away from the table and went to the kitchen to draw two fresh glasses of water he brought back to the table, although he didn't drink from either one. He didn't sit again. He paced, instead, his steps slow and measured. Hands on his hips. He reached the bathroom door and came back, stopped at the end of the kitchen bar and turning again before stopping abruptly. He pivoted to face them, but still didn't speak.

She had to sit, but not at the table across from him. Not in the side-piece seat, either. She settled into the couch, her back to Troy, her face to the fire. She didn't want any more wine but drank it anyway.

"When did you know Troy and I were married to each other?"

Elliott let out a long, hesitant sigh and replied in a low voice. "I knew it before I met him."

"What?" Troy's chair rocked as he twisted in it. "What does that mean? I don't understand."

Claire thought she did. "When did you move?"

"Thirteen months ago. When my divorce was final."

Troy let out another surprised, startled grunt. "You're *married?*"

"I was married. I'm not married anymore."

"You never," Troy said to Claire. His voice sifted into a strangled silence. He gripped the table for a moment, then drained a glass of water. "You don't...we never. The getaways are not supposed to be *married*, Claire. What the hell?"

She was not going to break down into tears. She. Would. Not. Claire did her best to draw in a slow breath, meant to keep her voice steady. Calm.

"I know. This was the first time," she said.

Troy pinched the bridge of his nose. "Why, Claire?"

"I don't know!" she cried, frustrated with herself. Furious with Elliott. "He kept texting me. He made me laugh. I don't know what else to say. I made a mistake!"

"No, Claire. Don't say that. Please!" Elliott moved closer to her. "I promise you, this isn't a mistake. We aren't."

"There's a reason why we don't fuck around with married people," Troy said to her, ignoring Elliott. "You know that."

"I know it," she said, miserable. "I told him that, too. He just didn't...listen to me."

Troy looked at Elliott. "Yeah. He can be persistent, can't he?"

"When I want something, I go for it," Elliott said.

Claire pushed up from the couch and took her wine to the kitchen to pour into the sink. She took a look out the back window to the darkness beyond and saw only an occasional eddy of snow. The glass was frosted. She pressed her fingertips to it, leaving bare circles.

She had no excuses for it. No defense. She'd made it clear to him from the start that *she* was married, and that was not going to change. "You told me you weren't happy."

"I wasn't happy. Heather and I were at the end of things. She was sleeping with someone else already, but she didn't know I knew about him. I met you, and it all felt so right, Claire. Can't you understand that? I never told you I was splitting from her because by that point, it had become so clear that you liked the fact I wasn't free to make us something more permanent. I didn't want to lose you."

"So you fucked my husband? Damn it, Elliott, what were you thinking?"

"I wanted to see the man who had so much more of you!" Elliott sounded anguished. He pounded a fist into his palm. "I wanted to see what he had that I didn't! And once I met him, I totally understood."

"You left your wife and moved to my town, where you stalked the gym my husband goes to until you met him. What else did you stalk? Did you watch our house?"

"No. Never. And I didn't *stalk* anyone," Elliott protested.

"So how'd you find out where Troy goes to the gym?" Claire demanded.

"You mentioned it once." He was lying. She'd very rarely, if ever, spoken of Troy with Elliott. He must have seen what she was thinking, because he put in quickly, "You said it the night we met. You mentioned it, off-hand. I remembered, that's all."

"How'd you know who I was?" Troy asked in a low voice.

Elliott sighed. "You were at the same party she and I met at. I remembered your face."

A chill rippled through her. She regretted pouring her wine down the drain and thought longingly of the gummies that had been in the package Elliott had not sent. She didn't dare trust them, and getting high would be stupid right now, with no idea if Jay was coming back or what he might do when he did. But she wanted to be woozy and dozy and drifting; she wanted to have some kind of veil between herself and all of...*this*.

"I know it must sound a little *Fatal Attraction*," Elliott began, but Troy interrupted him.

"More than a little."

Elliott dragged his hands through his hair. "I met Claire at the party and fell for her right away. She gave me her number, but I didn't think she'd really answer my texts. But she did."

"Why wouldn't I?" She shot back at him. "At the party you acted interested. I found you attractive. Troy and I have an agreement —"

"I had no idea you and I would hit it off the way we did. But it makes sense, doesn't it? Why wouldn't I fall for the guy the woman I love fell in love with?" Elliott asked.

"This is too twisted for me to follow," Claire said. "I'm too tired right now. Too upset."

"I didn't mean to upset you, Claire. Believe me, I wanted something entirely different from this weekend."

Claire's heart hammered. She rubbed the coldness of her fingertips together but didn't leave her place in the kitchen. They were three points of a triangle, now, and she didn't want to be the one to break it. "I'm sure you did."

"You lied to me." Troy sounded hurt, and although Claire couldn't blame him, the raw emotion in his voice set her teeth on edge.

Troy was not supposed to be the feeler. Troy was not supposed to be the one who got swept away by his emotions. Troy was...

He was supposed to be *hers*.

Elliott crossed to him, breaking the triangle. "You want to talk about lying? Neither one of you ever mentioned your little agreement to *me*. Both of you made me feel like I was your dirty little secret, when all along, you both knew there was no reason for us to hide anything."

Her head spun so much that she thought she probably ought to sit down and put her head between her knees. She looked across the cabin at Troy's stricken expression. But there was something else there too, wasn't there? Something in the glow of his gaze when he looked at Elliott.

"Ok. Let's all just calm down. Take a few steps back from this."

There was the Troy she knew and loved, the one who knew how to keep everything under control.

"In all the years we've been having getaways," she said quietly, "you've never had a steady.""

"I guess I fucked up, didn't I?" Troy said.

"No!" Elliott shouted. "Damn it, both of you. Just listen to me. You didn't fuck up. And yes, I lied to you, but it was because I wanted you both here with me this weekend. I wanted to tell you how much I want to be with you *both*."

TWENTY-TWO

"THE TWO RINGS," CLAIRE SAID, SUDDENLY REALIZING. "OH, my god."

Elliott looked surprised. "You found them?"

"They were in your bag when I was looking to borrow your hoodie. I saw them and thought one was for me, the other for you," she said. "What else could I have thought?"

Troy tried to get up from this chair but fell back into it with a pained groan. "Rings? What the hell is going on?"

Claire looked at Elliott. "When we hiked out to the waterfall, you got so upset because you'd planned a perfect moment. But it was more than that, wasn't it? You also thought Troy stood you up."

"I was going to show you both how great it could be if we could all be together." Elliott raked a hand through his dark hair. "But when Troy didn't show up, I thought it meant he'd reconsidered. He wasn't answering my texts or calls —"

"Because I was tied up in a goddamned basement," Troy interrupted. "You said you'd set up check-in for whatever time in the morning. I thought I'd get here early and surprise you. I was...excited. For the weekend."

Claire rubbed her grainy eyes and did not allow herself to think too much about her husband's self-described enthusiasm. Troy had never been a giver of gifts, a presenter of surprises. He'd always been practical, not what anyone might consider traditionally "romantic." At least, not with her.

She sighed. "What we all need is some sleep. We have no idea if or when Jay intends to come back, and Troy's not in any shape to try trekking through the snow, especially not with the storm still going."

"I could try," Elliott said.

Tears of frustration and disappointment burned in her eyes and throat, but Claire fought them back. She could not, would not lose control. When all of this was over and they were all safe, then she could unpack her feelings, then she could let herself break down. Right now, she had to keep herself as cold as the weather outside.

"Go ahead, then. If you really think you'll make it to the road, in the dark, without your boots or coat or gloves. Go out there and die!" Her voice broke and she cut herself off, turning away so she didn't have to look at him. She shrugged his hand off her shoulder. "Don't touch me."

Troy cleared his throat. "Claire's right. We have a good six hours until daylight, and even if we can find some cold weather gear, there's no point in going out there in the dark. We should all get some sleep and tackle this problem again in the morning."

Elliott stood between them, every line of his body tense as though he could not decide which direction to move. Troy shifted to lean with his elbows on his knees, his face in his hands. Claire made it easy for both of them.

"Both of you," she said, "can sleep out here."

Troy lifted his head to look at her. "Claire —"

"The couch pulls out." She crossed her arms and lifted her chin to stare him down. "I don't want to sleep anywhere close to either one of you right now."

Troy sighed in a familiar way, the one that irritated her because it meant he was placating her. "If that's what you want."

"I'm going to take a shower. Do either of you need the bathroom before I get in?"

"I do." Troy pushed up off the chair but staggered as he tried not to put weight on his injured ankle.

Elliott grabbed him, slung Troy's arm over his shoulder. Supported him. "I got you."

His eyes caught hers as he helped Troy toward the bathroom. Emotions flickered in them, an entire cascade, but she didn't want to see any of them. Claire shut the bedroom door so she didn't have to watch her lover help her husband to the toilet.

When they'd finished in the bathroom, she locked both the bedroom and the bathroom doors. Keeping the lights off, she turned on the shower and, without waiting for the water to get hot, slipped into the stream. She opened her mouth to let the water fill it. To choke her, overflowing, to strangle the sobs trying so hard to rip up and out of her throat. The water warmed, but Claire still shivered. In the darkness, she knelt on the floor of the shower and pressed the heels of her hands to her mouth, biting hard on her own flesh.

A horrible low keen slithered from between her clenched teeth. Claire tipped her face back up to the water, trying to drown herself into silence. It didn't work. She fell back against the shower wall in a splay of limbs.

She'd have stayed in there longer, but the water started going cold again. She subjected herself to it for a few long minutes until the icy spray began to prick like needles. She combed through her hair, wincing at the tenderness in her scalp. She probed the lump at the back of her skull until the dull ache flooded into her stomach, and she had to fight off a gag.

She was exhausted.

Making sure to unlock the bathroom door that led to living room, in case either Troy or Elliott needed to use it, she shut herself away into the bedroom. She wanted to put on comfy pajamas but didn't risk it — if Jay came back, she didn't want to be any more vulnerable than she already was. Instead, she slipped into a fresh pair of jeans, thick socks, a long-sleeved shirt. She was still cold. Maybe she was never going to be able to get warm again.

Burrowing under the blankets, Claire pressed her face to the pillow Elliott had been using and breathed in his scent until she couldn't stand it any more. She threw the pillow on the floor and dove back beneath the covers. Sleep would evade her, she was sure of that, but found herself drifting anyway. The wind pushed at the roof and tapped at the windows, but although the closed door meant the fire didn't warm this room, she was snug and cozy in the bed, especially being so fully dressed.

What were they going to do when Jay came back?

Claire had been asleep, or almost there, when the thought slapped her fully awake. Her heart pounded, pulse throbbing in her temples. A headache screwed its way into her eye sockets, going deep. She rolled onto her back to stare at the ceiling. She had no idea what time it was, but outside was still dark.

Her bladder insisted she get up. Claire stumbled to the bathroom in the dark and used the toilet. At the sink, she gulped some water cupped in her palm. She hadn't turned on the lights, and it took her a few minutes to realize they'd left the door to the living room ajar. The fire had died down to a low glow.

She heard a moan.

Her heart lodged in her throat, tight as a gripping fist. Claire put her hand to her chest, pushing against her sternum and the sudden sharp pain there. She crept to the door and peeked around it, hating herself for giving in to this curiosity. Knowing she wasn't going to enjoy what she saw.

From this angle she had a clear view of the foot of the mattress pulled out from the couch. She could see long, bare legs and feet. Two pairs, tangled together.

She had no idea which belonged to who.

Another groan pushed her a step back. She shouldn't be watching this — but she didn't look away. She could hear the creak of the pullout couch's mattress springs moving in a steady rhythm, but she couldn't see what was going on. But did she really have to? She knew what a blowjob sounded like. Did it matter who was giving or who was getting?

Men, she thought with sudden, fierce vehemence. A broken ankle, being trapped in an isolated cabin, discovering your lover has been sleeping with your spouse...nothing got between them and a hard-on, did it? She thought she might never want to have sex again based on what had happened so far this weekend, and her husband and her lover were banging on a sofa bed.

She would have wept, if it didn't make her want to laugh. Or maybe she had that backwards. Either way, she needed to stop being a voyeur and get herself back beneath the warmth of the blankets.

"I'm sorry..." Elliott's voice rose.

A figure sat, silhouetted in the firelight. Another joined it. She could barely make out features, but at least now she had the voices to help her discern who was who.

"You should have told me," Troy said.

Elliott put a hand on his shoulder. "It wasn't supposed to be a trick, not for either one of you. I wanted to surprise you. I'm the one who fucked up. I know that."

Troy groaned and fell back onto the mattress. The couch arms hid everything but his feet from view. Elliott got off the sofa bed. In the firelight, his lean naked form wore the shadows like a tux. He pulled one of the throw pillows from the nearby coffee table and slid it under Troy's injured ankle.

"Keep this elevated." He got back onto the mattress.

"I thought this was going to be a great weekend with the only two of us. Beer, blowjobs and backgammon, like you said. Then I get here, some big guy has no idea that I'm supposed to be showing up, and he hits me over the head and knocks me down the stairs. *Then* I find out you're the man who's been sleeping with my wife, and there's some kind of plot to...I don't even know what. Blackmail all of us. I thought you were going to ask me to leave her for you," Troy said. "I was...I might have said yes."

Troy, steady, unflappable, reliable, unemotional Troy had betrayed her.

Claire stifled her cry. She reeled away from the door and staggered into the bedroom, locking the bathroom door behind her. She fell into the bed. Shoved the pillow into her mouth. No matter what happened after this weekend, this was the end of her marriage. Three decades of a partnership that had worked for them, all gone.

Over the sound of the angry winter wind, she heard the roar of snowmobile engines.

TWENTY-THREE

The two men moved apart from each other when she opened the bedroom door. Both of them dressed quickly, as though she wouldn't notice they were naked. Or that maybe she'd think they'd stripped down for sleep, not fucking. She didn't care.

"I heard something outside." Claire went to the front windows to twitch aside the sheets and look out, but all she could see was darkness.

"Snowmobiles?" Elliott asked from behind her.

Troy added, "he's coming back."

The roughness of his voice turned her from the window. "I can hear more than one. Could be that pack of kids that were here the first night."

The night she and Elliott had made love on the floor above Troy's head. She wanted to ask if he'd heard them, but decided she really didn't want to know. Her husband had been hit on the head, shoved down the stairs, tied up and left in the cold, all while she and Elliott had been indulging in their decadences. It was not her fault, but guilt still sawed at her, doing its best to cut her in half, and then she was angry. Why should she be the guilty one?

"Can you see them?" Elliott joined her at the window.

He stood too close to her, his shoulder brushing hers, and Claire moved deliberately away from him. He noticed, but said nothing. She didn't care if she'd hurt his feelings.

The roar of the snowmobiles got closer. A series of lights swept across the outside of the sheets for only seconds before disappearing. She thought she heard the whoop and holler of voices.

"It is those kids. I'm going out there." Elliott sounded determined.

He'd opened the front door before Claire had a chance to react. She followed him onto the porch. The wind came up and stole away her breath with a gasp at the cold. She wrapped her arms across her chest, but that didn't do much.

The same as they'd done on Friday night, the pack of snowmobilers spun in large loops through the snow-covered parking area and the field beyond it. They were already riding around the back of the cabin by the time she and Elliott got out there. When he jumped off the porch, he sank almost hip deep into a snow drift.

"Just wait until they come back!" Claire cried out, but Elliott was ignoring her.

He struggled out of the drift, trying to get to the side of the house. No coat, no hat, no boots. He had to be freezing. He'd only made it a step or so when the pack came around again. This time, they stuck more to the field and farther from the house.

"Hey!" Elliott waved his arms

The snowmobilers were too far away to hear him, or else they didn't care. They hollered, shouting, but maybe they were afraid of getting in trouble, because they didn't come any closer.

More lights shone, this set coming up the long, unplowed road leading to the highway. Another snowmobile roared toward them. A single vehicle this time, one rider. As it blew past the cabin and through the square of light coming out from the front door, Claire caught sight of a bushy beard and a familiar black snowsuit. Jay didn't slow as he passed them, but a spray of snow from his snowmobile's treads got caught by the wind and hit Claire in the face. It stung her cheeks and got into her eyes.

Elliott didn't shout at Jay. He moved back toward the porch, climbing the first step covered in snow, then the upper one that had been slightly cleared off from the wind. He met Claire on the porch. Even in the small splash of light, she could see that his lips were blue.

Out in the field, Jay's snowmobile had caught up to the pack of kids. Claire didn't know if it was because his vehicle was bigger or more powerful, or if he simply handled it with more skill, but he managed to circle the group so fast he cut off the ones in the lead and forced them to change direction, back toward the access road.

A gun shot rang out.

"Holy shit." Elliott tripped up the stairs and fell onto the front porch, almost knocking Claire over.

"Get inside." She shut the door behind them. Another shot rang out. The sound of the snowmobile pack faded quickly. They were leaving. One vehicle, however, came back. The headlights threw up a beam onto the sheets over the front windows. Then it went dark.

"Lock the door. You're closer," Elliott said.

"He knows the code —"

"It'll only keep him out for a minute or so. We need some extra time," he snapped.

Claire punched the lock button, hearing the grinding noise that indicated it was locking. "Extra time for what?"

"To think."

From outside came the thump of heavy boots on the floorboards. The door handle moved and the door rattled. She and Elliott backed away from the door. Beeps sounded. This time, the little interior light turned green as the lock ground again, releasing. The door opened, and Jay's big form filled the doorframe.

"What the hell are you —" he started.

Troy's shout cut him off. He came out of the kitchen, a small saucepan in his hand. He hit Jay over the back of the head with it, sending the bigger man stumbling forward. Jay fell onto his knees.

Troy hit him again.

This time, Jay hit the floor, face-first. His nose made a sickening crunch that mingled with a revolting squelch. Claire recoiled.

If he had a gun with him, he hadn't brought it inside. Elliott stepped over Jay's prone form and slammed the door shut. He didn't bother locking it.

Jay groaned and tried to roll onto his back. Troy kicked him, shrieking at what must've been a horrific burst of pain from his injured ankle. Jay grunted and curled into a ball. Troy hit him with the saucepan again. And again.

"Stop!" Claire shoved herself between Troy and the man on the floor. Troy's chest heaved beneath her palm as she held him back. To her shock, he hocked a gobbet of spit onto the floor near Jay's head.

Her relentlessly rational and emotionally steady husband looked... enraged. Hair and eyes both wild. Mouth agape as he panted. A strand of silver drool leaked from the corner of his lips, and he wiped it away with a shaking hand.

"That son-of-a-bitch," he said, "that *prick*, attacked me. Tied me up. I could have died in that basement."

Before Claire could stop him, he hit Jay again. The saucepan-turned-weapon connected solidly, moving the bigger man's entire body from the force of the blow.

Elliot was the one who pulled him away this time. He held Troy as he struggled, wrapping his arms around him. They were well-matched in height, but Troy was broader through the shoulders. Elliott, though, had a lean, athletic strength, and being fifteen years younger didn't hurt, either. He easily pulled Troy away. Embraced him. All Claire could do was watch as he stroked his hand firmly down Troy's back, over and over, while Troy shouted hoarse words muffled against Elliott's chest.

At her feet, Jay groaned again. He didn't try to get up, but he did turn his head to the side. "...bitch."

She stood over him, her hands in fists. The impulse to hurt him worse than Troy had nearly overcame her, but she held herself back. Instead, she crouched in front of him.

"Where is your gun?"

Jay had the audacity to laugh at her. "I left it outside. You think I wanted to take the chance of one of you yahoos getting shot?"

"You didn't seem to care too much when you were shooting it off outside around those kids."

"I didn't aim it anywhere close to them. Besides," he added. "It's just rock salt. It's to scare them from coming back here and making trouble. Not to hurt anyone. Anyway, it's all gone."

"You don't have a problem hurting people though, do you?" Troy snarled from the kitchen where Elliott was still restraining him.

Jay rolled onto his back and put his hands up in front of him as though he expected Claire to hit him. "All of this is a real pile of steaming shit, I ain't gonna pretend otherwise. But this isn't going to get you anywhere. C'mon, let me up. We can talk about this."

"You weren't interested in anything I had to say when you shoved me down the stairs and left me to starve or freeze to death!"

Troy shook off Elliott's grip and hobbled toward Jay, but Elliott grabbed his wrist and held him back. The only way Troy could have continued moving was if he unbalanced himself. Jay mumbled something.

"What did you just say to me?" Troy tried again to get free of Elliott's grip.

"Troy, you're going to hurt yourself," Claire began.

Jay cut her off. "I said, 'what a fucking pussy.'"

Troy let out an incoherent roar. Elliott shushed and soothed him again. He went quiet, his expression seething, his breaths heaving.

Her husband would not have done that for her, Claire realized. Something dark unfolded inside her. Something...jealous.

"Little baby piss pants," Jay said.

"Are you trying to get your face busted?" Elliott pushed past Troy. His stance threatened, despite his calm voice.

"It's already busted," Jay said.

Claire was in no mood to get out the ruler for all the dick measuring that was going on in here. "Get his phone. Call for help."

Elliott bent over Jay, digging into the man's snowmobile suit pockets. He let out a frustrated yell and tried for another few seconds before stopping. Jay laughed. Elliott made as though to hit him but didn't. He stalked a few steps away before turning back to Claire.

"He doesn't have it."

"Check the rest of him," she said.

Jay laughed again. "You won't find it. I left it in my truck, along with the rest of your phones."

"Then get the key," she said through gritted teeth, "to his fucking snowmobile."

Jay had enough fight left in him to struggle when Elliott bent over him again. He slammed his head into Elliott's, sending him back with a shout of pain. Jay got to his feet, ungainly and lumbering, but big and pissed off. He didn't go after Elliott, though. He grabbed Claire, instead.

"Back off," the big man warned. "Or I'll hurt her even worse."

His hands squeezed her upper arms. Claire didn't fight him. She could feel the shakiness of Jay's grip. She had no doubts he'd do his best to hurt her, but it also seemed clear that he was in a lot of pain, maybe even woozy from being hit in the head. And, it would be three against one.

"Let her go," Elliott said.

Jay shook her a little. "Not until the two of you agree to back off."

Claire tensed, waiting for either of them to move. When neither of them did, she let out a long, slow sigh. Jay's grip tightened again on her upper arms.

He laughed, and she hated him for that laughter.

She slammed her head backward, pushing up on her toes at the same time. Pain vibrated through her skull as it connected with Jay's face. She cried out and repeated the motion. Jay let her go. She stumbled a few steps forward, expecting his grip to reel her back and falling to her knees when it didn't.

Behind her, Jay hit the floor with a thud that shook the cabin's walls.

She'd passed out a few times in her life. Low blood sugar, anemia while she was pregnant with Aviva, the fainting game they'd played in middle school. This was different. The pain swelled and rose through her head, squeezing her brain. It took her breath away. She put a hand to the back of her head and felt heat. Wetness. Her blood or his?

Elliott was there beside her in a moment, helping her up. He murmured words of comfort she was sure would have made sense if her entire mind hadn't been so scrambled. She clung to him, afraid she'd fall if she didn't. When she looked back, Troy knelt over Jay's prone form. His fingers pressed Jay's wrist. Troy looked up at her.

"I think...he might be dead."

Twenty-Four

The three of them stood over Jay's body.

"How can we be sure?" Claire asked, voice hoarse.

"If he never wakes up," Troy said, "then we'll be sure."

It was not the time for humor, but that rarely stopped him. Weddings, funerals, nothing was safe. Usually, he could get her to laugh too, even when she didn't want to. This time, Claire didn't so much as crack a smile. Elliott didn't, either.

"Should we just leave him there?" Claire asked.

Elliott's fingers squeezed her bicep. "First, let's get you cleaned up."

"He's bleeding," she pointed out.

Troy pressed his fingers to the big man's neck. "I can't feel a pulse."

"He's bleeding," Claire repeated. "You don't keep bleeding after you're dead."

She had no actual idea if that was true, or something she picked up from one of those true crime shows she sometimes had on in the background while she cooked dinner. At any rate, Jay was bleeding from his crunched nose and split lips, but the flow was slow and seeping. Nothing gouted or spurted.

"He could only be unconscious," Elliott said.

"We should tie him up. The way he tied me up." Troy's voice rasped, harsh with fury.

Claire half-expected him to hit the bigger man again, but Troy only nudged his body before pushing himself up. He put all his weight on his good foot, keeping the other lifted, toes barely brushing the floor. He wasn't steady, either.

"Go sit down," Claire told him. "Before you fall down."

"How about that old joke," Troy said. "The one about the hunter who calls the 911 operator. Says 'there's been an accident, I think my buddy's dead. Operator says, 'first thing you need to do is make sure he's dead.' Next thing you know, she hears a gun shot, and the hunter says — "

"'Okay, now what?'" Elliott finished the joke.

Troy didn't move. He swayed. "We could make sure he's dead."

For a moment, neither Claire nor Elliott said anything. He spoke first, murmuring Troy's name in a way that she supposed was meant to comfort him. It wouldn't work, she thought. Troy was *feeling*, and if she wasn't used to that, she could only imagine how it must be affecting her husband.

"We can't *kill* him, love," Elliott said.

She recoiled at the endearment meant for Troy, but one Elliott had often used with her. "I might have already killed him."

Troy swayed again. His hands clenched. "Fine. So we don't try to make sure he's *not* dying, then."

"We're going to get Claire cleaned up. We're going to have something hot to drink. We're going to get you off that bad ankle," Elliott said. "And we'll tie him up, just in case he does regain consciousness. Okay? Troy?"

Troy didn't answer, simply hopped himself over to the open sofa bed and fell onto it with a grunt. He propped his foot on a throw pillow and leaned against the back of the couch. Elliott squeezed her shoulder again, gently.

"C'mon, love. Let's get your head taken care of."

"Don't call me that," she said but allowed him to guide her into the kitchen, where he pulled out a clean dishtowel from the seemingly endless supply and pressed it to the back of her head. She hissed with pain at the pressure.

Elliott took away the cloth and showed her the spots of blood on it. "His teeth must've cut you. But it's not too bad. I don't think you'll need stitches. You're going to have a helluva headache, though. Let me clean off the blood and get you some ice."

"You don't have to take care of me, Elliott."

"Of course I have to take care of you," he said, bending back to the task of dealing with her wounds. "I love you."

She closed her eyes, hoping that would fight off the dizziness she couldn't be sure was because of hitting her head so hard, from exhaustion, or from this entire situation. A few tears slipped free and traced their way over her cheeks and onto her lips.

He bent close to brush his lips over her ear. "I love you."

Claire's hand found her way to his and held it, linking their fingers tight for a few seconds before she let go. Elliott shook some ice into another dishtowel and pressed it carefully onto the back of her head, placing her hand over it to hold it in place. The cold stung but also provided some relief.

"I'm putting the kettle on. Do you want to sit here or move to the living room? You'll be more comfortable in the chair there, I think. The bar stools are really high."

"I'll be fine. I want to sit here for a few minutes. I feel dizzy and a little sick to my stomach. I don't want to move too much."

He lifted the hand not holding the icepack and kissed it. "I'm going to check on Troy. You sit tight. Yell if you need me, if you think you're going to pass out or throw up."

He filled the kettle with water and set it on the burner. She watched him go to Troy and lean over him, murmuring into his ear. Elliott's adjusted the pillow under his ankle. He leaned to kiss Troy's temple, and when he started to pull away, Troy grabbed his wrist. Pulled him closer. They kissed on the mouth, nothing sexy about it, but tender and emotional and she forced herself to watch it because looking away would mean she could tell herself it wasn't real.

And it was very, very real.

Elliott next went to Jay, who still lay on the floor, quiet and unmoving. He used a kitchen cloth to press onto the man's nose. Crimson flowers bloomed, but although Jay's face looked exactly as if it had been pummeled by a saucepan, fists, and the back of a furious woman's head, when Elliott took the cloth away it seemed as though the blood flow had stopped.

Elliott got a throw pillow and tucked it beneath Jay's head. He turned the big man onto his side, grunting with the effort. He took off Jay's boots and unzipped the snowmobile suit, peeling it off and putting the suit aside, leaving Jay in jeans and a thermal shirt. He stood, looking around, and, spotting the rope Claire had kicked off herself earlier, he picked it up. He made swift work of tying Jay's ankles to his wrists, tucked behind his back. By the time he stepped back to survey everything he'd done, the kettle was hissing.

He made her tea with the same swift efficiency he'd used with everything else, and Claire could not stop herself from being grateful for it. This might be fuckery of the highest order, but she couldn't deny that if any one of the three of them would be able to figure out a way for them to get through this, it was probably going to be Elliott.

"There's something hard in you," she whispered.

He turned from the stove, kettle in hand. "What?"

"Nothing."

She watched him pluck a mint teabag from one of the boxes he'd brought along, drop it into a mug and add the boiling water. The mug steamed. Her throat ached — well, everything did. She looked into the living room and could see Jay's prone, still form.

"What am I going to do if he dies? That will mean I killed him!"

"Hey. Shhh. Don't think about that right now. He's not dead." Elliott put the mug in front of her. "Be careful, that's really hot. Do you want an ice cube? Keep that ice on the back of your head."

She'd let it down onto the table, her arm tired from holding it. His concern washed over her, and she wanted to sink into it like a warm bath. Most of all, Claire wanted to trust him, but how could she?

"I'm going to check on Troy," Elliott began, but stopped when she reached for him.

She searched his face, his eyes. There was an element of satisfaction in his expression, of something she could not quite name but seemed something like gratification. He enjoyed this. Taking care of her, taking care of Troy. Having both of them need him at the same time. Maybe it had something to do with proving himself to them. Maybe it was something else.

Claire let go of his wrist. "Thanks for the tea."

"You're welcome." He bent to press a kiss to her temple, but gently, so it didn't hurt her head.

She couldn't hear what he murmured to Troy, but their voices both pitched low, with some urgency in the rise and fall of their words. They were deliberately trying not to let her overhear them. Claire closed her eyes and let the steam bath her face, the minty smell caressing her and opening up her clogged nose.

A gust of wind knocked against the cabin. The lights flickered. Went out, but came back on within a blink.

If the power went out, they'd be fine. They'd be warm. They had food. Hell, they could melt snow if they needed water.

How long would Jay have to be missing before someone showed up to find him, and them? She supposed that even if someone else was monitoring the camera system, a power outage would mean nobody could check them, but that might prompt someone to come out to make sure everything was all right even sooner. At the very least, eventually, someone could come to plow the road. They could sit tight, if they had to....

She shuddered at the thought. No. They had to get out of here.

That meant finding the key to the snowmobile.

Claire had never driven a snowmobile, nor a scooter, a dirt bike or an ATV or a jet ski or anything similar. She'd never even learned to drive a stick-shift car. Troy was in no shape to be riding anything.

"Elliott."

He looked up. "You okay?"

"You need to get the snowmobile key."

Elliott frowned and stood. He looked down at Jay, who still wasn't making any kind of sound or movement. For a second or so, Claire thought he was going to argue with her, but then he knelt and picked up the black snowmobile suit. He patted it all over, digging into the pockets.

"Nothing." He bent and did the same with Jay's jeans and shirt front, then stood. "Nothing there, either."

"It's probably in the ignition." Troy's voice grated, croaking and harsh.

Claire looked at the clock on the wall. Almost two in the morning. She'd entered that twilight space of being so exhausted she couldn't function but also could not relax enough to sleep. She couldn't recall when it would be dawn, but surely not for a few more hours. Maybe more than that. "You should wait until morning."

"No. I'll go now. The sooner I can get help, the better. It's got a headlight on it." Elliott picked up the snowmobile suit. "I'll use this. And his boots. If I can't get into his truck to get to our phones, I'll just keep riding until I can flag down a car or something. They've got to have the plows out. The salt trucks, too, at least on the main road. I'll get help and come back."

"What are we supposed to do with him in the meantime? What if he wakes up?" Troy gestured at Jay. "I'm sure as hell not untying him."

"I'll tell the police what happened, so they won't be shocked when they get here," Elliott said, already pushing his legs into the snowmobile suit. Next, his arms. He zipped it. The suit was voluminous on him, far too long in both the legs and arms, and so bulky around his body he looked like —

"You're Ralphie's little brother, whats-his-name. From *A Christmas Story*." Troy snorted softly, laughing.

Sometimes, they were so in sync it was scary.

"I've never seen the whole movie," Elliott said.

"When we get home, we'll have to watch it. All of us," Troy said.

She honestly hadn't even known Troy had ever seen that movie. They didn't watch the regular Christmas classics, why would they? The idea of it, the three of them snuggled up together on the couch as though they were some merry trio, did not seem like reality. Then again, nothing about the past day or so seemed real, it was all a nightmare, and she was desperate to wake up.

With a small groan as her sore muscles protested, Claire got down from the bar stool and went to help Elliott finish suiting up. The boots, too, were huge on him, so big even tying the laces tighter around the ankles didn't do much to keep them on his feet.

"You'll need to stuff the toes. Let me grab you some extra socks."

In the bedroom, she hunted quickly through his duffel. The box was in there. The one with the rings. She didn't want to look at them, but did, lifting the lid with the distinctive creak of a ring box. The rings shone in the light coming in from the living room, and her hands shook as she closed the box and tucked it away back into the duffel.

He couldn't really think…he couldn't *really,* she told herself.

Even with the toes of the boots stuffed with extra socks, walking on the cabin's flat wooden floor looked difficult. Getting through all that snow was going to be even harder than that. Elliott gave a frustrated mutter as he galumphed across the room.

"I'll be on the snowmobile the whole time, anyway. It's not like I'll be running through the snow. It's better than leaving my feet bare, even if I put multiple layers of socks on. It's going to have to work."

"You don't have to go now," Troy interjected. "Stay until it's light, at least. Have something to eat, or let Claire pack you something. What if something happens?"

"We are no more than a few fucking miles from that main road." Elliott cut him off. No "sweetie, honey, love" in his tone this time. "I could run the fucking distance in under an hour, if there wasn't any snow. The sooner I can get down to the road and get some help, the better off we're going to be."

Silence.

"Right. You're right," Troy said.

Again, Claire noted the difference between in how her husband spoke to his lover and how he usually talked to her. She and Troy rarely argued. She'd learned to temper her tone, even when she was frustrated. It had been a struggle in the early years, with Claire determined never to let a man tamp down her feelings again and Troy as steadfast and steady as a rock except when he felt as though he was being yelled at. If she'd ever spoken to Troy in the tone Elliott just used, he would never have backed down.

"I'm going. I'll be back as soon as I can."

The cold wind that blew in when Elliott opened the door gusted the fire into a flare. He shut the door behind him, leaving the two of them alone. Claire didn't wait for Troy to speak. She went onto the front porch despite the frigid temperature so she could make sure Elliott was able to start the snowmobile. The wind bit at her face, took her breath away, left her without a voice. It didn't matter. He was already starting the engine and revving it, pulling away from the angled parking spot Jay had left the snowmobile in and heading for the main road before Claire would even have had time to shout something after him. Not that she even knew what she wanted to say.

"Be careful!" The wind tore her words from her throat and shredded them like lace. They disappeared into the darkness the same way Elliott did.

She wanted to watch until she couldn't see the headlight any longer, but her fingers, nose and toes were already numbed. She went back inside and shut the door, locking it, just in case. Her teeth rattled as she went to the fire to warm up.

"Claire," Troy said from behind her.

She didn't turn.

"I'm sorry. I don't know what to say, other than that."

"What are we going to do, Troy?" She didn't have to clarify what she meant. He would understand. She knew he would.

Whatever Troy might have said was cut off by Jay's sudden, choking shriek.

TWENTY-FIVE

THE BIG MAN WRITHED ON THE FLOOR, DOING HIS BEST TO fight his bonds. He let out a series of screams that got ever louder until he was clamoring like a fire alarm. Then he went silent and still again.

His shoulders rose and fell as he panted, and she could hear him breathing. He'd tried to roll onto his back but remained on his side, hands still tied behind him and connected to his ankles. He'd stopped struggling.

"Let me up," he said finally, "or I swear to Jesus, I will hurt you."

Troy forced himself off the couch, holding onto one arm of it to keep his balance. "Shut your fucking mouth, or I'll *kill* you."

Jay deflated like a pin-pricked balloon, slow at first, then all at once, and with a squeal. "I never meant to hurt anyone, okay? I'm in as much in trouble as you all."

"We're not in trouble," Troy said. "We haven't done anything to get in trouble for."

Claire was smart enough not to get too close, but she eyed Jay's face, trying to gauge his injuries. "We're not going to let you up until the authorities get here."

The big man writhed again, letting out more grunts, groans, and squeals before finally going still. He panted. "I need to pee. C'mon, don't make me piss myself."

"You didn't seem to give a damn if I had to use the bathroom," Troy said. "As far as I'm concerned, you can wallow in it."

Claire gave him a sharp look. The way he acted with Elliott confused and upset her, but how he'd been with Jay truly disturbed her. "I can't let you up, Jay. I can't trust you. I'm sorry."

"Can't you at least bring me a bottle or something?"

"You want my wife to hold your dick for you so you can piss in a bottle? Haven't you done enough to her? I should kick your teeth in for even saying a word to her. In fact, the next time you so much as blink in her direction, I think I might."

"Not with that broken ankle, you won't," Jay said, sounding grim but pleased.

"Troy," Claire said sharply. "Enough."

To Jay, she added, "He's right. Pee in your pants for all I care. I'm not untying you."

"Could you at least give me some aspirin? I'm hurt."

"I'm not giving you anything. Elliott's going to be back soon. I can't trust you not to try to hurt me or my husband."

"I promise I won't!"

"Not two minutes ago, you were threatening her," Troy said. "You can lie there and shut up, and if you can't manage that, I'll stuff something in your mouth."

Jay went quiet.

Troy sank back onto the couch, and after a few seconds, Claire joined him. It felt as though it was sit or fall for her by that point. Her eyes had gone gritty and grainy with the need for sleep. Her injuries throbbed. She curled her fingers back and forth. They hurt the worst.

"Your hands?" Troy asked in a low voice.

She nodded, wanting to cry.

"Come here." He held out an arm to pull her close so she could snuggle against him.

It felt good to be there with him. Comforted. She closed her eyes, hoping maybe when she opened them it would turn out to be a dream, but of course, it wasn't. Jay's sly voice drifted over to them, shattering any illusions she might have about this situation being a nightmare.

"How cute. You seem to be such the perfect couple. How come you're fucking around on your husband? What's the matter, you can't get it up? Or you can't get it up for a *woman*—"

Troy erupted off the couch and grabbed a throw blanket from the back of the arm chair. Claire twisted in her seat to shout out at him, but too late, he'd already stuffed the corner of the blanket in Jay's mouth. The big man screamed again, much the way he'd done when he first woke up, but the noises were muffled. His face got red and sweaty as he struggled.

"Choke on it," Troy said.

Jay went still. His eyes closed. Claire couldn't be sure if he'd passed out or was simply, for the time being, giving up.

Troy hobbled back to the couch and fell onto the cushions with a sigh that became a groan. He held out his arm, but this time, she only looked at him. With another sigh, he put his hand in his lap.

"Did you bring your special meds?" he asked.

She'd packed her vaporizer pen, but the flower she'd brought was definitely more for recreation. It would get her high, then knock her out, and despite her longing for sleep, Claire didn't want to be incapacitated. She thought of the gummies that had been in the box. She should be able to trust them, and a quarter gummy would be enough to ease her joints and settle some of her anxiety, too.

"I have something. Yes."

"You should take it. It could be a while before Ell gets back, and I don't want you hurting if you don't have to. Maybe it'll help with your head and stuff, too?"

"Is that what you call him? Ell?"

Troy hesitated, then nodded. "Sometimes. Don't you?"

"No."

They stared at each other without speaking before Troy hung his head. Guilty? Tired? Sad? Claire couldn't tell.

"I should have told you I'd found someone," he said finally. "I meant to. I wanted to."

"So why didn't you?"

He met her gaze again. "I kept thinking that one of us would end it, and then it wouldn't matter anymore."

She could understand that, since she'd had similar thoughts. The difference was, she'd always felt more comfortable with longer-term affairs. Troy had preferred hookups, or short-term, physical flings. At least, that's what she'd always believed.

"I guess you were wrong," she said.

Troy sighed. "Yeah. But honestly, Claire, would you have really wanted to know?"

"No. We don't talk about them. We don't let them interfere with what we have. Doing this was never supposed to get in between us."

"You know the first time you suggested it, you said that if I was so unhappy, maybe all I needed was a 'little getaway.' That's what you called it."

She remembered. Aviva had been a squalling, fussy baby. Claire had been at the end of her rope in the aftermath of a difficult pregnancy and childbirth. Not quite suffering postpartum depression, but definitely in the doldrums. She and Troy had been arguing, the smallest imagined insults festering. Their sex life, one thing that had seemed as though it would never falter, was almost non-existent, and not because of the old stereotype that a ring and a kid had made Claire stop wanting to screw.

Troy had been the one going distant and withdrawn, avoiding even the smallest semblances of affection. He'd finally admitted to her that somehow becoming a father had made him see the importance of being happy and fulfilled in every part of yourself, the way he saw Claire being with their daughter. And that a part of him that would always, so long as he was married to her, remain unfulfilled. He could be monogamous, he'd said, because that was what he'd signed up for. But —

"You weren't totally fulfilled," she said. "You told me you loved our life, you loved me and Viva, and that you could and would go without ever being with a man again, because you owed me that."

"And you said I didn't owe you living with a hole inside myself." Troy's voice cracked.

"You didn't. You don't," she added with a tremble in her own voice. "I meant it then. When you love someone, you want them to be happy. And I loved you."

His gaze sharpened. "Past tense?"

"I still love you, Troy."

"Do you love him?"

Claire became very aware of Jay on the floor, close enough to hear them, if he bothered to listen. She didn't care, really, but for the fact this conversation should have been private. It probably ought to have been one they'd already had.

"Do *you* love him?" she countered.

Troy's silence was the answer she'd already suspected. She couldn't help the tears burning in her eyes or the way her throat tightened. She ducked her head, not wanting to burst into sobs. Not sure, really, why she was even trying to hold them back.

"I love you, too," her husband said quickly. "I still love you, Claire."

She twisted toward him. "I heard you."

He tilted his head. "What?"

"I heard you talking to him," she said. "I heard what you said. That if he'd asked you, you might have left me."

Troy looked stricken. His lips moved, but nothing came out but a hiss of air. He sat back against the couch and let his head fall against the cushions. He stared at the ceiling not blinking.

"I would never, never have left you for him," she said. "In fact, I was getting ready to break it off with him. This was going to be our last weekend."

He sat up. "What? Why? Does he know that?"

"I didn't admit it to him, but I think he suspected it. He was getting too close. Asking for too much. I think that's why he orchestrated all of this." She waved a hand around the cabin.

Troy frowned and stared at his hands linked in his lap. "I thought..."

"It doesn't matter, now. We can talk about it when we get home. We can decide what we're going to do. Unless..." she trailed off, uncertain. "You already made a choice?"

He shook his head. "No. I mean, you're right. Of course you are. We can't possibly think about anything right now but getting out of here and figuring out what happened."

"He invited us both here on purpose. Do you think he set up the rest of this, too?" She regretted saying the words aloud the moment they came out of her mouth. The accusation felt disloyal, but more than that, also paranoid.

Troy turned to her, taking her hands. "Elliott would never hurt us. I'm going to find out who did, Claire, and I swear, they're going to pay."

It seemed impossible that she could have forgotten about Friday afternoon, but she guessed it was her mind continually trying to push away the horrible memory so it wouldn't overwhelm her. It rushed back to her, now, though, and she shuddered with revulsion. Her throat tightened again, this time with nausea.

"I'm going to get a gummy." She pulled her hands from his grip and went into the bathroom first, where she thought she might vomit. She managed to hold it back though, and instead cupped a handful of cold water from the tap. It didn't completely settle her stomach, but the gummy would help that, too.

She found the pouch and held it under the lamp, checking it carefully to be sure it was, in fact, still sealed and hadn't been tampered with. She could not forget the wine she was now sure had been drugged. The package was small enough to fit into her palm. When she tore it open, two gummies, each a different color, fell into her hand. She put one of them back and used her fingernails to cut the remaining edible into four small squares. She returned three pieces to the package and ate the single quarter. According to the package, this was a 1:1 product, which was likely to get her a little high, but it would also greatly reduce her pain. It wouldn't knock her out totally, but it might even let her sleep, if she let it.

At first, the noise from outside sounded like another furious spate of wind, but quickly she realized it was an engine. Claire shoved the small pouch into her pocket and ran to the living room. Lights swung across the front windows, highlighting shadows on the sheets Elliott had hung over the glass.

The engine cut out.

The wind howled.

The door lock beeped as someone outside typed in the code, and the door opened.

It wasn't Elliott.

Twenty-Six

Snow spun, twisting into the room all around him as Brent Allwein turned, grabbing at something upon the front porch. He heaved Elliott through the doorway ahead of him and tossed him down with force enough to send the other man sprawling. Blood dripped from various slashes on Elliott's face.

Claire gasped and took a step in their direction. Troy let out a cry and got up off the couch, but a threatening gesture and a shout from Brent stopped him from moving closer.

Keeping his eyes on Troy, Brent slammed the door. He didn't bother to lock it. His eyes quickly took in the entirety of the cabin's main space, his gaze lingering for a moment on Jay, who was struggling against his bonds again. At last, Brent fixed his gaze on Claire. His lips twisted into a smug smile that turned her stomach.

Tall, handsome, charming, from a wealthy family — Brent had all the ingredients of the perfect potential son-in-law, but he'd been Claire's least favorite of Aviva's boyfriends. She'd been relieved when Aviva broke it off with him. She and Troy had never talked much about it, nor about their individual feelings about the guy, but she'd always thought he'd been glad, too.

"Hello, 'Mom'," Brent said. "Fancy meeting you here."

"Brent, what the hell is going on?" This came from Troy, who took a single hopping step in Elliott's direction.

Brent ignored him. His grin stretched wider, his lips thinning over the gleaming expanse of his teeth. Incredibly, he gave Claire a slow and deliberate wink, like something out of a parody. She recoiled, but kept her eyes on him. He couldn't be trusted.

Elliott rolled onto his side, pushing up on one hand but failing to get to his feet. His face had taken a beating, skin bruising, one eye swelling shut. Crusted blood had mustached itself beneath his nose. His voice sounded as though he'd been punched in the throat. "Snowmobile wrecked. Something happened to it. I got about a half mile down the road, and it started to bump and shake. I lost control and went off into the trees."

"You shredded the belt," Brent said, his tone conversational and casual and completely out of place. He stripped out of his coat and hung it on the hooks by the front door but left his boots on. Snow melted around his feet, making dirty puddles that ran in rivulets toward the man on the floor. "You didn't take off the emergency brake. Newbie move, bro."

Jay's muffled squeals got Brent's attention.

"Sorry, Jay, buddy, but your ride is *wrecked*. Sucks for the snowmobile, but lucky for you, I guess? If he'd made it to the main road, he would've been able to flag down a plow. And then what would we have done?" Brent put his hands on his hips. His jeans were dark with wet from the knees down.

He gave a dramatic shiver and stalked toward the fireplace. Claire moved out of his way. He gave her another look as he passed by, this one with narrow eyes. The charm had vanished, replaced with a cold and calculating assessment.

"We'd have even more trouble than we do," Brent finished.

"What are you doing here?" Claire demanded.

"Jay called me." He held his hands out to the fire, rubbing them briskly together.

Elliott managed to get to his feet. He hobbled into the bathroom, leaving the door open, and ran the water in the sink. Troy went after him, slowly, letting out small articulations of pain with every step.

"Looks like neither one of them is going to be running a marathon any time soon. Or even walking one. But that's a good thing. Means I won't have to bother tying them up. Unlike some people I know, that isn't actually my kink." Brent turned his back to the fire and made a show of warming his rear. The devilish grin he shot toward Claire was meant to be charming, but it left her cold.

The gummy had kicked in, a little, warmth spreading through her and easing its way into the aches and pains of her joints. It mingled, too, with the exhaustion in her brain to make her slow and logy. Capable of thinking, but not quick deductions. She was trying to make a connection, but not quite getting there.

"Why did Jay call *you*?"

Jay wriggled and grunted. Brent's smile turned to a grimacing sneer when he looked at the man on the floor. "Because he's a fuckup."

The big man went still and closed his eyes again.

"How do you know him?"

Brent looked at her. His lips curved upwards again, but the smile did not reach his eyes. "How's Aviva?"

Claire frowned. "Why should I tell you anything about her?"

"Because I asked. Because I *care*," Brent said in a tone that clearly implied the opposite.

"She doesn't need the kind of caring you gave her."

He blinked rapidly, his expression twisting into a flash of hurt, a flash of what might have been regret, before he put on that shark's grin again. It was the first hint of real, believable emotion she'd seen from him, and it worried her more than the put-on charm and swagger. She could deal with arrogance and fight against an ego, but a person who felt genuine hurt was so much harder to reason with.

"None of this is going to make her get back together with you," she began, but Brent's laughter cut her off and into silence.

"Riiiight," he said. "Because Aviva Levy breaking up with me totally wrecked my life. Sure it did. Listen, Claire, I have women lining up to get a shot at being with me, I don't need to waste my time on some stuck-up bitch with Daddy issues who can't get her shit together enough to know a good thing when she has it."

For a moment, Claire thought he was talking about her.

"I was glad to get rid of her," Brent finished.

Hatred, thick as tar, hot as lava, surged through her. His words and the disdain in his voice revolted her. Claire wanted to throttle him for daring to speak of her daughter that way.

"*She* got rid of *you*."

"Ooh. Harsh. And here, I thought you liked me. No. Wait," Brent said before she could reply. "You never liked me, did you, Claire? You were always perfectly polite to me, but you never really liked me. You didn't think I was good enough for your daughter."

"You're not."

"Well," Brent said with a laugh and a wave of his hand. "Would anyone ever be?"

"What's that supposed to mean?" Claire swung her gaze into the bathroom. Elliott was hunched over the sink, Troy at his side. She could hear the soft splash of running water and low murmur of their voices, but no actual words.

"You and Daddy in there raised a real princess. How could anyone ever be good enough for her?"

Claire bristled. Aviva, an only child, had grown up with the privilege of parents who had enough money to provide for her. It was true she'd never lacked for anything, not financially or emotionally. But Claire and Troy had been careful to never spoil her.

"Princess Aviva," Brent continued before Claire could find the words to refute him. "Pretty Jewish Princess. Can't cook, can't clean, but she sure knows how to open a wallet. There's a reason why stereotypes are real, you know that?"

"You keep my daughter's name out of your mouth." Claire couldn't keep the disgust out of her tone. None of what he'd said was true, and it dug deep into her core to hear him toss out those accusations with the casual anti-Semitism of a man accustomed to getting away with slurs because nobody had ever held him accountable. It didn't even matter whether or not he really believed what he was saying about Aviva. He believed he could say it without reproach, and that was somehow even worse.

Brent held up his hands. "Of course. No offense."

"You toss around insults and say 'no offense' as if that absolves you," Claire said. "It doesn't. It makes you a disgusting, garbage person, Brent. It makes you tiny and small and useless. You're not worth a squashed piece of shit on the bottom of my daughter's shoe."

The edible had loosened her tongue, but it also gave her an eloquence she might not have otherwise had. Her words had stung him hard by the look on his face, and that small triumph warmed her.

Brent's jaw set. Brow furrowed. His fingers curled into fists. She lifted her chin, half-expecting him to take a swing at her, but Brent only looked back into the fire. His shoulders lifted and fell with angry breaths.

"Answer my question," she said.

"I told you —"

"*Why* would Jay call you, damn it?"

"Because," Brent said patiently, as though speaking to a child, "once shit started going sideways, he didn't know how to handle any of it. So he called me to come in and take care of it. He used his lifeline, so to speak. His free phone call."

She paused to count quickly to five and catch her breath. "Stop talking in circles."

"Jay has a little...problem, I guess you could call it. Maybe even an addiction? I can't say for sure." Brent shrugged, turning again toward the fire and rubbing his hands together before putting them back on his hips. "He gets off on watching people when they don't know it."

Despite her own proximity to the flames, a chill twisted inside her. "Yes. I know about the cameras."

"Do you?"

She didn't believe his surprise, not for a second. "I know he's been watching us."

"Not just him," Brent said.

Claire turned over this information in her mind, trying to force it to make sense. She regretted eating the quarter gummy now. It was going to stay in her system too long, keeping her duller than she needed to be right now. She imagined Jay selling footage to amateur porn sites; her heart lodged in her throat. She looked at the man on the floor. He pleaded at her with his eyes but made no noises.

"I brought your daughter here, Claire. You want to know what we did here? All romantic and cozy?"

"Shut up."

"I bet I could have Jay show you the footage if you really want to see it. I never asked him to delete it, even when I found out about the cameras. I'm sure he's got a lot of good stuff saved up."

"You're disgusting," she said.

Brent's laugh pitched low. Dark. "I thought renting this place sounded great. Nice and remote, romantic, perfect for a sexy weekend away with the woman I was intending to make my wife. How about that, Claire? Did you know that? Did she ever tell you that I was going to actually fucking *propose*?"

Claire said nothing.

Brent took a log and threw it into the fire hard enough to scatter sparks onto the floor. One flew far enough to land on a throw rug. It began to smoke, and for an instant, Claire had the panicked thought that they might all die in a fire. Brent stamped out the spark. Again. Then one more time, even after it had gone cold. He turned toward her.

"I guess you know what it's like to show up for a sexy weekend away — oh, sorry. What do you call it? A 'getaway.'" He used air quotes around the word. "So you show up for your sexy weekend, only to discover that the guy who owns the cabin has security cams hooked up all over the place, and they're not to make sure nobody breaks in. They're totally there to watch what you've been doing all weekend. *You* know how that feels, don't you?"

"Yes."

"Bad, right? Well, we were only here a few hours before I found one and figured it out. It's my dad's business, you know that, right? I spent hours and hours of my summer vacations helping him install this shit. I know how to spot hidden cams, especially when they've been installed by amateurs." At this, he made as though to kick Jay, who let out another series of strangled noises.

"If you knew there were cameras, why didn't you come home right away?"

He shrugged. "Maybe I'm an exhibitionist."

Claire twitched at the thought of Jay watching her daughter doing anything, much less having a romantic weekend with Brent. "You should have taken her out of here the second you suspected something."

"And ruin all my plans? No way, *Mom*. I had the ring and everything. Had it all planned out. I knew how to make it a big enough deal, you know what I mean? Aviva would have certain expectations, right? She wasn't going to settle for anything hokey pokey. She needed the whole thing. The princess treatment."

Brent dragged both hands through his hair, tipping his head back to stare at the ceiling for a few seconds. "A girl like that, you have to do it right."

He looked at her. Then beyond her, to the bathroom. Troy and Elliott weren't in there anymore. They must have gone into the bedroom. Brent's gaze returned to her, and his tongue slid over his teeth as he bared them.

"So I bring her up here, have it all planned out, and before I even have the chance to pop the question, we have a fight. She found some texts on my phone she misinterpreted."

Now Claire remembered. Aviva had told her about the texts from other girls. The notifications from dating apps. She'd cried in Claire's arms about it, angry and hurt and disillusioned. Aviva had stayed with Brent for another few months but had broken it off shortly after the Allwein's holiday party. Claire had never asked, but she'd imagined that he'd been able to beguile Aviva into giving him another chance, at least short-term.

"She told me all about that," Claire said. "You cheating asshole."

Brent's laughter spilled out of him sounding genuinely full of humor. He gave her a long, wide-eyed stare and shook his head. "I hardly think you're in any position to judge *me* about cheating. Are you? Considering that you've been coming up to this place with someone who's not your husband for like, almost two years?"

"That's none of your business. And it's not cheating."

"Right, right, right. Of course not. You and hubby have an *arrangement.*"

Now, she thought. Now they were getting to the heart of things. She frowned at him. "I should have known the second you walked through that door what this was about."

"You think you know? I guarantee that you don't."

"So tell me then," she challenged.

Brent looked toward the closed bedroom door and, with a frown, crossed to yank it open. "What're you two fuckboys doing in here?"

From around him, she could see Elliott curled on his side on the bed. Troy sat next to him, a hand on his shoulder. Brent backed up a step or two.

"Door stays open." To Claire he said, "This doesn't bother you?"

"All of this bothers me."

His expression smoothed into something mimicking sympathy. "If I'd known he was going to end up pulling this sort of shit on you, Claire, I would never have told him about you. Like, I know it's not cool to offer an alcoholic a glass of wine, but I was pissed off at you, you know? So I offered you something I was pretty sure you wouldn't be able to turn down."

"What are you talking about?"

"Oh, right. You have no idea. The night you met Elliott at my parents' house. I'd told him to see if he could meet you. Get your digits. Get you up here for the weekend. He wasn't supposed to pull all this other bullshit."

"I don't understand. How...how do you know Elliott?"

Brent laughed. "He's my brother."

TWENTY-SEVEN

"HALF-BROTHER," BRENT AMENDED AT CLAIRE'S STARTLED gasp. "Our father married my mother when Elliott was in grade school. I came along a short time later."

Claire sat on the couch and put her face in her hands, trying to process all of this. "You don't have the same last name."

Unless Elliott had lied about that, too.

"He has his mother's last name."

"You set me up."

"I tried to. How was I supposed to know you were going to fall for him? I figured you'd do your thing and be done with him. Isn't that what you usually do?"

Furious and frustrated, Claire shook both her fists at him. "You have no idea what I 'usually do,' Brent. You have no clue who I am. No clue about my marriage or how it works. You saw me out one night, one goddamned night, and you assume you know me and my life. You don't. You're an ignorant, greedy and entitled little prick."

He crossed to her and had the front of her shirt fisted in his hands before she could even think about trying to get away. He hauled her to her feet and shook her hard enough to rattle her teeth. He got so close she could see her own face reflected in his eyes.

"You're angry because I fell for Elliott instead of you?"

"You weren't *that* good a lay," Brent said. "And I told you, tying people up isn't my kink."

Her entire body crystallized. Ice. Searing cold swept over, around and all through her. The pieces her medicated mind had been trying to put together all pressed into the right places, and there it was. The full picture.

"You sent me the box. You were here on Friday."

Brent let her go with a shove hard enough to send her back onto the couch. "It seemed like something you really wanted, by the way you talked to him about it. It was only supposed to get you in trouble with Elliott, though. Make him realize what you are, that he wasn't the only one, or at least think so. He'd know he didn't send you anything like that, but he'd wonder who did, right? I wasn't planning on...but then I came in there and saw you, all ready for it, and I just...couldn't stop myself."

Claire gagged and clapped a hand over her mouth, certain she was going to vomit and ready to do it right there on the floor, honestly. Her stomach lurched, bile rising in her throat. She swallowed the burning flavor, but it seared her voice into a hoarse whisper.

"I knew it wasn't Jay." Another, more horrible thought struck her. "You used a condom. You did plan it."

Brent grinned.

"You caught me." His "aw shucks" expression turned into a grimace and he spoke through gritted teeth. His breath smelled of mint and licorice. "Of course I fucking used a condom. I met you in a hotel lobby trolling for dick. You think I'd go in raw?"

She heaved, but nothing would come up.

"You took me upstairs. I thought we had a good time. You wouldn't give me your number, though. I guess you can't really ghost someone if you don't even give them your number in the first place. And then, a few months later, my brand-new girlfriend wants me to meet her parents, and guess who's there? The MILF who didn't like me enough to go for a second round. And you know what's even worse, Claire? You know what really, really pissed me off even more?"

"I didn't remember you." She pressed her fingertips to her eyelids, gently, until whorls of color made her ease off.

"Do you know what that's like? To realize you once fucked your girlfriend's mother, her *still-married* mother, and she doesn't even think it was memorable?"

"It was out of context," she told him. "And it had been months and months."

"You fuck so many guys you can't keep them straight, huh?"

She didn't answer that. It wasn't true, but she also didn't owe him any explanations. Brent and the hotel lobby had been an anomaly and not her usual habit. Her father had just died. She'd thought she'd try the casual thing because it worked for Troy, but her brief few months of one-night stands had left her feeling too vulnerable and too often unsatisfied. It took her time to settle into feeling comfortable enough with someone to have good sex, and for something that was meant to be only good sex and nothing more, why would she bother wasting her time without being satisfied?

"Slut," he said.

Claire laughed, and she could see her reaction surprised him. "Do you really think that's going to hurt my feelings? Do you think I care about what a rapist thinks?"

For the second time, she thought he was going to hit her, but even though Brent was an entitled, arrogant and manipulative little pustule, he did not seem like a woman-beater. He could be, though, she thought as she watched him stalk away from her and stand again in front of the fire. If she pushed him hard enough. He would hit her, and he would hurt her.

She would have to hurt him, first.

"You were ready for it," Brent said. "I'm sure the wine helped. Your favorite, isn't it? See, I pay attention. I didn't rape you. You were totally willing and ready for it, the same as that first time."

He wanted to believe that. She could hear the conviction in his voice and see it in his eyes. But there was something else there, too. He knew what he'd done was wrong. He knew she could ruin his life if she told the authorities about it — the same way she knew it was entirely possible that he'd get off with a slap on the wrist because to some people, she was exactly what he'd just called her.

She was going to have to be clever.

"Why were you here in the first place?"

"I was as surprised as Jay was when Troy showed up. I figured he'd found out about you and your fucktoy —"

"Stop calling him that."

"Your lover? Is that better?"

She clenched her fingers together so hard the ache that had been subdued by the edible flared again. She rocked a little, trying not to completely lose her shit about this. "Just call him by his name."

"Fine. I figured Troy had figured out about you and my big bro, and he came up here to confront the two of you. That was going to totally fuck with my plans, but what could I do? He surprised Jay, who went all pinwheel arms on him, but I had nothing to do with that." Brent bent to pick up the poker and stirred the logs. The fire brightened.

"Your plans to..." She couldn't bring herself to reference the box and Friday afternoon aloud again.

"I *didn't* plan that. It just happened. I already told you that."

"So...you thought you could blackmail me?"

"It seemed possible, yeah. I had plenty of footage of you and Elliott. Jay was afraid I'd go to the cops about what he'd done. I promised him some of the money if he helped me. But he wasn't supposed to attack Troy and tie him up in the basement. That was totally out of line, bro." He shot those words at Jay. "So I got up here to check it all out. And then I saw you. And then..."

He shrugged.

"Elliott and I have been coming here for two years. Why not threaten me with the footage of us after that first time?"

He didn't answer her at first, and the silence drifted between them, soft as a sigh. Brent tipped his head back to the ceiling, hands on his hips, and let out a small groan. He looked at her.

"You never told him. Did you?"

"Told who what?"

Brent frowned. "You never told Troy that you picked me up in a hotel bar and spent the night with me."

"No. I never told him." Claire said.

His brow furrowed, eyes narrowing. "Why not?"

"I had no reason to. We don't talk to each other about our...we don't talk about it."

"I guessed you'd never said anything. I mean, a man who can shake the hand of a guy who fucked his wife...and who's also fucking his daughter —"

"Do you have to be so crude?" Claire snapped.

Brent's eyes widened a little, and he laughed. "Golly gee, Miz Fitzgerald, I never thought you were the shy type."

Claire sighed heavily.

"I liked watching you," Brent said flatly. "Every time I watched you up here, every time I got to see you doing all the things you did when you thought you were alone, it felt like I was getting even. I liked that. A lot."

Repulsive.

"Do you do this to every woman who rejects you?"

He smiled. "Only the ones who are dumb enough to fuck around on their husbands in cabins where I have access to the surveillance tapes."

"Did he know about this plan? Elliott?" She swallowed another rush of bitterness.

"I wish I could tell you that he's been in on it from the start. That would cut deep, huh?"

She saw no reason not to tell him the truth. "Yes."

"No, big bro never knew about the cameras. He knew you were Aviva's mother, sure, but I made him promise not to tell you he knew that, and he went along with it because he owed me one."

Brent had set her up to meet Elliott, and Elliott had gone along with it. All that bullshit about waiting his whole life for her, his persistence. It had never been about her, at all.

"I'm sensing a pattern," she said. "What did you have to hold over his head?"

"It would kill our father to know the golden boy is into dick," Brent replied with a nasty grin. "I mean, I've known forever that he's into dick,

I just had no idea he was into your *husband's* dick. But I guess, neither did you."

Claire didn't answer.

"Aww, don't look like that. I can tell it bothers you. Does it make it better if I swear to you that I never, ever told him about the surveillance up here? Lucky for you, Elliott had nothing to do with any of the rest of it."

"What do you want, Brent?"

"I want," he said, "the money. It's always been about the money."

It took her a second or so to find a reply. Blackmail, of course, was usually about money. But the way he'd said it made it sound...big. Important. Vast.

"Money. From...me and Troy?"

"I thought about asking the tooth fairy for it, but she didn't come through." He flashed a grin at her, his tone jagged as broken glass.

Claire shook her head. "Your parents are the ones with money."

"My parents," Brent replied in a voice thick with scorn, "decided to cut me off."

"I can't blame them."

"I want the trust fund money," he said. "Stop being stupid."

She bristled at being called stupid and didn't try to hide it. Brent's laughter this time had a sharp, mean edge to it. It didn't surprise her. She'd always known his charm hid a capacity for nastiness.

She didn't ask him how he knew about it — he and Aviva had dated for almost a year. It made sense that she might have told him about the trust that had been set up by Claire's father for his only grandchild. The money he'd deliberately used as a final fuck-you from the grave, bypassing the daughter who'd so egregiously disappointed him.

"The money you're so sure I'm going to give you is Aviva's, and she can't touch it until she's thirty. Even if I wanted to —"

"But you don't want to. Do you, Claire? You don't want to give me a goddamned thing." Brent snatched her by the upper arms again and jerked her a couple of stumbling steps close to him. His other hand grabbed her breast, squeezing. He thumbed the nipple, which tightened, although not from passion. He pinched it, hard, until she gasped.Then he released her arms and fastened his fingers on her chin, squeezing her mouth into fish lips. "And you never fucking did."

She struggled in his grip until he let her go. "I can't get you that money."

"Break the trust."

"Let me rephrase it," she said. "I *will not* get you that money."

"I'm going to show her the footage, Claire. You know that, right? Baby Princess Aviva is going to find out exactly what kind of marriage her parents really have. Oh, and that her daddy is into dudes."

Claire lifted her chin and fixed him with a steady gaze. "Go ahead."

It was the wrong answer. She saw it in the darkness that clouded his gaze and the sudden stiffening of his expression. She'd taken away the ace up his sleeve and pushed him into a corner. Without something to hold over her and Troy's head, Brent was going to lash out. She should have lied, Claire thought, but damn it, she was tired of men thinking they could decide the moral code for everyone but themselves.

"I need a drink. I'm going to make some hot tea." She stood on unsteady legs and, without looking at Brent, went to the bedroom door. Troy looked up at her, gesturing quickly that Elliott was sleeping. She nodded and went back out, pulling the door half-closed behind her and holding up a hand when Brent started to protest. "Elliott's asleep. Just leave the door like this, okay? They're not going anywhere, and they're not doing anything. Troy's only sitting with him."

Again without waiting for permission, she stepped over Jay and went to the kitchen to put the kettle on. She ran water in the sink to splash her face and rinse her mouth of the taste of blood and vomit and fear and anger. When she glanced into the living room, she saw Brent bent over Jay, muttering something to him. Brent looked up. Saw her watching. He came into the kitchen.

"They're in the bedroom together. Neither one of them came out to help you, not even when you shouted. How does that make you feel?"

She couldn't remember shouting, although she didn't doubt that she had. Claire shrugged, though, trying to keep herself focused on what she might do in these next few moments. How she was going to get out of this. Her mind tried again to pull her back to memories of Friday, of that unseen mouth on her, the phantom hands. Knowing it had been

Brent did not make what happened feel any less like an assault, but there was a solace in learning the truth about who it had been. In knowing, she supposed that she could understand his reasoning, as foul and disgusting as it was. If it had been a stranger, she might have feared for the rest of her life about what could happen when she let herself be vulnerable.

"It looks like Troy-O made his choice, huh?" Brent murmured, standing too close to her now. "And it's not you."

Claire's back and shoulders tensed and stiffened, but she kept her voice calm. "That's between him and me. We'll figure it out. We always do. Do you want some tea?"

"What?"

She turned a bit toward him. "Do you want some hot tea?"

"The fuck would I want —"

"Let me make you some tea, and we'll talk about how we can solve this problem. I can't break the trust," she lied smoothly, "but I can put my hands on some stocks and bonds I can sell."

Brent's confusion was palpable. "You said you weren't going to give me the money."

"I said I wouldn't give you Aviva's money. I won't take that away from my daughter. She's got nothing to do with this." In Claire's pocket, the pouch of gummies pressed her thigh. Small curls of steam wafted from the kettle's spout, but it wasn't yet whistling. "Go have a seat. I'll bring you some tea. We'll talk. Okay? We can figure it out."

She was using her "mom" voice on him, and it worked. He nodded and backed away from her. Claire forced herself to meet his gaze without blinking or cutting it away.

"I'm going to make sure those two in the bedroom aren't getting into anything. Then I'll drink tea with you and talk about how you're going to give me what I want. Sure."

She waited until he'd gone into the bedroom before digging out the pouch. As fast as she could with suddenly shaking hands, she shook out the one and three quarters remaining gummies into her palm. She put them into the biggest mug she could find and poured hot water over them as she searched the cupboard for a fruity tea that would disguise the flavor.

Damn it, they weren't melting the way she'd hoped they would. She stuck her fingers in the mug, hissing with pain at the burn, and grabbed a spoon to scoop them out. They'd softened into a mass, but only slightly.

Brent's voice rose from the bedroom. Mocking laughter. Troy's voice rose, angry.

Claire shoved the mass of slick, hot gummies into her mouth. She chewed, chewed, fast as she could, swishing the saliva around in her mouth but not swallowing. She almost gagged but held it back. The candies dissolved. She chewed faster. She spit the goo into the bottom of the mug and tried again with more hot water from the now-shrieking kettle. The noise blocked out noise from the bedroom, so she had no idea if Brent was coming back. She dunked a Peachy Dreams teabag into the boiling water. Stirred.

Prayed.

She turned to see Brent settling in at the table with an expectant look on his face. "Wait a second. It's really hot. Let me grab an ice cube."

She spun the spoon in the edible-infused tea and pulled it out. Clean. Her heart hammered. She put a couple of ice cubes in the tea and took both steaming mugs to the table.

She set one in front of Brent.

He sipped it. Set it down. Gestured at the chair across from him.

"Is the tea okay?"

"It's fine," he said. "Now sit."

From beneath the table, he pulled out a gun.

Twenty-Eight

but she was not leaping to obey.

Her subtle objection didn't seem to matter to Brent, who fixed her with a steady expression. His mug steamed slightly in front of him, but he didn't drink any more. She sipped hers, hoping to prompt him into doing the same. Hoping, too, to rinse any residual edible out of her own mouth — she'd done her best not to swallow any. Her eyes were heavy and head buzzing from tension and exhaustion already.

"It's my brother's," he told her. "I was watching the cameras from Jay's place. When I saw you guys go outside yesterday, I got up here by the back road. Went in through the outside basement doors and snagged it out of his bag. You know. Just in case something went wrong. I thought for sure you'd see me, but I guess the two of you were too busy playing with each other. Nice snowman, by the way."

"How did you know about the gun?"

"Because I know my brother carries," Brent said. His "duh" was silent, but she still heard it. "Our dad always insisted we go with him to the gun range, so we could learn how to be safe. I know Elliott doesn't keep it loaded. But I also took the ammunition, so don't think about trying anything."

"I don't know how to use a gun."

"I am sorry about all of this, Claire. I know you don't believe me."

She had no answer for him. She sipped hot tea instead, and met his gaze with as steady a gaze as she could manage. She had no real plan beyond getting him to drink the drug-infused tea, but she needed something better. Her mind worked, rusty gears grinding. She kept her expression as steady as she could, trying her best to give him the impression she was totally, utterly invested in paying attention to him.

He'd get off on that.

"If things had gone the way I'd planned, you would never even have known I was involved," Brent continued.

"But you got yourself involved. Very, very involved."

His gaze flattened. "You need to get over that. It was nothing."

Icy rage filtered into her. She fought to retain her neutral expression, but she mustn't have done a very good job. "It was *not* nothing."

For a split-second, she considered trying to act as though she'd loved what he'd done to her. That she wanted more of it. Seduction might get him vulnerable enough for her to get past him. The urge passed almost instantly.

Giving him even a moment's satisfaction in thinking that what he'd done to her was all right, that she'd wanted more of it...her throat burned at the thought of it. She tried to wash away the bitterness with more hot tea. She was almost finished with her mug. His was still almost completely full.

"No," Brent said after a pause. "I guess it wasn't. But you're still going to have to get over it, Claire."

"When were you going to ask for the money?"

"*I* was never going to ask you for anything. Jay was —"

"When," Claire interrupted, sick to death of this young punk's endless circling.

Brent leaned back in his chair, creaking it. He laced his fingers behind his head and studied her. "You were going to break it off with him, weren't you? Elliott, I mean."

She refused to answer.

"Don't tell me you were going to leave Troy." Brent's chair came down with a thump, and he leaned forward with a gleeful smile tempered by his lowered brows. He moved his head, searching to pin her gaze with his, and sat back again once she gave in and met it.

"I would never leave Troy. That was never what any of this was about."

"What was it about, then?"

"I don't owe you an explanation," Claire told him, "and it's not any of your business, anyway."

From his place on the floor, Jay let out another flurry of muffled shouts and began writhing again. Claire twisted in her chair to look at him. Taking the gun, Brent went to the older man.

"They really got you tied up good, don't they? That had to be my brother. He was an Eagle Scout. Where's your knife? C'mon, Jay, I know you always have a big pigsticker on you." Jay made another series of grunting screams that Brent pretended to understand. He leaned close, his expression concerned, before popping back up straight with a grin. "What's that? You were a total tool and left it down at the truck? Figures."

Brent went to the kitchen and grabbed a knife from the block. He used it to slice the rope tying Jay's wrists to his ankles. "C'mon, then. Get up. We need to get all this straight. Make a plan."

Jay was taller, broader and heavier than Brent, but Brent got him to his feet anyway and marched him to the table, where he sat him down hard in the wobbly chair usually pushed off to the side. Tea splashed from the mug Claire had prepared for him. Her throat closed, but Brent pulled out his chair and sat. He still had the gun, but he held it on his knee. He drank, making a small face.

"Still hot." He looked at Jay. "You want some tea?"

Jay shook his head.

Brent looked at his watch. Took another sip. He pushed the mug away from him with a grimace, and her heart seized. Did he taste something wrong with it? She tried to see how much he'd actually consumed, but the shadows in the mug prevented her from seeing.

"All right, Claire. Let's get this worked out. God damn, it's almost four in the morning." He gave a jaw-cracking yawn.

Only almost four? This night was endless. She warmed her hands on her mug, watching him carefully. She hoped he was going to nod out, but it took a while for edibles to kick in. Could be close to an hour.

"I can't break the trust. The only way I could access that money is if..." The only way she get to that money was if her daughter pre-deceased her. She didn't even want to say it aloud. Didn't want to put the idea in his head. Murder was a leap from rape, assault, blackmail, extortion. But not big enough for her to assume he wouldn't attempt it. He had taken the gun, after all.

"What?" Brent said sharply.

"It doesn't matter. I can't do it. It's impossible."

"Nothing is impossible, if you try hard enough." Brent grinned.

She shook her head. "My father set it up for Aviva. He was a very, very good estate lawyer. But I'm sure we can work out something else. If you let me talk to Troy, we can find a way to get you the money."

They could refinance the house. Dig into their retirement. Sell some stocks. At least, she could convince Brent that's what they meant to do. Claire had no intentions of actually giving this little prick a single cent. She only needed to keep him talking long enough for him to pass out.

"You can get your hands on two hundred thousand bucks, easy as that?"

Claire's brow furrowed. "Two hundred...that's not even...No. Of course I can't."

She paused, a slow realization taking over. "How much do you think that trust fund is worth?"

Brent scowled. "Two hundred K?"

"Did Aviva tell you that?"

He looked genuinely surprised. Then he laughed. "No. You did."

She wasn't sure what to say.

Brent leaned toward her. "You don't remember at all, do you? The night we met in that hotel lobby. You were tossing back shots. You offered to buy me a drink —"

"Stop."

"You told me your father had died, but you didn't care," Brent went on, relentless. Cruel. "You said he'd been a real dick to you for your whole life, and he was trying to screw you over even after he died. You said he put all the money in a trust fund for your daughter so you couldn't touch it. You told me it was two hundred thousand dollars. Then you offered to suck — "

"Stop it," she said. "I don't need a play-by-play."

All of this had come from that night.

"It's not even close to being two hundred thousand dollars." She wanted to drop her face in her hands and weep and laugh, all at the same time. "I don't even think it'll be close to that when it comes due, not even if it's invested brilliantly."

"Why would you tell me it was?"

"At the time, I had no idea how much money it was. My father had died. I don't know, Brent," Claire said. "Maybe I was just bragging. It's not like I ever thought I'd see you again."

He grimaced. "How much is in the account?"

"I haven't looked at it this month, but the last time I saw the statement, it had just under fifty thousand dollars in it." It was a nice nest egg, a down payment on a house, money to pay off a master's or PhD, if Aviva pursued one.

Jay coughed. "...less than fifty thousand? That's *all*?"

"What do you mean, that's all? That's a nice little chunk of change, especially for someone like you," Brent put in.

"It might be enough for your bail," Jay muttered. "I'd never have agreed to any of this if I knew you weren't even going to get fifty grand."

"You agreed so I wouldn't take your ass to the police and tell them you've been peeping on your renters," Brent retorted. He shoved the gun into the back of his jeans, then slammed back another glug of tea and got up from the table to stalk to the kitchen, where he threw the mug into the sink hard enough that Claire heard it shatter.

"We can still get you something." She twisted in her seat to stare after him. "It'll take some time."

"Right, right, it'll take time to get the money, and meanwhile, I'm supposed to do what. Let you go back home? You'll go right to the cops." Brent yanked open the fridge door and grabbed out a block of cheese. He pulled a knife from the block and began cutting it. "You got crackers or something?"

"Everything we brought is in that cupboard next to the fridge."

He pulled down a box of crackers and dumped some into a bowl.

Sliced some more cheese. He shoved some into his mouth and faced her, waving the knife.

"See, the thing is, Claire, it's all fucked sideways now. So I need some time to think about how to make sure you don't have the chance to tell anyone about this. You want some cheese?"

"No."

It was too early for the munchies to be kicking in. Or was it? He didn't seem impaired yet. Aviva had once told her mother that Brent was kind of a stoner. Maybe his tolerance was keeping the gummies from affecting him.

"Jay? Cheese?"

The big man had been so silent Claire had wondered if he was still conscious. He shifted in the chair now, shaking his head. His cough sounded thick and wet, hacking. Disgusting. She eyed him. Bruises spread across his face, and blood crusted his upper lip. His nose looked squashed and bent. Gingerly, she touched the back of her head and was glad she'd hurt him.

Jay looked at her, eyes half-lidded and gaze unfocused. He slipped out a tongue to run across his lips. She thought he meant to speak, but his gaze went to Brent in the kitchen, and he stayed quiet.

"They never cut *him* off. Elliott, I mean." Brent said this with his mouth full, chomping cheese and crackers. He came back into the living room with the plate in his hand. The gun was still stuck in his waistband. She hoped it would go off. "Bet you didn't know that, did you? He quit his job to move to your town, and Mom and Dad had to step up and basically fund him. They paid for his divorce, too. His rent, utilities, car payment, all that, for eight freaking months until he got another job. Because he wanted to get closer to you. But I'm the one who gets cut off, I'm the one kicked out of the house. How fair is that?"

"Sounds like you need to blackmail your parents," Claire said.

She wasn't going to let herself dwell on Elliott's poor financial choices, or what holes he'd dug for himself in his pursuit of her. His bank account had never been her business. Brent scowled at her. Without explanation, he went into the bedroom and slammed the door behind him.

Even with the door shut, Claire knew very well how not-soundproof this cabin was. She didn't know how much time she had before Brent came back, but she was going to use it. Jay's head hung, his shoulders hunched. A strand of bloody drool or snot hung from his chin, but she forced herself to concentrate on his face. His eyes were closed.

"Jay." She leaned close. "Can you wake up?"

He didn't move. She tried again, this time with a gentle hand on his knee. She shook a tiny bit.

His eyes flew open. His hand slapped down on hers, gripping it. Twisting. Her fingers screamed with an agony compounded by their already fragile state. She gasped, choking, and he yanked her forward.

"Don't let him hear you," Jay muttered. His eyes rolled, wild in his skull, and looked beyond her to the bedroom door. "Don't you let that crazy son-of-a-bitch know I'm talking to you."

"Please let go of my hand..."

He squeezed it harder. Claire bit back a cry of pain. Bright flashes were tickling the edges of her vision, but she forced them away. Jay let her go abruptly, almost flinging her hand from his. She sat back with a gasping sigh.

"You need to get the snowmobile. Okay? Get down to my truck. It's not locked. Keys are under the mat. Your phones are in the glove box."

"I can't drive —"

"Shut up for once in your big-mouthed life," Jay ordered.

Rage curled her aching fingers into fists.

"I am so fucking tired," she said, "of men telling women they have big mouths just because they can't be bothered to listen to what we have to say."

Jay spat a gobbet of phlegm onto the floor and looked at her. "You have a filthy mouth."

"Yeah. I do. And guess what, Jay? I don't care if it bothers you. Instead of puffing up your chest and trying to put me in my place, tell me how to operate the snowmobile so I can get us out of here." She sat back, out of his reach. If he came at her, she was ready to punch, kick, bite.

Jay didn't come for her.

He blinked, that big bushy head swinging back and forth, a bison ready to charge. He didn't look chastened, but he'd definitely been put in his place, and he was feeling it. He hated her, that was clear all over his expression, but Claire didn't care. She hated him, too.

"You'd better do it fast, because I don't think he's going to be in there much longer," she said.

Jay frowned and looked again toward the bedroom. "It's got a pull start. Shit. You need to get one of the men to do it. You're never gonna be able to start it. It's a bitch even for me."

Voices raised in the bedroom. She and Jay looked at each other. He leaned forward, unsteady even while still sitting. She reached a hand to catch him, certain he was going to topple over.

"You're gonna grab the pull cord. It's got a T-shaped handle. You put your foot on the running board, and you yank that cord, hard as you can. It'll take a couple of tries, if you can even manage it at all. She's gonna start up rough —"

"What about the thing that Elliott didn't do. The parking brake? It made him wreck."

Jay's eyes drifted shut. He swayed in place. "Shit. Yeah. He might've put that on, I don't know. You have to check that. Let me think how to describe it to you."

They'd taken too long. Troy came out of the bedroom, Brent following. Jay and Claire pushed away from each other the same as magnets with different polarities. Brent gave Troy's shoulder a shove that sent him stumbling a few steps.

"Tell her," Brent said.

Claire groaned, but mentally. What else could possibly happen tonight to upend her world? Troy looked sheepish, but also a little defiant. He shrugged off Brent's touch.

"I can get him the money he wants," Troy said.

"I know we can, but we should talk about this." She gave Brent a glance. "It'll take time to work it out."

"No," her husband interrupted. "I can get it to him now. Tonight. I just need access to my phone so I can send it to him."

"How are you going to do that?"

"With Ca$hMe. It's an app," Troy said.

"I know what it is. But we don't have enough cash in any of our accounts." Her mind was already calculating overdrafts and unpaid bills. The penalties for withdrawing money early from their retirement accounts. This would break them.

Brent laughed. "Oh, he's got a real surprise for you."

"Troy?"

Troy sighed and gave her that strange expression again. "I have an account you don't know about."

More lies. More secrets.

"How much is in there?" Claire asked.

Troy hesitated before answering. Brent shoved his shoulder again. His grin spread across his face like an oil slick.

"Tell her," he said.

Troy sighed, looking caught out more than he had from anything else, even the revelation that they'd both been sleeping with the same man. Brent laughed. He shrugged.

"I've got a hundred and sixty thousand dollars in it."

TWENTY-NINE

She'd misheard him. He'd said a hundred and sixty *dollars*. Right?

"Well, it isn't two hundred," Brent said, "but I'll be happy to take it off your hands."

"Troy," she began but her voice crackled and sputtered the same as static on an old radio.

Troy crossed the room and took her shoulders in his hands, his grip gentle. "I took the money my parents gave me when we got married —"

"You said you spent that on your school loans —"

"I did. Some of it. But most of it, I put away. I made some good investments."

Claire swallowed against the lump in her throat. For more than twenty years, she'd believed the generous gift from his parents had been long gone. The years when they'd struggled, barely making ends meet. The really, really bad year after Aviva was born, when Claire had been unable to work and they'd refinanced the house to stay afloat. There'd been so many nights she'd bent over the checkbook, bleary eyed, the baby at her breast while Troy slept and Claire tried to figure out how they were going to pay for diapers.

And he'd had money, a lot of it, all this time.

"Guess you've always been a liar, huh, Troy?" Brent asked.

If Troy had told her about the money, they'd have spent it, and what would they have done now? Instead, the secret he'd kept, like so many they'd each kept over the years, was going to save them now from far greater harm. She'd never loved him as much as she did right then.

"Oh, thank God," Claire said.

Her reaction seemed to stump Brent, who gave her a curious look. "I thought you'd be pissed off at him."

"I knew she wouldn't be," Troy said calmly, not giving Brent even the barest glance.

Brent frowned. "I don't get it. Any of this. My mother might not care who my dad's sleeping around with, but she would lose her freaking mind if he hid money from her."

"I told you before. You have no idea about who I am. Or who we are, together." To Troy, Claire said, "will you be able to transfer all of it tonight?"

"I don't know. I have to log in to my account and see what the transfer limits are. And for that, I need my phone. And I'll need to get on the internet." Troy's voice was steady as stone, no emotions in it at all.

Claire wanted to weep with the relief at the return of the Troy she knew. Imperturbable and unruffled. He had a plan. A goal. She trusted him. No matter what happened next, Troy was going to make it all work out okay in the end.

Her body sagged. All she wanted was to sleep and sleep, but despite her exhaustion, she knew there was no way she'd be able to until all of this was resolved. She forced her body out of her chair and hugged Troy, who held her tight.

"Once I get my phone," he whispered in her ear, so faintly she almost couldn't hear him. "I'll call the police."

She gripped him tighter for a few seconds, clinging even though it hurt all her muscles. She wanted to tell him about drugging Brent, but Troy gently pushed her away from him with a kiss on her cheek. His eyes shifted infinitesimally in Brent's direction, then back to hers. He didn't want Brent suspecting anything. She understood.

Claire cleared her throat, pitching her voice loud enough to be sure Brent could hear her from the kitchen. "How's Elliott?"

"I think he's got a concussion." Now, Troy gave Brent a full look. "I should be monitoring him. Brain injuries can be really serious."

"That's so sweet. You two make a great couple. Can't wait to see you both at the big family barbecue." Brent said this in a sticky-sweet voice lacking sincerity.

Troy's expression barely shifted when he looked at Claire. "My phone is probably still in the basement. I had it with me when you called me Friday morning, and I put it my pocket after that, but I think I remember it falling out when Jay threw me down the stairs."

"I didn't throw you. You fell," Jay piped up.

Troy ignored him, his gaze steady on Claire's as he addressed Brent. "Brent, if you go get my phone, I'll be able to log in to my Ca$hMe account. I can check the transfer limits and get the process started. You can have the first payment by morning."

"How about I log out of my account and you use mine?"

Troy's mouth thinned, only for a second. He kept his voice light. Unconcerned. "I don't remember my login information. Ask Claire. I have to have everything autofilled, or else I'm always resetting my password. Unless you want to let me also log into my email, but even then I have it set up to send a two-step verification text —"

"Yeah, fuck that mess. I'll go look for your phone." Brent tossed his plate into the sink with a clatter and wiped his mouth with the back of his hand.

He wove a little as he crossed the living room to the basement door. Troy noticed. Claire wished she could tell him with her eyes what she'd done, but there was no way to explain. She and Troy moved closer again. His hands found hers. She winced when she squeezed them.

"Sorry," he mouthed.

Brent opened the basement door and went down the steep stairs with heavy, lumbering steps. Once he'd disappeared, Jay got out of his chair. He was also unsteady on his feet, but he managed to keep his balance and stand up straight. He tweaked aside the sheet to look out front, and spoke to them both over his shoulder.

"I wanted him to come up here and fix this mess because it was all his idea. I never wanted him to go batshit. Are you two listening to me? This is all this fault. He's blackmailing me, too!"

Troy let go of her hands and turned to Jay. He snorted his disdain. "At this point, what he's doing is technically extortion. He told me if I didn't get him the money, he was going to kill you. Tell me why I should care about that."

Jay goggled, eyes and mouth both wide before he shut them. "Damn him, damn him. He's out of his mind. Why would he have threatened to kill *me*? Why not *her*?"

"He's not going to actually kill anyone," Claire said firmly.

"He's got a gun!" Jay whisper-shouted.

"Killing someone requires effort. Brent has never had to work that hard for anything in his life. He doesn't have the fortitude."

The big man covered his eyes with one hand and gave a long, low groan. "I never should have told him to come here."

"But you did," Troy said.

"He used my second sled to get up here. If I can get out there, I can get down to the main road."

"You're not going anywhere," Troy told him.

Jay looked up. "Your buddy in there totaled my other sled, you think I'm going to let one of yinz take this one? No. I'll do it."

"You," Troy repeated, "are not going anywhere. I don't trust you. You'll get down there and head off to who knows where."

"I want out of this as much as you do!"

"You told us yourself that he's blackmailing you. You want to convince me that you're going to the cops and admitting you've got this place rigged up with cameras you've been using to spy on people? You're going to lose your business, first of all, not to mention the lawsuits. You'll probably go to jail, too." Troy said all of this quickly, without raising his voice. "So you're not going anywhere. I'll do it."

Claire reached for him. "Your ankle. If something happens, you won't be able to walk on it. You could freeze out there and die, and we wouldn't know about it."

"I don't want you doing this, Claire. Elliott —"

"Hard no to that. He's not wrecking another one of my vehicles," Jay cut in.

"Elliott has a head injury. He can't do it." Claire drew herself up. "I'll have to. But we're going to have to put Brent out of commission somehow. Knock him out, tie him up."

Jay leaned heavily on the table. "Just give him the money. You said you have it. Just give him what he wants, and we can all go home."

"I'll never give him what he wants," Troy said in a voice so flat and cold it made Claire shiver.

"You gonna try to trick him?" Jay whispered fiercely and stabbed a finger in Troy's direction. "You don't have the money? Shit, I knew it was too good to be true."

"I have the money. I'm just not going to give him any of it."

She and Troy faced each other. He wasn't putting weight on that bad ankle, and lines of strain had etched into the corners of his eyes and around his mouth. He looked worse than she even felt. She put his arm around her shoulders, trying to offer him support.

"When he comes up from the basement, I'm going to hit him with a log," Troy said grimly.

Jay burst into laughter.

Claire ignored him. "I'll help you."

"No. I don't want you anywhere near him."

"This is not a cave," she said, "and you are not a cave man. You can barely stand on that ankle. I'm going to help you."

Footsteps on the basement stairs turned them both in that direction. There wasn't time for Troy to hobble over there, much less carrying a log. Claire moved, fast, trying not to overthink. Trying only to act. She went first for a log from the pile near the fireplace, but they were all too big and heavy.

She grabbed the poker, instead.

It weighed in her hand, dragging at her muscles, but she forced her fingers closed around the shaft and hefted it as she limped as fast as she could toward the open basement door. She got there at the same time Brent appeared. He was red-eyed and red-faced, with spiderwebs and dirt clinging to his previously pristine preppy haircut.

He stepped through the doorway and into the living room, Troy's phone held up in one hand. She swung the poker. She'd intended to aim for his head, but hesitated at the last second. Killing someone took effort, she'd been right about that, and she didn't want to kill him, only knock him out and get the gun from him.

Her weak fingers could not hold the heavy iron instrument, especially not in motion. The poker slipped from her grasp and she reached for it, but she lost the grip. The poker fell, hitting Brent in the foot. He let out a holler, more surprise than pain. He grabbed her wrist as he fell backwards, his other arm flailing to catch his balance.

Brent fell down the stairs.

He took Claire with him.

THIRTY

Together, they rolled down the steep and narrow basement stairs. Brent took the brunt of the fall, but even with his body cushioning her, the landing jarred her into a daze. At first, Claire couldn't move. With its single bare overhead bulb, the basement wore more shadows than light, but she could see Brent's face.

His eyes were open, staring, but he wasn't moving.

"Claire!"

She rolled off Brent and managed to get to her hands and knees on the bottom stair. Looking up, she saw Troy silhouetted there. He looked as if he was trying to get down to her.

"I'm okay," she called out. She pushed up onto the bottom stair, testing herself for damage. Nothing seemed broken.

Behind her, Brent groaned and sat up. "Motherfucker."

In high school, Claire had been part of a friend group that partied. A lot. Nothing heavier than weed and booze, but their weekends had often included a lot of both. One night, she'd gone to a party at a kid named Kevin's house. His parents were out of town, and their friend group gathered to do the usual. For whatever crazy reason, that night, Claire had wanted to hook up with Kevin. She declined a ride home with a few of the other friends, and although Kevin had turned out to be a huge mistake, not taking that ride had been a good choice.

The driver had nodded out at the wheel, sending the car off the road into a tree. The car had been totaled. Every single kid in it, all of them drunk or high or both, had walked away from the accident with nothing more than bruises. The general consensus had been their intoxication had left them boneless and supple enough to escape serious injury.

Brent got to his feet in much the same way she'd always imagined her friends tumbling out of the wreckage. He moved a little like a puppet, jerking one way and the next, but kept his feet. He focused on her, but Claire wasn't going to wait for him to grab for her.

On her hands and knees, she scrambled up the stairs. She got there with Brent close on her heels. At the top, Troy grabbed the back of her shirt and hauled her out of the way, but they didn't have time to close the door or hit him with anything.

Brent slammed the door behind him to keep himself from being pushed down the stairs again. He advanced on Troy and Claire, but stopped short. He rolled his head on his neck, cracking it.

"God damn it, that hurt like a son-of-a-bitch."

"Yeah," Troy said. "I know."

Brent scanned the room. "Where's Jay?"

Claire hadn't noticed the open front door before now. Brent saw it, too. He lumbered toward it, not staggering but not running, either. He screamed Jay's name.

From outside came a harsh, ratcheting noise that stopped abruptly. The pull start, she realized, shocked to discover she was capable of coherent thought. The noise came again, along with an engine rumble that also stopped right away. Jay's faint shout drifted to them through the open door.

The knife Brent had used to slice away the ropes tying up Jay was on the table. He took it. He went outside. All the noises stopped.

"Where's the gun?" Troy asked.

Claire shook her head. "Maybe he dropped it in the basement."

From outside came a high-pitched scream of agony.

Moments later, Brent came back into the cabin. Blood spattered his face, and his hands were covered in it. He went right to the kitchen and began scrubbing them.

Troy and Claire looked at each other. He tried to hold her back from heading for the door, but she shrugged him off. She ran out onto the front porch and slipped in the icy snow. She caught herself before she could fall.

Jay sprawled in the snow, face down. Crimson had splashed the white drifts all around him. Claire teetered on the steps, but a hand came from behind and pulled her back inside.

Brent shut the door. "Don't bother. He's dead."

"He might not —"

"He's definitely dead," Brent told her flatly. "I stabbed him in the eye, all the way to the hilt."

For a moment, nobody said anything.

Finally, Troy spoke. "Good."

Brent laughed. "My man!"

"I need to use the bathroom." Claire spoke so softly neither man heard her. She made her way into the bathroom and ran the cold water, first to cup a handful to drink and next to splash her face.

She assessed the damage. Of all the things that had happened since Friday, falling down the basement stairs had surprisingly done her the least harm. Her reflection showed dark shadows below her eyes, bruises or simple exhaustion. She turned her face side to side. Cuts. Dried blood. More bruises. Experimentally, she worked her fingers into fists and released them. Her hands hurt, yes, but they almost always did.

Claire braced herself on the sink and concentrated on her breathing. She counted slowly, one through five. Held it. Then let the breath out slowly too, counting again. It wasn't helping; she wasn't calmer, she wasn't soothed. But it gave her something to do to stop herself from collapsing.

She could not believe Brent hadn't passed out already, or at least gone into the munchies and giggles zone. She'd lost track of time, but a couple of hours *had* to have passed. Yet when she leaned to crane for a glimpse of the clock on the living room wall, she was stunned to see that it had only been fifty minutes or so since she'd made him the tea. It was similar to being ill with the flu — the nights were always endless, with morning holding out hope you'd feel better, if only you could get through the next few hours.

Well, she wasn't sick, and she *was* going to get through this. Carefully, since she felt as though she might topple over if she tried to walk too fast, Claire went into the bedroom. Elliott lay motionless on the bed. Her heart seized even as she reached for him. She expected to find his body cold, no pulse, but she let out a sobbing sigh of relief when he was warm. Breathing. Not dead.

She'd been planning to end things with him, and so she'd contemplated how it would be to lose him. To have an empty and aching open space in her world that had once been filled with Elliott. She'd imagined her grief, but knew she'd survive it, because, after all, he would still *exist*. Until this moment, she had not allowed herself to really think about how would feel to know that the entire world had moved on without Elliott as a part of it.

"Elliott. Sweetheart." She tasted tears when she spoke. She leaned close and listened to the soft in-out hush of his breathing. Should she wake him? What were you supposed to do for head injuries, anyway? She'd always thought you were supposed to keep the person awake.

If she had her phone, she'd simply tap tap tap and search for the answer. If she had her phone, she could call for emergency services. If she had her phone, if, if, if...

Elliott sighed and shifted. His eyes opened. "Claire."

"I'm here."

"Where's Troy?"

"He's in the living room. He's fine," she added quickly at the sight of Elliott's distressed expression. "He promised Brent some money. They're figuring out how to make that happen."

Elliott grabbed her wrist with surprising strength. "Don't give him anything."

"He killed Jay." She choked on the words. "I tried drugging him, but it's not working yet."

Elliott fell back against the pillows and closed his eyes. His grip loosened. "I'm so sorry, Claire. I should have told you long ago that he and I were related. I never thought he would do something like this."

"I'm not sure why it came as such a shock. He's an asshole."

He looked at her. "He wasn't always. I know you don't have a high opinion of him, but believe me, I never suspected he'd be capable of doing this. And to *kill* someone…you drugged him?"

"You can't possibly be blaming that on me. Drugged or not, he actively threatened and went after Jay, and he stabbed him in the eye." Her breath wheezed out of her. "How can you defend him?"

He sighed. "He's my brother."

"He sent me the box." She said nothing more than that for a moment, letting him digest that information. "It was him on Friday."

Elliott shifted again on the bed, pushing up on his elbow. "I think I have to puke."

It had been a long number of years since Claire had been on stomach flu duty with Aviva, but some instincts never faded. She grabbed the trash pail next to the dresser and had it by the side of the bed in seconds. Elliott leaned over it, emptying his stomach while she rubbed his back and tried not to sympathy vomit. Finished, he fell onto the bed again. She put the can in the bathroom and got him a cup of water from the sink, pausing at the door to the living room to listen.

"…it's broken," Brent said.

"Let me try again." This came from Troy.

"The screen is cracked, man, and it won't even stay on. You're at 1% battery. It's never going to work. Just go get your damned planner with all your login information on it, like you said you could."

"I'll just try again. One more time."

Troy was stalling.

She returned to Elliott's side with a damp cloth and the water. He sipped it and put the cup on the nightstand. He used the cloth on his face.

"Thank you."

Claire pressed a hand to his forehead. "I think you have a fever. We need to get you some help."

"I'll be okay. Claire, I'm sorry. I'm so sorry. I can't believe he'd do that to you."

She had no trouble believing it. "You knew all along. Didn't you? About me and him, the hotel."

"Yes," he said after a long, long silence.

I hate that I was just one of many.

That's what he'd said to her, and those words held so much more meaning, now. "You agreed to meet me. To pursue me, to get me to sleep with you."

"That's how it started, but it's not how it is now. Claire, I —"

She cut him off before he could finish. She couldn't bear hearing him say he loved her. Not now.

"He says you owed him one. He wouldn't tell me why." She paused again, giving him the chance to answer, but he didn't. "What does he have on you, Elliott? What could be so bad that you'd willingly use someone else, anyone, to satisfy him? You used *me*."

"That's not how it is!"

"That's how it started, you said so yourself!"

"I didn't know you when I agreed to it. I thought, why not? You were attractive. Smart and funny. It wasn't as if it was a hardship to get to know you. If you'd shown me no interest, I wouldn't have been able to do much more about it, but you did. I thought I'd see how far it would go, but by the time it went somewhere, Claire, I swear to you, it wasn't about him anymore. I hated thinking about you and him together. Can't you understand how much I hated it?"

"It was years ago, and it meant *nothing*." She grabbed at the sheets. "Don't you understand that? It had nothing to do with you, Elliott, but you...damn it, you had *everything* to do with him!"

Raised voices turned her toward the bedroom door.

"Troy is stalling him. He told me he's not going to actually give Brent anything." She leaned close to whisper in his ear. "But I don't know what he's planning, exactly. I need to go out there and see. Do you need anything else? Are you going to be sick again?"

"No. I'll get up."

She doubted he could. Dismissing him, she stood. "Do whatever you want."

"Claire...please...."

She left him without another word. The moment she stepped into the living room, Brent had hold of her arm. He yanked her forward. She couldn't see Troy at first, then spotted him on the couch. It looked as though his hands and feet were bound again.

"I'm done with this bullshit," Brent told her. "You're coming with me."

THIRTY-ONE

Brent shoved her through the shed door and forward a few stumbling steps. Claire managed to catch herself, but her head spun. Keeping her feet took everything she had. The walk through the deep snow had worn her almost into catatonia. He'd dragged her by the hair for the last few feet. She couldn't feel her hands or feet, both bare. Icicles had frozen from the snot dripping out of her nose. She shuddered, over and over, certain she was going to pass out.

"Alone at last," Brent said. Her chattering teeth wouldn't let her answer. He looked her over, up and down. "You look like shit."

She sank slowly onto her knees, trying to draw her body as tight as she could in an effort at warming herself. The shed wasn't heated, but it cut the wind and wasn't as cold as outside. She could see her breath, but her shivers eased. Brent studied her without bending, his gaze fixed hard. Eyes narrowed. Mouth pursed.

With Troy's phone broken, he'd agreed to log in through Brent's. The planner, supposedly in Troy's car, also supposedly held all the password and account information he'd need. She'd warned him multiple times about keeping all of his information in a place that could be so easily accessed from someone else, but he'd never listened to her.

"Why did you bring me out here? You don't need me to look for

Troy's planner." The individual words spit out of her between the clatter of her teeth.

"Maybe I wanted to give the lovebirds some time alone to figure out how they're going to get rid of you," Brent told her. When she flinched he added, "Hits home, huh? Feels right? Well, Claire, maybe I thought you wanted to get away from them, so you didn't have to watch them slobbering all over each other. That has to suck, big time. I'm only trying to look out for you."

"Spare me the fake solicitousness," she told him. The cold concrete pressed her knees through her jeans, but she didn't feel capable of getting to her feet. If anything, she wanted to curl into a ball right here on the shed floor and take her chances at freezing.

Brent waved his hands. "Oooh. You've alway had such a big mouth, I guess I'm not surprised you use it to say big words."

She didn't answer him.

Her silence annoyed him, she saw that on his face. He didn't call her out on it, though. He backed up a few steps and looked around the shed. A long row of fluorescent overhead lights lit the space with a bright, bluish glow that hurt her eyes. The low, barely audible buzz irritated her ears, too.

Troy's car had been parked haphazardly at an angle. Brent ran a hand over the hood. A fresh dent in the front bumper matched a scar in the shed's wooden wall. Troy would be upset, she thought before realizing the stupidity of that idea. If they all got out of here alive, harmed no more than they'd already been, a dent would be the last thing he'd care about.

Brent saw her looking. "I'll give Jay some credit. He *tried*. I mean, the man was all in for the idea. He lied to you when he said this was all because of me, because he sure as hell never told me he'd turn down his share of the money."

"You weren't ever going to give him any."

He laughed. "No. I wasn't. But he didn't know that. Anyway, my brother really fucked it all up, didn't he? Making plans we couldn't predict. Too bad Jay turned out to be as stupid as I thought he was. I shouldn't have trusted him."

"No," she corrected. "You shouldn't have *killed* him."

"Probably not. It wasn't part of the plan. And I did have one. A plaaaan." He dragged out the word, exaggerating it to go along with the sneer twisting his lips.

His words had begun to slur. He definitely seemed to be moving slower as he crossed the room to stand over her. Please, Claire thought, please. Knock him out. Her teeth chattered again, more with fear than cold this time, and she clenched her jaw to stop them. After a second, though, she let the chattering start again. It couldn't hurt her to look weak in front of him. He would enjoy that.

"You're cold. Come over here and I'll warm you up," he said.

Claire didn't move. Her entire body shook with cold and anxiety. Brent shrugged and kicked a coffee can that scattered screws and nails as it rolled away. He turned back to her.

"Jay was stupid, but he was right about one thing. None of this was supposed to happen. I guess none of that matters now, though, does it? Because now I have to deal with the mess. And you know what, Claire? That pisses me off. I had plans for Spring Break. I was going to Cabo, baby."

She blinked. "You're serious."

"Of course I'm not *serious*." Brent's voice dripped with disdain. "What am I? A villain from some moronic teen movie? I killed a man, Claire! The fact he was dumber than a box of rocks and a scumbag voyeur who got off on watching other people fuck isn't going to matter to a jury, is it? Do you think they'll care that this was *just* supposed to be blackmail? Hell, I'm a white male in my early twenties. They're going to use me as the poster boy to prove how woke they are."

"Do you expect me to feel sorry for you?"

He pivoted on his heel in an unsteady half-spin. "No. Not that you would even if I did."

Brent raked a hand through the fall of his hair, pushing it out of his eyes. He took a moment to stare up at the ceiling, shaking his head. He advanced on her and bent to grab her upper arms, but he did it gently enough not to hurt. He rubbed his hands up and down as though he was trying to warm her. It didn't work.

He frowned at her lack of reaction. "It didn't have to be this way."

He sounded so sincerely and genuinely upset that for a second, a stupid, single second, she felt a scrap of pity for him. He was young. And privileged. And, as he'd said, none of this was supposed to have happened.

Her sympathy didn't last longer than it took for her to blink, but it had been there, a reminder that although he was not, in fact, a movie villain, he was still an entitled asshole.

"You could let us all go. We could tell them that you didn't mean to kill Jay. We could say it was an accident, Brent."

"It won't matter."

"It could," she insisted softly. "If we all agree to the same story. But if you keep us here...if you hurt me or Troy or Elliott, you won't be able to explain any of that away."

His hands squeezed. He let her go but didn't move away from her. Whatever he saw in her face was not reflected in his eyes, which were narrowed. Cold. He wasn't sneering any longer, but the faintly smug smile that played on his lips was somehow worse.

"Think of your parents," she said. "He's your brother."

It was the wrong thing to say. Brent scowled. "My parents are the ones who made me do this. If they just kept up their end of the bargain, we wouldn't be here today."

Claire stifled her urge to shout at him that his parents didn't owe him a lifetime of financial support. Brent was twenty-five years old and should be out on his own. She swallowed her words.

"We could convince them Jay attacked you first. But we can't convince anyone of anything if you hurt us."

"I still won't have what I wanted in the first place."

"My marriage is over. You've seen to that. It's what you wanted, isn't it? You wanted to make me suffer." Claire kept her voice low and as steady as possible, which was hard to do when she wanted to shriek, to howl, to slap at him with her voice and her hands, to punch the self-satisfaction off his face. She wanted to hurt him in ways that would never heal.

Brent laughed, incredulous. "You really are a dumb bitch, aren't you? You really think I care enough about you to give a damn if your *marriage* gets fucked up? Not. Even. Close."

With every word he inched his face closer to hers. In the harsh white light from the shed's overhead lamps, his eyes were very blue and very bright, but the whites were pinkish. His pupils were dilated. All she had to do was wait him out.

"What was it then?" she asked.

"C'mon. What are you, stupid? It's all about the money. It's always been about the money. When Aviva introduced me to you, I remembered you telling me she had that trust fund. I'd never have believed it if you hadn't told me yourself. I mean, you and hubby are not the sort of people who have a trust fund."

"You shouldn't be so quick to judge other people by what you think you know," Claire said.

Brent pulled his face into an expression of pseudo-apology. "Right, right, right. Of course I shouldn't. I mean, I thought I knew something about you, and it turned out I was wrong, wasn't I? Tell me something. What did it feel like when you found out your boytoy has been fucking your husband for what, a year? How does it feel to know they're in *looooove*?"

"I feel betrayed." She saw no need to lie.

"I thought you two had an 'arrangement.'"

Oh, how she hated air quotes.

She had to unclench her jaw before she could speak. "We did."

"And he broke it." No nastiness this time. No smugness. Only curiosity. "How can you not hate him?"

"I don't hate either one of them," Claire said, which might have been a lie. She wasn't sure.

Brent grinned. "I bet you hate me, though."

This time her refusal to answer him did seem to get under his skin. He leaned in again. Those wide-pupiled eyes searched hers.

"Would you kill them? Because they betrayed you, I mean."

"What? No!"

"Not even one of them? If you were going to kill one of them, which would it be? I bet it would be hubby. You'd be a hot widow. And hey, if you marry my brother, we'd be related."

"I would never kill anyone, no matter how they betrayed me," Claire said. It wasn't any of his business, but the words, that truth, came out of her anyway.

"I never thought I'd kill someone, either. Until I did."

Claire shivered and wrapped her arms around herself. "I'm freezing. Let's get Troy's planner and go back to the cabin."

He moved toward her. For a horrible moment, Claire thought he meant to kiss her, but he only pushed his face so close to hers she could count his eyelashes. He fixed her with a long, solid look. His breath tickled her skin, but she didn't so much as flinch.

She considered biting him.

"Why didn't you ever want me again, Claire?"

She jerked her head away from his intended caress of her cheek. "How can you even ask me that?"

"I want to know." Brent stood up and backed away a few steps toward the car.

He listed like he was on a ship plowing its way through stormy seas. He spun on his heel and turned in her direction, catching himself before he could lose his balance and totally topple over. He held out his arms.

"What was wrong with me, Claire? Huh?"

"We had one night together. We were always meant to be strangers, that's all —"

"But we weren't sssssstrangers," he slurred. "We could totally have had a thing together."

"You were my daughter's boyfriend. She was in love with you. Why would I ever sleep with you again?"

"Because you sleep with everyone else!"

Claire recoiled at Brent's shout but then squared herself to face him.

"That's not any of your business, and it's also not true. But even if I trawled myself up and down Main Street hopping on any dick that drove by, it would not obligate me to fuck *you* just because you wanted it."

"You think you're funny and clever. Don't you? You think you're so beautiful. Well. You're right. Why do you think I stayed with Aviva for as long as I did? You always judge the daughter by how her mother ages, right? You're beautiful, Claire." He lurched a step her way but spun again, arms still out, a parody of Maria from *The Sound of Music*.

She crossed her fingers, hoping he was going to pass out at any second. "I know."

"You're supposed to say thank you when someone compliments you. Not say you *know*." His lip curled. "Like some stuck-up bitch."

"Okay, there it is. 'Stuck-up bitch.' That's what men call women who don't kiss their ass for being told something they already know about themselves. Guess what, Brent," she said. "I also know I'm funny. And smart."

For a moment she was sure he was going to hit her, and she readied herself to duck away from him. Brent teetered, instead, and went very, very still. He glared at her.

"You never approved of me. Did you? You never...never wanted me to be with Aviva. Too goy for you, huh? Afraid our kids would believe in Sssssssanta?"

He flung his arms out again, expansively, every word a mushy garble. He swung his head around to look at her with what seemed to be great effort. His eyes were redder, now. The cold didn't seem to be bothering him at all.

"I wanted my daughter to be happy. If you made her happy, then I was happy," Claire told him. "But you didn't make her happy, Brent. You were a selfish, cheating prick who gaslighted her and tried to make her think it was her fault when you treated her like shit. So, you're right. I did not like you."

"She broke up with me because of you! You told her — "

"I *never* told her what happened with us."

He spun again, staggering. "Liar. If you didn't tell her what happened with us, why did she break up with me?"

"She broke up with you because my daughter, like her mother, is beautiful and funny and most of all, she's smart enough to know when she's not being treated the way she deserves."

Claire rubbed her arms faster, trying to warm herself. She went to Troy's car and tried the passenger side door. Locked. She went around the other side to the driver's door. It opened.

Brent doubled over, laughing hysterically. Ignoring him, she leaned across the driver's seat to look at the passenger side. Nothing. She looked in the back seat, but couldn't see much from that angle. She opened the back door and found Troy's laptop bag on the floor behind the passenger seat. His planner was in it. She hesitated before slipping it free.

If she got the information Troy needed to transfer that money, it meant only a temporary reprieve. Nobody would plow the road until someone noticed Jay was missing, and she had no idea how long that would take. She no longer believed Brent wouldn't kill them all, not after seeing what he'd done to Jay.

"If you're so smart, how'd you get yourself in such a mess?" Brent demanded.

"Brent, it's over. You're not going to get away with this. You've made that impossible for yourself."

"I didn't kill Jay. Hubby dearest did. Or maybe it was loverboy. I haven't decided yet. But it was definitely one of them. Not me." Brent's grin stretched wide and wider, revealing straight teeth so white they almost glowed in the fluorescents. "A love triangle gone wrong, right? And in the aftermath, maybe a murder suicide? Whattaya think?"

Brent shrugged. With that casual, careless gesture, Claire lost the final, lacy shreds of hope. He would kill them, and it seemed possible he might get away with it.

"I think you're out of your mind if you believe you can do this."

"Nobody knows you're here. It'll be days, maybe even a week before anyone finds you. And nobody knows I was ever here at all. There's nothing to connect me to any of this."

"There are cameras," she said desperately. "Footage. Someone will see it."

He laughed silently. "I deleted all that footage. I disabled the cameras before I got here. I made Jay give me complete admin access to the entire system, Claire. There's no record of me ever being here or anything that happened this weekend. Or ever. Hell, they won't even... know...they won't even know Jay was watching everyone else. I'm going set it up to make it look like a lover's quarrel he got in the middle of. Shit. What the...?"

He wasn't moving, but he staggered anyway. He laughed again, wheezing, bent over and craning his face toward her. " I am very, very fucked up. What did you do to me?"

"Nothing yet," Claire said as she followed him and used both hands to shove him backwards. "But I'm sure as hell about to."

THIRTY-TWO

HER HANDS WERE SO NUMB SHE BARELY FELT HIS BODY WHEN she shoved him. Brent toppled back, already off balance. His hip hit the trunk edge of Troy's car. Brent snatched up her wrist faster than she expected him to be, considering how out of it he'd been acting.

His grip twisted, grinding the bones together while Claire cried out. His other fist came up to clip her jaw in an indiscriminate blow that nevertheless would have sent her reeling if he hadn't been holding onto her.

He dragged her closer. Their knees banged together. He took her by the throat.

"I'm going to fucking kill you," Brent said. "Ffffuck...and. Fuck and kill you?"

Claire believed he meant to, but she was not going to let him. She would not die today. Not here, not at the hand of this...bro...this kid, this manipulative piece of human trash.

She kneed him straight into the nuts. At the same time, she hit him directly in the Adam's apple with the hand he was gripping. Agony flared in her fingers, but she didn't care. Brent choked out a scream and let her go. She fell back. So did he. He hit the car. She hit the floor.

The fall knocked the wind out of her, but she managed not to slam her head on the concrete. She rolled onto her side, curling into herself from the pain and also trying to make herself a smaller target in case Brent was able to get himself under control enough to go after her. Her hands swept the floor as she tried to get purchase enough to balance herself. Eternity passed while she tried to get to her feet. Her ears rang from Brent's punch. Blood streamed into her eye and over her cheek, into her mouth, it flooded over the bruises she could feel forming on her throat from where he'd choked her.

Claire wiped her face with one hand and used her other one to support herself as she rolled onto it and her knees. She was going to throw up. Pass out.

No.

No.

No, she was going to get up on her feet and get herself out of this shed, and she was going to...

She didn't know what she was going to do, but the sound of Brent's wheezing curses got her moving. He'd slid down the side of the car and onto the concrete, where he lay in the fetal position, but she couldn't be certain he would stay here.

He wasn't unconscious, but he looked as though he was feeling really good. Claire had been there a time or two before she'd gotten the hang of medicinal quality edibles. Better than his obvious impending unconsciousness was what she spotted on the concrete not far from him.

His phone.

The screen had cracked, but when she swiped the glass, it lit. It was passcode protected, of course, but the emergency calling should still work. No service here in the shed, though, and she couldn't tell if he'd connected to the hidden WiFi Jay had bragged about. She shoved the phone in her pocket anyway.

She needed something to tie him up. Spotting a pegboard along the back wall behind Troy's car, she got there as fast as she could. The cold that felt as though it had sunk into her bones was still there, but now a heat rose within her, a combination of desperation and delirium. Everything hurt, especially her head, but she pushed herself anyway.

Brent muttered something that sounded like her name, along with a string of mumbled curses. He rolled onto his side, hands flat on the concrete, and made an attempt to get up. It failed, but he would try again, she could see that. Maybe she'd underestimated a frat boy's stamina and his tolerance for THC.

Various tools hung on the pegboard, along with empty spaces outlined in permanent marker that showed where missing tools had once been. No rope, no shears, nothing she could use to stab him or tie him up. She plucked a hammer from the hook.

Behind her, something scraped on the concrete. She turned, hefting the hammer, and saw that Brent had managed to get onto his feet. His eyes drooped, but he swiveled in her direction and took a couple of determined steps toward her.

"What're you do with...ham? Mer? Hammer," he said.

"I'm going to hit you with it, if you don't back off!"

Brent put up his hands and made several small pushing-away motions. "I am sooooooo baked."

"You'll be fine in a few hours," Claire said.

She thought he was going to come at her, but Brent whirled away and headed for the door of the shed. He wrangled it open and wobbled through it, leaving it open behind him. She followed.

He might be stoned, but he'd retained enough of his wits to wait for her right outside the door. When she came through it, he swung at her, but Claire easily ducked his fist. She shoved him back against the shed's outside wall. Brent fell down into the drift that reached to her hip.

If she left him there and he passed out, he might die from exposure. A mother would lose a son. Claire would forever carry the knowledge that her inaction killed him.

"Fuck you," she said into the dark and the wind and the pile of snow under which Brent had disappeared. "Fuck you."

The lights of the cabin were her guide as she fell into the snow herself. The places where the earth had been scoured bare by the wind gave her a few seconds of respite before she had to get back to slogging, but it was enough to keep her going. By the time she got back around to the front porch, she couldn't feel her hands or feet. It was like walking on blocks of wood. She couldn't get her fingers to work on the long series of numbers for the door code, so she pounded on it, instead.

Nobody came to open it.

She tried again, leaning against it with both hands. Her entire body wracked with shudders that slowly eased. Unexpected warmth began to fill her. This, she thought drowsily, was how it felt to freeze to death.

The door opened so abruptly she fell through it. Her hands came up automatically to catch herself from hitting face first. She had no sensation in them as they hit the wooden floorboards, but the vibration of her fall racked her entire body. She rolled onto her side, her wrists aching. She hoped she hadn't broken anything.

"Claire, baby, oh no…" Troy bent over her to chafe at her hands. Even in the firelight's fading glow, he looked pale. Drawn. Deep shadows below his eyes had nothing to do with the dim light.

"I'm okay. I'll be okay." She struggled to sit. "Where's Elliott?"

"He's in the bedroom. He's in and out of consciousness. I got him to drink some water. He might have some broken ribs, too. Where's the little asshole?"

"I left him passed out in a snow bank." She'd lost the hammer somewhere along the way, only realizing it this moment. A sob burst out of her.

She and Troy clung to each other for a moment before she thought to check and see if he'd been putting weight on his injured ankle. He'd stuck his leg out in an awkward position to protect it, but his head hung. Sweat dripped from his face.

"I am really, really fucking up this ankle."

"You need to get off it."

"Let's get you warmed up," Troy said.

The cabin was already noticeably colder. The power had gone out. Together, they managed to get themselves in front of the fireplace. Troy, with a groan, got a log from the bin next to it and laid it on the fire. Sparks flew out, scorching the floor. The fire itself looked as though it made a heavy sigh, the embers glowing brighter for a few seconds, but the log didn't catch. Troy leaned forward to blow on it, every breath sounding harsh and weak.

"Let me help you."

Claire lent her breath to his. Breath, breath, blow. A small curl of flame eased along the fresh log. It crackled. It was catching. She leaned back, the floor so hard on every sore and complaining inch of her, but she didn't have the strength in the moment to get onto the couch.

"See what happens when we work together?" Troy said. "We've always been such a good team."

His voice held a hint of desperation. Claire looked at him. She wanted to lean into his embrace and let him comfort her the way he'd done so many times, for so many reasons. She wanted him to tell her it was all going to be okay. They were going to be fine. But she didn't believe any of that, not anymore.

"Claire. Do you forgive me? Can you ever?"

"I don't know," she told him.

She expected an argument, but Troy only nodded. Something pinched in her pocket, and she shifted. She'd almost forgotten about Brent's phone. She pulled it out, now, and laid it on the floor in front of the fire. The cracked screen glistened with melting snow.

"Here." Troy shrugged out of his long-sleeved shirt, leaving him in a t-shirt. He dried the phone and tapped the screen. "Shit. Needs a passcode."

"See if it can connect to the WiFi."

He tilted it from side to side, then shook his head. "I don't see any signal at all. No bars. Maybe he's not connected."

The phone screen went black, and this time when Troy swiped it, it didn't come on. He wiped it again with the shirt. Claire sagged, trying to get herself warm and incapable of doing much more at the moment.

"Battery's low," Troy said. "But I don't think it got too wet to work. Here, baby, put this shirt on. You're freezing."

She accepted the warmth of his shirt. It smelled of sweat but also of laundry soap and Troy and she pressed the damp sleeve to her face. The extra layer helped.

"I never thought I'd be warm again."

"Let me see your hands."

Reluctantly, because she knew any touch was going to hurt, she held them out. Troy took them gently, pulling her more into the light and inspecting her fingertips. He kissed them, which hurt, and she pulled away. It seemed like an analogy.

"I don't think you have frostbite. But you need to warm up slowly, I think. Hell. I don't know. Elliott's the one who knows all that kind of thing."

Both of them looked toward the bedroom.

"Do you think he's going to die?" Claire asked.

Troy shook his head. "No. He's hurt. There could be internal bleeding or something. But he's not going to die, because we're going to get out of here. We're all going to be fine."

A noise at the back of the house had them both sitting up, eyes wide. It could only be Brent. Another thud against the back of the wall had Claire shoving his phone into her pocket before scrambling to her feet. She swayed but kept her balance.

"Brent's trying to get into the basement."

She pointed at the door and struggled to her feet to move toward it. There was no way Troy could keep up with her. She was limping and slow, but his ankle wouldn't let him move with any speed.

The door she'd always thought was an owner's closet could not be locked without a key, but the heavy bookcase next to it could be shoved in front. She pulled, then hobbled around to the other side and pushed. The bookcase moved half an inch. She thought she heard footsteps on the stairs.

She shoved harder.

"Let me help — "

"Gun. Is. In. Basement!" She gasped out the words, hoping he could understand them.

Finding strength inside her, she shoved again. The bookcase moved another half an inch. It was nowhere near entirely blocking the door, but when she gave another final, heaving shove, she had to hope it would be enough.

"He's going to come through this door, and you need to be in a place he can't get to you," she said. "You need to get into the bedroom. Bar the bathroom door and the bedroom doors, both of them. I don't understand how he's even able to stand, much less walk..."

"I'm not leaving you out here with him!"

"I'm not going to stay here. I'm going to use the snowmobile."

"Claire, no —"

More noise. Definitely footsteps on the stairs. Slow. Thudding. But moving closer.

"I love you." Claire kissed him. She held him tight. "I love you so much. I'm going to get the snowmobile. And Troy...do whatever you have to so you can keep you and Elliott safe from him."

He nodded. They kissed again, faster this time, but with no less sentiment. Claire forced herself away from him. She had to move. Her body was already protesting the cold outside, already fighting her to stay here, where it was warm. She didn't allow herself to think about what lay ahead of her. She concentrated on what Jay had told her about how to turn on the snowmobile and how to run it.

She flung the front door open and yanked it shut behind her. The snowmobile was canted at the bottom of the three steps leading to the porch. She flung her leg over it, hands already searching for the pull cord Jay had told her about. There was a little light coming from the cabin windows. A hint of the coming dawn in the sky. It wasn't enough for her to see what she was doing.

Cursing, Claire tried again. Slower this time, forcing herself to take her time so she didn't screw it up. She found the T-shaped bar and curled her numb fingers around it. She braced herself. She'd seen her dad do this with a lawnmower, back in the day. He'd push the mower and call for her to bring him a beer, and he'd ruffle her hair and tell her she was quite a kid. That this, a good memory of her father, should infiltrate her now seemed ironic. Fateful. She could do this. She had to do it.

She pulled as hard as she could, but she couldn't get the vehicle to start.

Shadows moved across the sheet-covered windows. Fighting. She heard, or imagined, the sound of shouts. One of the figures went down. The other loomed, monstrous. She couldn't let herself focus on what might be happening inside. She had to get this thing started.

The door flew open. She didn't dare look to see who stood in the doorway. She fumbled again, her fingers numb. The sound of her name turned her head involuntarily toward the cabin door. Relief flooded her at Troy's familiar silhouette, and she hoped he'd knocked Brent out.

She did not dare to hope he'd killed him, that seemed too much even now.

Troy shouted her name again, but whatever else he was trying to tell her got whisked away by the wind. Behind him, a shadow rose, followed quickly by a figure. Claire tried to scream a warning, but her voice, too, was shredded in the wind and torn away. She got off the snowmobile but didn't make it to the steps before Brent hit Troy on the side of the head, knocking him back. He bent over him. Punching. Kicking. Claire screamed again.

Brent turned toward the doorway as the wind slammed the door shut.

She heard a shot.

THIRTY-THREE

seconds, revealing the shambling zombie form of the bro who would not die, but for the moment, nothing happened except a gust of frigid wind whipped her hair into her face. She let go of the pull cord and got off the snowmobile on stiff and desensitized legs that immediately buckled. She stopped herself from falling face-first into the snow only by accident — her out-flung hand caught the snowmobile and kept her half-standing. The rest of her landed on something solid. Unyielding.

Snow had covered Jay's body, including the blood that must have shot from his stabbed-out eye. The blade bristled there, and Claire considered grabbing it, but she couldn't stomach the idea of pulling it out of Jay's head. Even if she had a knife, Brent would have to get too close to her before she could use it, and at this point she was trying her best to stay as far from him as she could.

The door stayed closed. She couldn't wait to see if Brent had fallen down, passed out, been knocked out. She couldn't trust that he wasn't going to come after her. What, then, could she do?

She had always been the kid who traumatized herself watching scary movies when she was supposed to be in bed, then giving herself nightmares, or worse, being unable to fall asleep as she lay, wide-eyed with terror, waiting for the closet door to swing open and reveal the monster waiting to eat her.

Stanley Kubrick's *The Shining* had done her in more than many of the horror movies she'd terrorized herself with. The father who'd turned from loving to abusive had been scarier than a naked rotting corpse ghost, and she'd identified too closely with the little boy Danny who'd been about the same age as she'd been when she'd watched it. She had never forgotten the final scenes, and they came to her now as she stumbled away from the snowmobile and into snow so deep she sunk all the way to her hip.

The wind had blown it into a drift here at the corner of the cabin, but it wasn't much shallower beyond the porch. The wind that had slapped her before came around the corner of the cabin and pummeled her so fiercely that for a moment, she couldn't even draw a breath. Her lungs burned. Her eyes watered, tears freezing her to blindness. She pitched forward, arms out and fell into the snow.

She lost Brent's phone.

Spewing a flurry of profanities, Claire swept her hands through the snow in front of her. Praying her fingers had not gone too numb to feel, she tried again. She found it, grabbed it up and shoved deeper into the too-shallow pocket of her jeans, cursing the women's fashion industry for never making them deep enough.

She forced herself to take another few steps toward the road. Each one needed an exaggerated length in order to get her foot entirely free of the snow before she put it down again, but she needed to be sure Brent saw which direction she was going.

Same as the little boy in *The Shining*, she needed him to follow her before she could trick him.

Every instinct shrieked at her to simply run, run, run, but Claire forced herself to move slowly. To think. At any second, he was going to fight down Troy again and come out that front door. She had no doubts. Troy had done his best, but Brent had beaten him. The wind tossed her the faint noise of his furious screaming, or maybe she was imagining it. She had to move.

Her ultimate goal was not the access road. No way for her to get there on foot with snow up to her knees in places, even deeper than others with the drifts. She needed to head the opposite direction, into the forest, toward the waterfall. There was a signal there, a faint one, but that was all she had now. Hope.

No boots, no gloves, no coat, no hat. Miles from help. Stalked and attacked by a man who'd tipped over the edge of rationality.

Facing away from the cabin, Claire fell down into the snow again, this time making an exaggerated outline of her body as she forced a flailing struggle to get up. The snow angel she made had eight wings and wheels for legs, far closer to the biblical description than the gowned seraphim of childhood snow days. She rolled over, denting the white drifts all over, then got to her feet.

One step at a time, backwards, settling her steps as best she could into the footprints she'd already left. Another howl of anger drifted to her on the wind. It sounded louder and closer, but so far, the front door stayed shut.

No more time for being careful. Now, Claire ran. Here and there the wind had swept the field clear of snow almost down to the bare grass, but there were plenty of places she had to navigate through deeper piles. Her breath tore at her lungs. Snot ran freely from her nose, freezing on her upper lip. Her eyes had nearly frozen shut.

She pushed on toward the tree line. She didn't know how close she had to get to the waterfall before there'd be a signal, but she wasn't going to allow herself to think even for one second that she wouldn't be able to find one. Nor would she let herself imagine the snow staying as deep under the cover of the forest as it was out here in the bare field. It had to be easier to run there. It had to, or else she wasn't going to —

"Run," she urged herself through chattering teeth. "Run!"

She hated herself for wishing for the warmth she'd felt before, the heat and comfort and sleepiness that came with freezing to death. She tried to make herself wish for numbness instead, but her body had gone beyond that. Everything burned now, each step like razors slicing at her.

She could see now, barely, and she blinked hard to clear her eyes of the snow and frozen tears. For now, she had the advantage of semi-darkness to shield her, but morning was coming, and it would get here whether or not she was ready for it.

She heard more shouting behind her. Incoherent. Raging. And

then, the roar of the snowmobile engine. She dared look behind her to see the cabin door standing wide open, light spilling out into a golden rectangle on the snow.

She couldn't run anymore. Not a single step. Claire pitched forward into the snow without catching herself. It was so deep it almost completely covered her.

The buzz of the snowmobile got louder, but farther away. She thought she heard the sound of Brent shouting her name over the noise, but she couldn't be sure. Couldn't be certain of anything, anymore, other than that she was going to die.

The thought of this got her to her feet. One step at a time, she staggered into standing despite the numbness and the soft, wet weight of the snow trying so hard to hold her down. If she was going to die out here, she wasn't going to do it because she'd given it up.

He was heading away from her, toward the road. Her trick had worked. She stopped herself from letting out a triumphant scream only because she had no strength to make one. In the next second she staggered again, hope depleting as the snowmobile's headlamp swung back toward her.

Brent steered it in a loop. Then it blinded her as he headed right for her. Claire yanked her foot free of the snow and stepped back. Then again. She was beyond the tree line now. The snow was still deep enough for a snowmobile to drive on, but not nearly as deep as it was in the field. She could move a little faster now, but she would never be able to outrun a snowmobile. She recognized this spot.

She wasn't going to make it to the waterfall and the possible cell service, either, not before Brent caught up to her. Was he going to run her over? Would he jump off it and grab her, try to choke her again? Maybe he'd stab her to death.

She was out of choices.

"Come on then," she said aloud, nowhere near loud enough for Brent to hear, hardly loud enough to hear herself. But she said it, then again, even louder until she was screaming it, her fists raised and ready. "Come on then! Come. On!"

He couldn't hear her, but he could see her. His howl cut through the night and sliced away at her, and if it contained actual words, Claire could not hear them. It didn't matter. She screamed her own animalistic shriek into the biting wind, right at him.

She ran again to stand between two trees, the opening too narrow for the snowmobile to pass through. It passed by, spitting up snow toward her. She had a single moment of seeing his face, distorted and monstrous, before the vehicle swung around and headed back.

Claire was already running as best she could. She couldn't see the path. Couldn't see anything more than a few inches in front of her face. She ran anyway, knocking away branches that tried to slap her down. She tripped and went to her knees. Got up. She knew this spot.

Brent was coming back.

Dodging and ducking again through the trees, she let him catch up to her as she ran between two trees. At the last second, she threw herself off to one side and fell into the snow. The snowmobile raged toward her. Then past her, through the trees she'd been standing between only moments before.

When what felt like hot rain hit her in the face, Claire stumbled back with a cry. She tasted metal. The snowmobile roared, veering off to the left of her and into a tree. It hit so hard the snow fell off and thudded to the ground. The vehicle itself stuttered to a stop.

Claire let out a gagging, guttural moan. Her knees tried to give out, but she refused to fall again. Instead, she stood motionless, unable to do more than stare. It took her some time to realize she could see Brent's corpse because the sky had lightened. The sun was coming up. In the dawn's gray light, the spray of his blood looked dark, close to black.

She could feel it on her face. Sickened, Claire bent to scoop up a handful of clean snow. She scrubbed away the blood. She spit away the taste of bile.

Brent had fallen off before the snowmobile hit the tree. He'd landed a few feet away from Claire — at least his body had. It spouted crimson from the stump of his neck, a red rain melting the white drifts.

His head rolled to one side and and half-disappeared into the bloody snow.

Thirty-Four

She couldn't look at him again, or behind him to the strands of barbed wire strung between the trees that had so capably and quickly decapitated him. She fumbled with the lock screen to bring up the emergency calling feature. She tapped in 911. Then, all she could do was hold up the phone and pray she could get a signal.

"...what's...emergency?"

At the sound of the operator's voice, Claire let out a sobbing sigh. She did her best to speak slowly and clearly, an near-impossible feat with the lockjaw of being so cold preventing her from moving her mouth. "There's been an accident."

She didn't know the address. Could not recall Jay's last name. The operator's voice crackled in and out.

Claire tried again. "I'm in a cabin. It's off Route 41. My car's parked at the bottom of the access road. Can you hear me?"

"I can hear you, ma'am. Please state your emergency."

"There's been an accident," Claire repeated, hesitant to say more than that. "Please send someone right away. We need an ambulance. But the road isn't plowed."

The operator didn't speak, or if she did, Claire couldn't hear her.

Claire held the phone away from her ear to look at the screen. The call had failed. She tried again, but this time when she swiped the screen, the phone didn't light. The battery had died, or the extreme cold had killed it.

Overhead, the sky had lightened enough that she could see clearly. She shoved the phone in her pocket and geared herself up to make it back to the cabin. She didn't look at the snowmobile as she passed it, or the body, or the hole in the snow.

Somehow, she made it back to the cabin. She pressed her hands against the front door, leaning. Forehead against the cold, painted wood. She watched her own breath steaming out of her. The door was locked, and she did not have the fortitude to press the long string of numbers she wasn't even sure she could remember.

Next to the door, below the kitchen window, was a pile of wood. Claire took the top log, hefting it in both her hands. Splinters pierced her, and her weakened hands lost their grip, so she clawed the log to her chest. Using the last bit of strength she could muster, she heaved it through the front windows.

Glass shattered. The sheets hung over the inside of the windows tore down. Claire reached inside, avoiding the jagged shards still sticking into the window frame, and gathered a handful of the fabric to protect her hand as she knocked out the rest of the glass. She swung a leg over the sill, caught up for a moment by her own exhaustion. The table was in the way on the other side, and she let herself fall onto it. It creaked and rocked, but held. She stayed that way for a few minutes until the cold air prompted her to get up and head for the fire.

The living room was empty. The bedroom and bathroom doors, closed. She heard no voices. No sounds other than the crackling of the fire, now fighting the influx of chilly air coming in the broken window.

The power was still out, but with the sun up, plenty of light came in through the windows. Obvious signs of a struggle were everywhere. Overturned chairs. The couch had been shoved at an angle. The coffee table, broken and pushed aside. Pictures had fallen from the walls.

Claire got herself into the kitchen and filled half a glass of water, which she gulped greedily. Her stomach lurched, and she hung over the sink but managed to stop herself from throwing up. She stayed that way for much longer than she'd expected, but at least the counter was propping her up. If she tried to step away, she didn't fully believe that she wouldn't fall down.

She heard a noise and whirled to face the front door, certain it would slam open to reveal a risen corpse. Brent or Jay, it wouldn't matter. One of them had come back to life and was coming for her. Harsh gasps panted out of her, but in seconds her brain managed to wrestle her terror into submission. The front door was closed. Snow blew in now and then from the broken windows, but no figures loomed there.

The creak of hinges turned her toward the living room. The bathroom or bedroom doors had opened, but from this angle she could not see which one. It was enough to get her moving though, a few faltering steps to the bar, where she clung for support. Another few beyond that, into the living room side of the bar she still used for support. From here she could see that the bathroom door was cracked open.

She listened for voices, but heard nothing. Using the bar as a guide, she hobbled toward the bathroom door. It creaked when she opened it. The bathroom inside was dark, no windows, but through the door to the bedroom she could see light. Shadows shifted. Someone was moving in the bedroom.

Before Claire could do anything else, the door from the bedroom to the bathroom swung open, slow, slow, slow, to reveal a figure silhouetted in such deep shadow she couldn't be sure who it was. It moved forward, bare feet slapping the tile floor. It slipped, went to one knee with a hoarse shout.

"Elliott," Claire cried at the sound of that voice.

He looked up. The way his body had twisted put his face in the light coming from the bedroom. Blood streaked it. More blood covered his shirt front. His hands, shaking as he lifted them, also looked dark and sticky with it.

"Elliott...what happened? What did you do?"

He slumped on the floor and stared at his bloody hands. He looked up at her. From this distance, she couldn't see if he had an obvious wound that she didn't already know about.

"Whose blood is that," she asked, thinking she was shouting but hearing only a whispered question.

He blinked, head nodding as though he was trying to stay awake. He looked up at her again. "It's Troy's."

THIRTY-FIVE

CLAIRE DIDN'T WANT TO GO PAST THE MAN IN FRONT OF HER. Elliott wore Troy's blood like Halloween makeup. She wasn't going to get close enough to him to let him do anything to her.

She went out the bathroom and into the bedroom through the other door. Troy lay on the bed, the blankets beneath him saturated with blood. She staggered across the room and crawled onto the bed from the footboard up. Troy didn't move when she bent over him and said his name. She shook him, gently. He didn't respond.

Her husband's name rose to her lips but without breath behind it, could not be screamed. The noise that came out of her was a hissing, stuttering sigh, air let out of a punctured tire, except it was her heart that had been punctured. Slowly, she turned to face the man standing in the doorway.

"Did you do this?" Claire demanded.

Elliott leaned in the doorway, head hanging. He put a hand to his face. Covered his mouth. Mumbled something that she couldn't understand.

She flew at him, fists raised, to pound on his chest. She didn't care that she sent him falling backward, his hands raised to fend her off. She didn't care that she was hurting him. She wanted to hurt him.

"Did you kill him!"

Again, he tried to speak, but she slapped his mouth. His head turned with the blow, as weak as it had been. Elliott put up a hand to stop her. Claire stepped back.

"Did you," she asked, "kill him?"

Brent was Elliott's brother. He'd agreed to meet her for Brent's sick and twisted fantasy fulfillment. He'd pursued her. He'd stalked her. He'd seduced her husband. Infiltrated her family.

He had made her love him, while all along, everything he'd ever done had been one betrayal after another.

When he pushed abruptly past her, Claire lost her balance and fell against the wall. She grabbed at him, trying to keep him from reaching the bed, and Troy, but her fingers slipped uselessly off Elliott's shirt. She hopped forward to grab again, pulling him.

"Is he dead?" Elliott shouted hoarsely. "Troy? Love, are you...wake up. Is he dead, Claire? Oh, my God, is he dead?"

On the bed, Troy stirred. Groggily, he spoke a name. He sat up.

He had not asked for her.

Elliott gave her an accusatory glance over his shoulder. "He's not fucking dead. Why would you say that? Why would you, how *could* you ask me if I'd *killed* him. What the hell is wrong with you, Claire?"

"I'm okay," Troy said. "I'll be fine. Fucker hit me in the head, that's all. Broke my nose, I think. But I'm okay."

Her knees gave out. Her pounding heart had not yet slowed, and she pressed a hand over her breast to calm it. Claire let herself fall into the chair in the corner of the room. Troy wasn't dead, but nothing would ever be okay again.

THE POWER HAD COME BACK ON.

Claire had used the shower and dressed in fresh clothes, then given over the bathroom to the men so they could do the same. She hung up the sheet over the broken window to prevent at least some of the freezing air from coming inside, but it didn't help much. She turned up the furnace, instead, not caring what it would do to Jay's propane bill. Jay couldn't care about anything, anymore.

She made hot tea and sandwiches and served them on the kitchen counter, since every other table in the cabin had been overturned or somehow broken. She wasn't hungry, but she forced herself to eat. When Troy came out into the kitchen, supported on Elliott's shoulder, she left them to the food and drink and sat by the fire so she didn't have to talk to either one of them.

They spoke in soft whispers that drifted to her over the sound of the crackling fire and the soughing wind. She heard the single syllable of her name but wasn't sure which one of them had said it; at this point, Claire didn't care. She curled on the couch under a blanket and drifted into a thin and shallow sleep without the comfort of dreams.

Neither of them had asked her what happened to Brent.

The light coming in from the outside was brighter by the time she felt awake enough to sit. Late afternoon. Claire moved slowly as she sat up. Careful to stretch each limb and twist neck and back before she got to her feet. Every part of her ached, every muscle stiff, and she wanted to be sure she would be able to keep her balance on the way to the bathroom. The first few steps were agonizing, but she made it to the toilet without falling over.

Troy and Elliott were in the bedroom, both on the bed. She could see them through the open door. They faced each other. When she got up to wash her hands, she could see that Troy, at least, was awake. His eyes caught hers over Elliott's shoulder, and Elliott turned to look at her, too.

"Claire," Troy said. "Come here."

She shook her head. "No."

Troy sat up. Cleaning up had done him good — bruises littered his face and his nose looked as if it might be broken, but she no longer would have assumed he was dead. Elliott, too, looked similar with obvious bruising and swelling, and a still-oozing slash on his forehead that had been covered with an adhesive bandage. He sat up, too, and drew his long legs in close to his body, linking his hands at the knees.

"There's room for you," Elliott said.

"No," Claire repeated. "There isn't."

"Hello?"

The three of them looked to the bedroom door. Claire got there first. She looked around the doorframe to see a uniformed police officer in a bulky winter coat, in the front doorway.

He had a gun.

After that, everything happened so fast that Claire was never sure what went wrong. The cop saw her in the doorway and looked surprised. She held up her hands and stepped through it. Maybe speaking, maybe not, maybe trying to explain, maybe simply crying out in relief.

Elliott was close behind her. The officer saw him before Elliott saw the cop. Troy shouted from the bedroom, or maybe Elliott was the one shouting, but he was the one with his hand on Claire's shoulder, yanking her back toward the bedroom. Claire fought off his hand, aware of two things at the same moment — first, Elliott was trying to protect her from the threat he assumed she was under. Two, the police officer was doing the same thing.

"He has a gun!" The cop screamed.

The bullet sounded and felt like a furious hornet as it passed her.

Claire went to her knees to cover her head. Elliott fell forward, also landing on his knees. Blood welled between the fingers of the hand he held over his chest. He cried out, wordless, and pitched onto his side where he curled into the fetal position.

"Oh shit," the cop said.

THIRTY-SIX

What had once been a guilty fantasy had become her reality, but Claire no longer harbored any pangs of conscience. Sure, there were sad nights when she drank a little too much wine and wept in the shower, but most of the time, she indulged in a long and decadent bath and a book when she went to bed and slept alone. She woke every morning with a sense of satisfaction, and that was worth the occasional bout of tears.

As she put the finishing touches on the table on her back deck, she paused to admire the flowers she'd planted in pots all around the space. A water fountain trickled, splashing. Hummingbirds zoomed around a series of feeders she did her best to keep full.

The party would start in a couple of hours. Aviva was leaving next week to go overseas, where she'd be supervising students taking a gap year. She'd be gone for a year and a half. Longer, if she decided to stay on with the program. It was a world away, and Claire already missed her.

"Claire?"

She turned at the sound of a familiar male voice. "The gate's unlocked, come on in."

The gate opened, and Troy came through it. He had a few grocery bags in one hand and a bunch of flowers in the other. He waved them at her and crossed the flagstones to the deck.

Claire greeted him with a kiss, the way she always did, although this one didn't linger. She added a squeeze, suddenly sentimental. Troy, his arms full, did his best to return the hug.

"Where's Viva?" he asked when they parted.

"She ran out to pick up some ice and a few bottles of champagne. Some last-minute friends texted to say they were going to make it, after all." She studied him, looking up and down. He wore fitted charcoal trousers and a slim-cut button-down shirt in dark gray with blue accents. He had a new haircut, too. She touched one of his buttons. "You look handsome."

Troy laughed. Pink crept into his cheeks. "Thanks."

"Put the flowers there. You can bring the bags inside. Do you want a beer? Glass of wine?" She gestured as she took him into her kitchen.

He put the bags on the counter. "Beer, I guess."

Claire pulled out a bottle of a local IPA from the fridge and handed it to him. A new figure silhouetted in the sliding glass doors. She grabbed another beer in anticipation.

"Now that's what I call a greeting," Elliott said as she handed him the bottle.

He kissed her, his lips drifting over hers in a way that promised something deeper, if she agreed. Claire did not agree. Not this time, anyway, although she was open to the idea of changing her mind. For now, she stepped away from him.

The separation she'd asked for from Troy had no end date, but neither had they filed for divorce. It turned out that nearly three decades of a marriage, a good marriage, could not be undone so simply and easily, not even by betrayal. She and Troy had not lasted as long as they did without learning how to forgive each other.

Elliott had forgiven her for believing he might have killed Troy, but Claire knew he hadn't forgotten. How could he? How could anyone forget that the person they loved was convinced they could be capable of murder? How could you ever trust someone who you believed could kill?

"You look good," she told him. "You both look good."

He'd fully recovered from the gunshot that had gone through his shoulder, fortunately missing anything important. Shadows haunted his eyes sometimes, although Claire suspected he usually hid them from her. She bet he shared them with Troy, but that was not her business. Like the kissing, someday that might change. For now, the three of them stepped very carefully around each other. Negotiating. Navigating.

No more secrets.

Claire who lived alone was not as happy as Claire who had not lived alone once imagined she would be. She was *happier.* And for now, Claire thought, that was enough.

About the Author

Mina Hardy writes books. Usually, they feature good people making bad choices, but sometimes they might be about bad people making good choices. Either way, everyone is basically a mess, and you shouldn't trust any of them.

From twisted tales of domestic suspense to darker stories of bumping in the night, you can expect some thrills and a few chills. Follow her on social media, if that's the sort of thing that melts your butter.

She's also known as Megan Hart.

facebook.com/MinaHardyWritesBooks

instagram.com/MinaHardyWritesBooks

amazon.com/stores/author/B089X773H1

threads.net/minahardywritesbooks

tiktok.com/@readinbed

www.ingramcontent.com/pod-product-compliance
Lightning Source LLC
Chambersburg PA
CBHW061808190726
48289CB00007B/2122